Praise for Laura Bacchi and Bonnie Dee's
Butterfly Unpinned

"Butterfly Unpinned is a deeply dark tale which touched the recesses of my heart. There are not enough superlatives to talk about this beautiful story or the wonderful writing team of Ms. Dee and Ms. Bacchi."
~ *Two Lips Reviews*

"Laura Bacchi and Bonnie Dee tell an emotion driven story with Butterfly Unpinned."
~ *Romance Junkies*

"This story does a great job of showing both the worst and the best of the BDSM world, and the line is very clearly drawn by the authors. This is one you want to add to your keeper shelves, I know I am!"
~ *Coffee Time Romance*

"The balance of Butterfly's fragility and Bryan's savior complex is a careful one, as is the dark sensuality prevalent in the first half with the deeper, heart-stopping eroticism of the second."
~ *Book Utopia & Uniquely Pleasurable Review*

"What a horrifying, powerful and beautiful story authors Bonnie Dee and Laura Bacchi have created with Butterfly Unpinned. I was gripped hard from the very beginning and I couldn't put it down until I'd read the very last word."
~ *Fallen Angel Reviews*

Look for these titles

Butterfly Unpinned

Laura Bacchi and Bonnie Dee

A Samhain Publishing, Ltd. publication.

Samhain Publishing, Ltd.
577 Mulberry Street, Suite 1520
Macon, GA 31201
www.samhainpublishing.com

Butterfly Unpinned
Copyright © 2010 by Laura Bacchi and Bonnie Dee
Print ISBN: 978-1-60504-555-9
Digital ISBN: 978-1-60504-535-1

Editing by Linda Ingmanson
Cover by Scott Carpenter

First Samhain Publishing, Ltd. electronic publication: May 2009
First Samhain Publishing, Ltd. print publication: March 2010

Dedication

To Stephen, for making me believe again. And to Sarah, for insights into Navajo culture. — LB

To all my readers, thanks for continuing to support my writing addiction. — BD

Prologue

Butterfly scrubbed the stain on the floor with a toothbrush, the bristles whisking over the carpet fibers, working stain remover into them. She paused to blot the area with a damp rag then stared at the result. Her heart pounded in her throat. The purple stain was almost removed from the carpet—and so was all color. A filmy white patch like a cloud covered a section of carpet about the size of her palm.

She covered her mouth with her hand, but a whimper escaped nonetheless. Master would be so angry. Not only had she ruined the carpet, she hadn't received permission to have that glass of Cabernet. The crime of disobedience was far worse than a carpet stain.

Her skin crawled with dread of his disappointment and the inevitable punishment she'd earn. Butterfly considered hiding the evidence. The stain wasn't in the center of the room, but near the wall. By moving the couch slightly, she could hide her sin. She surrendered the idea almost immediately. Concealing the stain would only compound her transgression—and her penalty when Master eventually found out. But mainly she gave up the idea because, unlike the other girls, she found it impossible to lie to him.

She lived for him. He was her entire world. She had no desire but to please him in every possible way, and complete honesty was number one on his list of commandments. Butterfly was to be open to him at all times, both body and mind. She was allowed no inner life that Master couldn't view—

literally. Her journal, in which she related all her dreams, desires, mental struggles and moments of rebellion, was written for him so that he could possess her thoughts and feelings as well as her body. She'd signed a contract surrendering her entire being to her Master and giving him the authority to dictate every aspect of her life. It was no longer her life, but *his* life.

Butterfly sat back on her heels and stared at the damage she'd done. The white stain was a black mark on a nearly flawless record of obedience. There was nothing to do except own up to her mistake. She could only imagine what demeaning punishment he would invent for her. He always knew exactly what she needed for her correction. While some of the other women might be whipped, bound or beaten for a transgression, Butterfly was more likely to receive psychological chastisement that touched her far more deeply.

Perhaps it would be best to greet him at the door with the truth and a penitent posture. But no, he was often bad-tempered after a day of dealing with the hassles of his work. Maybe she should wait until he'd relaxed with a drink and a blowjob then admit her mistake.

Would it be best to wear one of his favorite dresses or only her tattooed skin and piercings? She knew he appreciated the vulnerability of the naked female form prostrate at his feet. Yes, nude would be better. She'd wear her garnet nipple rings and the gold hoops in her labia with delicate gold chains connecting them. Master loved the way they dangled, enjoyed giving a tug on one of the chains. A shiver of desire mingled with dread and fear in a potent cocktail of emotion that shook her to the core.

As she put away the stain remover, rags and toothbrush, Butterfly played out every scenario she could imagine, rehearsed every combination of words that might alleviate some of Master's anger, guessed every conceivable reaction he might have and its consequence. Her head spun with the possibilities. It was too much. She wasn't used to thinking so hard, only obeying his orders to the letter. She hadn't been punished in such a long time that she'd almost forgotten how severe Master could be. And it was all her fault for stealing the wine. Why did she force him to teach her this lesson again when she knew perfectly well complete obedience to her Master was the only way for a slave to be content?

"B, what are you up to, another exciting afternoon of cleaning house?" The voice from behind made her jump. Butterfly turned from the supply cupboard to face Jasmine. The dark-haired girl was red-cheeked and smelled like sweat and fresh air. She'd just come in from the outdoors.

Jasmine stared at her with an expression of both curiosity and disdain. She was the newest of Master's acquisitions and made no secret of her lack of respect for Butterfly's seniority in the household or her contempt for her. In fact, Jasmine's earlier running commentary on why Master no longer preferred Butterfly was the reason she'd needed some wine in the first place.

"Don't you ever get tired of being such a little mouse creeping around this place? You know, Master might not be so bored with you if you showed a little rebellious streak now and then. That's what he loves. It gives him a challenge, and every man loves a challenge."

Butterfly remained silent, closed the cupboard door and walked past Jasmine, but the girl followed her down the hall. "I may be new, but I've already got the man figured out. How many years have you been with him and you don't have a clue about what he really needs from you?"

"Jasmine, please go shower then come to the kitchen to help prepare dinner." So far Butterfly's tactic in dealing with the opinionated young woman was to ignore all her jibes and snide comments. Spunky Jasmine would settle down after she'd been in the house a while and Master had quenched her fire with stringent discipline.

"Seriously, you have to get a little naughty sometimes to keep his interest. Trust me. Master might hold you up as a model slave to the rest of us, but he finds you as bland as tapioca."

Breathing slowly, Butterfly suppressed the dart of irritation that pierced her calm. On some level she thought the girl might be right. Well, today's incident with the wine would certainly put a spark back in her relationship with Master.

Jasmine pressed close to her side, crowding her, exuding sweat and pheromones and the scent of a healthy young female. "Don't you miss it? Hasn't it been too long since he tied you up and whipped you or put you in the stocks and paddled your bottom raw?" Her breath stirred Butterfly's hair as she whispered with fervent excitement.

Butterfly felt a surge of desire at her words. She wasn't particularly fond of whipping, but being tied in intricate positions for hours at a time... She shivered and her pussy clenched at memories of being bound, gagged and kept in a small, tight space. "Don't you ache for it?" Jasmine's husky, seductive voice chiseled away at her composure as the girl's hand slid around her waist. "Don't you miss the hurt? Crave the pain? What time and attention does he give you these days? You're no more to him than a faithful old dog sent to fetch his slippers, while the rest of us have all the fun."

Jasmine's right. He's losing interest in you. You're not the most attractive of the women. You have no special quality to entice him. You're nothing. The cool, reasonable inner voice that sounded exactly like her mother whispered insidiously.

Butterfly stopped in the middle of the hall and pulled Jasmine's arm from around her waist. "Please go and do as I told you—clean up and report to the kitchen." She kept her voice polite yet firm. "I don't want to have to reprimand you."

"Or punish me, God forbid." Laughing, Jasmine walked backward down the hall in front of her, hips swaying from side to side. "You know, I could help you stir things up a bit. How would Master deal with you if he found out you aren't able to manage the household? I might get punished for acting up, but you... He'd find a different way to show you his displeasure, wouldn't he?"

Butterfly's calm exterior was being chipped away from the inside. She'd had years of practice in keeping her expression unruffled no matter what was said to her or what harm words inflicted, but Jasmine was sorely trying her patience today.

"No whippings for you," the girl continued with a saucy grin. "He knows what hurts you the most. Maybe he'd take away your precious piano for a while or force you to stand in a field under the open sky. Maybe drop you off on a city street for a few hours." She laughed again. Butterfly's fear of open places and crowds was a weakness that could easily be exploited. "Or perhaps he'd humiliate you. Lots of ways he could do that. Can't you picture them?"

She could, and had over the past hour as she'd scrubbed at the carpet stain. Master might make a lesson of her in front of the others. Show the girls that even a model slave like Butterfly occasionally had to be reminded of her place. He might have her lick all their feet to demonstrate her debasement or wear diapers to illustrate she'd been a naughty baby. Or she might have to return to square one, the ultimate mind-breaking punishment he'd inflicted on her in the early days of her captivity, the thing he knew was guaranteed to bring her face to face with her demons... Master might force her to give an outdoor performance for a group of guests.

Sitting nude under the open sky, completely exposed to the stares of an audience while her fingers trembled on the piano keys was only the beginning of one of those humiliating concerts. At least, while she played, she didn't have to meet all those eyes, but after a few pieces, Master would have her sit on top of the glossy black grand piano, legs spread wide so everyone could see every part of her while she masturbated. He didn't allow her to keep her eyes closed. She must make eye contact with the guests while she moved herself to climax—not an easy trick when her heart pounded and her genitals felt hard and cold as stone, refusing to respond to her touch.

Only when her degradation was complete would he allow her to retreat back to the safety of the indoors, to lie shaking on her pallet, weeping in shame at her weakness.

Butterfly shuddered, physically quivering at the memory and, like a jackal, Jasmine noted the movement and tore into her. "Humiliation—don't like that do you, princess? You always think you're better than the rest of us. The way you talk, and sitting at that piano all the time. You imagine yourself a lady instead of a slave, which is all you are, just like everybody else here."

Butterfly's mouth thinned to a straight line as she pushed past Jasmine. "Just be sure you're in the kitchen in ten minutes or we'll see what kind of punishment you can bear when I tell Master you're not making any attempt to fit in here."

Once she was out of the new slave's earshot, she exhaled loudly, releasing the tension and frustration of the encounter. She hated confrontation. It wasn't in her nature to stand against anyone. She longed for the quiet tranquility of Master's home before Jasmine came. She missed the early days when there was only herself and silent Sapphire.

Now, with four "doves" as Master called them, including volatile Jasmine, there was drama brewing all the time. Peace was all Butterfly had ever wanted, but recently she wondered if serving him could give her that. Every time the traitorous thought of breaking her contract and leaving reared its head, she beat it into silence. His pleasure was her pleasure—as simple as that. It was all she needed to remember in order to be content.

But lately she felt like a butterfly trapped under a bell jar, beating its wings frantically against the glass, using up the last bit of oxygen before falling lifeless to the bottom of its prison. Was there no place where she could find elusive peace? No one who could bind her and keep her safe and still?

She suppressed the rising flutter of anxiety in her chest and the dream of a love she would never experience. The caring, nurturing feeling she craved didn't exist. There was only this— Master and pleasing Master. It was her life and her solemn vow.

Chapter One

Bryan looked around the bare study while sweat slicked his palms. Guys like him didn't usually get a shot at a project like this—the best supplies money could buy, the freedom to be artistic, naked women... His chuckle echoed in the almost empty room. Nope, nothing like carving a bunch of naked women to get his adrenaline pumping on a job.

After rubbing both hands dry on his jeans, he opened the packet of instructions from Gary Sanderson, the owner of this magnificent house. There wasn't much to go on, only some photos of the women to be carved and written instructions as promised. He spread the photographs out on the massive desk now covered by a drop cloth, and whistled long and low.

How the hell had Gary gotten these women to pose for him like this? The four beauties stared back at him. Well, not quite *at* him. More like off to the side or with gazes slightly downcast. All had long hair and pierced nipples, and a few had hoops nestled lower between the hairless outer lips of their pussies.

He pulled up a stool and sat. The photos had been done in sepia, probably by Gary himself. He was a photographer—the artsy kind with work in galleries in New York or LA and coffee table books about exotic places like Thailand and India. One thing was for sure... Gary wasn't hurting for money. Not with a place like this.

Bryan pushed the prickly twinge of jealousy aside and studied the photos. Faint highlights of color had been added to the women's eyes, cheeks and hair. The pictures reminded him of antique postcards he'd seen at flea markets on those rare days his grandfather would fire up the old Ford and venture off the reservation to Flagstaff. He shook his head. Grandfather had prepared him well for carpentry and carving—just not for this kind of subject matter. Maybe he'd send photos of his work back to the old man once the project was finished, let him know what his grandson was up to in the California. He laughed. No matter how badly Grandfather felt these days, he'd still get a kick out of that.

Next he pulled out the instructions, three short sentences typed in the middle of the page:

Capture the beauty of each, with a dove somewhere on every column.

Make the women appear to hold up the bookshelves in some manner.

Don't make them look too happy.

He reread the letter, but still it sounded like a fucking riddle. He'd expected something much more concrete. Which woman to carve where, that kind of thing. The last sentence struck him as strange—even a little cruel—but for the money he was being paid, Bryan wasn't about to quibble.

He hopped off the stool and inspected the four rough columns already in place around the room. The mahogany wouldn't be too much of a bitch to work with, but then again he would be doing this project solo. Gary had been adamant about that point, and Bryan let him win the battle, especially after refusing to work with teak as Gary had first requested. When he offered to double the pay, Bryan had held his ground.

"No endangered woods," he'd said, and the teak Gary had specified was definitely on that list. Bryan promised to find a compromise they could both be happy with. When he found out about an old lodge being sold off piece by piece, Gary didn't seem too convinced that the old mahogany pillars would be a good choice. But he paid for the wood anyway, probably because Bryan had agreed to start from scratch if he hated the end result. If Gary did hate it, Bryan would have to make room in a friend's garage for four naked ladies because he had a feeling he was going to fall in love with each creation after he was through.

He picked up the photographs, ready to slip them back into the envelope, but one image made him stop. All of the women were knock-out gorgeous: the full-breasted blonde, the raven-haired minx with a hint of a smirk curling her lips, the brunette with bold curves... He wondered if their coloring was true as he tucked each photo back into hiding. Except one. Another brunette, by the looks of her. What little he could see of her eyes told him they were a startling green. *Look up,* he wanted to say. *Don't be shy.*

She was petite, and her long hair reached her hips. He didn't usually go for delicate women—a big guy like him preferred something he could hold on to, a woman with a mouth that would reach his own as they fucked. This one would make him hesitant, protective even. He let go of the photo. Once it was safely inside, he fastened the envelope's clasp. *Time to get to work.*

Bryan found his pencil and sized up the first chunk of wood. He sketched the shape of a face then moved lower, listening to the mahogany as he drew. The sound of graphite against grain would lead him, tell him where to hack away and where to carve with care. When he was satisfied with the sketch, he dug a string out from his pocket and tied back his long hair to keep it out of his face as he worked. Next came the new chisels and gouges, courtesy of Gary, and the steady bang of his mallet against each tool. Except for his work, the house was quiet with nothing to distract him. Soon the smell of old wood filled the room, and chips and curls of it littered the floor to crunch beneath his work boots.

As the short morning shadows shifted into nothing, then stretched out again with the promise of late afternoon, he felt the first twinge of pain in his shoulders. A quick twist of his neck sent a cracking noise up through his spine. When he placed his U-gouge back into position, he noticed the time.

"Damn." He put down his tools. "No wonder my stomach was growling."

Bryan turned, ready to explore the kitchen that Gary had said was at his disposal, but stopped cold. The petite woman from the photo knelt in the hallway beyond, her shimmering chestnut hair covering shoulders and arms and thighs.

Covering too much, he thought. She held a platter in her trembling arms. Was she afraid of him? Or was the tray too heavy? He licked his lips, not quite knowing what to say to a woman he'd never expected to see in the flesh.

"Is that for me?" he asked.

She nodded slightly and lifted the tray higher. A thin band of silver encircling her neck glinted in the light as she moved. When a fork rattled on the metal tray, he rushed to relieve the woman of her burden.

"How long have you been here?"

"Not long, Sir." Her voice was barely audible, and he had to lean in to catch her last two words. Big mistake. She smelled of honeysuckle. His cock went from zero to full throttle in two seconds. And her little outfit of transparent scarves certainly didn't help the situation. Bryan stood there holding the tray like an idiot, as if he'd stepped into an episode of *The Twilight Zone*—the X-rated version. Was she a servant? A mistress? He forced himself to stop staring at her nearly nude body and gawked at his sandwich instead.

"Sir, if the sandwich isn't to your liking, or if you'd like fresh tea—"

"Fresh tea, eh? So you have been here a while."

She nodded then bowed her head lower as if she'd committed some offense.

"Next time, just come on in," he said. "No need to sit like that until I turn around, okay?"

More nodding. She didn't seem relieved, though. If anything, she seemed disappointed. He offered her a hand while balancing the tray in his other. She hesitated before accepting it. Her fingers felt cold and weightless in his palm. She slid her hand from his and, with a curt bob of her head, padded softly away on bare feet. He watched, hungrier for her than for the food. Four vivid butterfly tattoos in teals and deep reds decorated her back at the base of her spine in a tight geometric cluster and peeked out from behind the scarves as she moved. The bottoms of her small feet were dirty from going barefoot. He fought the urge to catch her. Carry her into the study and haul her lithe frame into his lap. He'd rub her feet clean with his bandana…

She must've known he was watching. As she turned toward the hallway that would take her farther into Gary's maze of a mansion, she slowed with one tiny foot lifted, its toes grazing the hardwood floor. She looked back. But she didn't look up.

It was the most erotic thing he'd ever seen.

The fork clattered on the tray again when he brought it close to his chest. The sound startled her into action, and she disappeared behind a corner.

Bryan took his lunch to the desk and gulped down a bite of the sandwich while his balls drew up tighter in his briefs. That's when he realized he'd never managed to look into her eyes.

The next day he was ready for her. Waiting for any small sound of her approach as his tools went deeper, carved faster. This was the easy part—removing chunks of wood on the sides to create a crude outline of the figure that would curve around the semicircle of reclaimed timber. It was a lot like peeling back layers, quick and impatient at first so he could get to the good stuff. Once the body was roughed out, he moved more slowly, careful not to go too far.

"Wood is not like clay," his grandmother had once told him. "You can put more clay on. Once wood is gone, that's it. *Ná'eeshnáád.*" Ruined.

He hadn't always appreciated her wisdom back then, or her recounting of the story about how clay came to his people, but now he missed those stories and understood all too well that one wrong move could result in days of work—and good materials—wasted. He forced his arm to slow then grabbed a smaller gouge. This pillar, the blonde, would be ready for the file soon.

The woman from yesterday had yet to make her appearance. He checked his watch. Not quite noon. His stomach rumbled, and his cock twitched in his jeans. He put his hands on the sculpture's shoulders, closed his eyes and felt for the places still needing work before moving on to the final stages of the process. His thumb playfully ran over a nipple, but his mind was on the barefoot angel he'd seen in the flesh. Last night he'd decided that she would be the last of the group he'd carve, and he had a feeling she'd be worth the wait.

His fingers trailed over a hip as he knelt to see how the bottom half was progressing. The blonde's legs were slightly spread apart, her weight resting awkwardly on the balls of her arched feet. A few rough patches here and there, but he'd make quick work of those. As he stood again, footsteps sounded in the hallway. He rose but didn't turn. Her steps sounded louder, more confident. He closed his eyes. Listened. He didn't want her to kneel today, and when she reached the threshold to the study, he turned around.

Disappointment hit him like a brick. It wasn't her.

An ebony-haired woman sank slowly to the floor. She kept her eyes downcast, but the haughty tilt of her chin didn't quite fit the picture of subservience. He recognized her from the photos. The smirking one. He couldn't help but grin—this one was trouble.

"Hi there," he said.

She met his gaze, which was having a tough time staying on her blue eyes. Unlike yesterday's maid, or whatever she was, this one wore no clothes at all. She knelt on the floor, tray upraised, perky breasts thrusting out proudly for his inspection.

"It's my pleasure to serve you today, Sir."

"Thank you, uh..."

"Jasmine," she offered.

Jasmine. His sketch of her sculpture flashed through his

mind. He'd need to go back and add the flower of her namesake.

"Nice to meet you, Jasmine." He leaned against the doorframe and watched as she lifted the tray higher while easing her legs apart. Her jaunty nipples pointed his way, their elaborate rings each dangling a tiny bell as she moved. He laughed to himself. Subtlety wasn't her strength. He took the tray, expecting her legs to scoot together again. Instead she placed a hand on the floor and leaned backward into a seductive pose. Her legs opened wider to reveal a trio of gold hoops, one at the hood of her clit and the other two emerging from the frilled lips below. His cock responded automatically, rising and hardening.

"Where's the woman who served me yesterday?"

Jasmine's eyes rolled. "Oh, Butterfly? Trust me, whatever she did for you, I can do better."

Modest, too, he thought. *Better set the record straight.*

"She only brought me lunch."

That seemed to lift Jasmine's spirits. And her body. She rose and walked right up to him then returned to kneeling.

"Good," she whispered. "That means I'll be the first in this household to serve you properly."

He nearly dropped his lunch when her hand found the outline of his erection through his jeans.

"Sorry." She giggled, took the tray from him and set it on the floor.

When her hand lifted for his crotch again, he caught her wrist. "Listen, sweetheart. You're obviously Gary's girlfriend or companion or something. I've been hired to do a job, and I don't want to blow it—"

"But I do." She grinned and unbuttoned his jeans. The metallic rasp of his zipper sounded too loud in the air. He looked to the hall for any signs of company. There were none, so he loosened his grip on her arm.

"Master instructed us to serve you in any way," she continued. "It will be my pleasure. Think of it as a perk that comes with the job." Her fingers worked their way into his briefs as the words she spoke finally made a connection in his head.

"Master?"

She nodded, her head bobbing like it would on his cock soon if he didn't stop her. Christ, he hadn't had a blowjob since Simone... He'd be a fool to pass this up. An image of Butterfly popped into his head. Made him pull back. He glanced down at Jasmine. Although she was naked and on her knees, an "I'm better than you" smirk curled her ruby lips. Even her pout reminded him of his ex—and anything that brought back memories of that stuck-up bitch wasn't worth the suck.

"Sorry, Jasmine. Maybe some other time." He zipped up and slid out from the tight space between her body and the doorjamb.

She had the nerve to look hurt. He bent down to her level. "I appreciate the offer but need to make sure this kind of thing is okay with your, um, master. It just doesn't feel right."

Her arms crossed under her breasts and lifted them higher. "Didn't Master say you could help yourself to anything in his house while you were working?"

"Yes, but you're not a thing. You're a person. There's a difference."

She shook her head. Long raven strands cascaded over her breasts. He stood before the temptation to touch her dark pink nipples won out over his common sense. You didn't go into a man's house and mess with his woman—or women.

"Not in Master's house," she whispered slyly. "Here I'm only a slave, and I am to serve you in any way you please."

"A slave? You mean like a sex slave?" His heart jolted with a mixture of dismay and lust. Should he be worried? Was he involved in something illegal just by being here?

"By choice," she added. "We've all signed contracts. We all want to be here. It's not like we've been kidnapped or anything. This is a lifestyle choice." She grinned, and when she moved the tinkling of the little bells made music at the end of their hoops.

He resisted the urge to bend down and grab one. To help her up and pull her into the study. She'd look like heaven spread out on the drape-covered desk, her pussy his for the taking. He closed his eyes and pictured her there. She'd smile as his cock pressed into her...

Butterfly wouldn't smile so easily. Her expression would be serious. The sex would probably be serious, too. Earning her smile would be a challenge, and when it came, it would be fleeting and elusive, like her name. The next time he saw Gary, he'd find out exactly what went on at this house. Bryan sucked air through his teeth as the woman began fingering herself. Hell, when he'd interviewed for this project, he knew something wasn't quite right. At first he assumed Gary got all his money from drugs or by some other illegal means, but the prestigious photography gig laid that theory to rest. He'd even looked Gary up on the Internet and, sure enough, his name was associated with galleries all over the world—and a few museums. But the guy had been so secretive, so cryptic, that Bryan swore he'd find a few skeletons in the closet once he got on site. He just hadn't expected skeletons of the naked, sex slave variety.

So he'd talk to Gary. Find out what the fuck was going on— not in a judgmental way, but with an approach that would uncover the full story about what he could expect as he worked on this project, and others. Gary had made it clear that if he did good work with these sculptures, other projects were up for grabs. Maybe he should go ahead and ask about those projects too. Then he'd ask for Butterfly—if she'd have him. Unlike Jasmine, Butterfly didn't seem too eager for his company.

"Thanks for lunch, Jasmine. I'd better eat and get back to work."

Her smile faded into a frown when he grabbed the tray from the floor and retreated into the study. As he bit into his sandwich, he heard her huff with anger, stomping down the hallway like a sullen child. At that moment he wasn't certain whether to envy or pity Gary. Sure, all those women would be fun to bed, but if Jasmine was any indication, managing four women would keep a man's hands full. In more ways than one.

Gary, my man, I don't envy you one bit. Because, slaves or not, a house filled with women could be a helluva lot of trouble.

Chapter Two

Butterfly had wiped every last smear from the full-length oval mirror in the hallway. She'd polished every inch of the ornate gold frame, even detailing it with a Q-tip, but still she continued to rub and polish, as one minute after another slipped by. She couldn't take her eyes from the reflection of the giant working in the other room. The mirror was angled to show the study where he carved one of the large pillars. When he stepped back to study it, his face and entire body were reflected in the glass, but he was so intent on his work, he didn't seem aware of her working quietly in the hallway and watching him. The man was less intimidating at a distance, where she could study him at her leisure.

The way his big hands handled the tools was fascinating. As the carving grew finer, the chisels he chose were smaller and he handled them even more delicately, shaving off tiny shreds of wood. There was a frown of concentration furrowing his thick, dark eyebrows. He leaned in to blow away a bit of wood from the carving, and his full lips pursed slightly. A shiver ran through her as she imagined what those lips might feel like pressed against hers.

Leaning back, he regarded his work, impatiently pushing his hair away from his face. Today it wasn't secured, but flowed long and loose down his back. What would it feel like to stroke? Soft and smooth as the raven's feathers it resembled or coarse and thick? And what was she doing imagining such things or even looking at the stranger?

She turned back to her work, rubbing hard at a little fleck on the surface of the glass. There was no reason for her to be here any longer. The mirror was as clean as brand new. Butterfly looked at herself in the glass: wide eyes, flushed pink cheeks, lips parted and damp from her tongue running over them. She looked feverish and hungry, like a woman anticipating sex. This was wrong. It wasn't what Master had meant when he told her to make the carpenter comfortable and please him in any way he desired. She was meant to fulfill those duties with non-attachment, as one of her owner's dictates, not with lust and longing in her heart. But she couldn't deny that arousal and sexual curiosity were exactly what she felt when she looked at the woodworker. When Jasmine had taken her place serving the handsome stranger his food yesterday, she'd wanted to storm in there and pull the girl out of the room by her hair. Today Butterfly would make sure she was the one to supply his afternoon break.

Once more she glanced in the mirror—just to see if the man looked like he might be ready for a snack. He was staring back at her, his dark eyes focused on her reflection in the mirror.

She froze, the dust cloth clenched in one fist and her gaze locked with his. What did she look like to him? Long, straight brown hair framed her heart-shaped face. Her eyes were too large for her face, her chin and nose too pointed. She must look like a little mouse to him.

Master had taught her well that demurely downcast eyes best illustrated subservience, but somehow it was impossible for her to look away from the man in the mirror.

He smiled at her, strong, white teeth flashing against his dark face, and lifted a hand in greeting. "Hey," he called from the other room.

Instinctively, she raised her hand in return, waving at him through the safe remove of the mirror.

"Want to come see what I'm working on?" His voice was low and cajoling, the timbre as warm as banked coals. When she hesitated, he said, "Come on."

She couldn't disobey a direct order. Dropping her rag on

the floor, she turned from the mirror and crossed the hall to enter the study. Now that she faced him, she could no longer hold his gaze. She examined the floor, the draped desk, the toes of his big boots. She raised her head slightly higher and took in his jeans up to where they met the hem of his T-shirt. "May I get you something to eat or drink, Sir?"

"No, thanks. I have my water here." He gestured to a bottle sitting on one of the bookshelves. "I don't need anything else. I just wondered if you'd like to see your portrait. And if you wouldn't mind not calling me 'sir'." He laughed. "Makes me feel old."

She started to explain that it was meant to show respect, but her eyes shot to the column he'd been working on instead. "Me?"

"This one is. The rest have roughed-in shapes of the other women on them. I was going to save yours for last, but I was inspired to work on it today." He shifted closer, more of him filling her view. "Are you... Do you, uh, work for Mr. Sanderson?"

"I serve him."

"Like a maid or housekeeper or something?" Ducking his head, he tried to move his face into her line of sight. She caught a hint of a teasing grin curving his generous mouth. He had to know what she was, especially after meeting Jasmine. The girl would've told him, flaunted it even.

She turned away, gazing at his artwork rather than at him. "He's my Master. I belong to him."

"Huh." The man didn't say anything for a moment, and her stomach tightened as she thought how strange it must sound to an outsider, someone who didn't understand. "That's what that girl Jasmine said. I thought maybe she was kidding, that it was some kind of game."

"No." Moving closer to the mahogany column, she examined the freshly carved surface. Butterfly's features were carefully rendered in the wooden woman, but none of her inner flaws were recorded. The artist's version was pure and angelic, not unworthy as she knew herself to be.

"So all these women living here seriously consider themselves slaves?"

She took a quick, deep breath. *Here goes.* "We've each entered into a contract with our Master. We're his by choice." She wondered if she'd spoken too much. It was hard to know how much she was allowed to reveal to this man. Master hadn't really told her.

"I'm not quite sure how to respond to that." He moved up behind her to study the carving, too, and changed the subject. "I haven't got this quite right. If you could pose for me, it would help."

She felt the heat his big body radiated from inches away and glanced sideways at him, her gaze lifting no higher than his waist. The hard bulge of an erection was visible at the fly of his blue jeans.

Master had told her to please him in every way. "The man is doing some beautiful work," he'd said. "I want to show him my appreciation and hospitality. Food, drink, sex, whatever he needs, you supply. Got it?"

Butterfly gestured to his crotch. "May I service you?" Her voice was low, barely a whisper. Even after all these years she had trouble offering sexual favors to Master's friends or business associates. She would do anything to please him, but offering her body to strangers was still terribly difficult. With this man, however, it was not so hard. Not when curiosity made her want to see what lay behind his fly.

There was a long moment of silence. The click of his throat as he swallowed was audible in the quiet room. "That's a...a very generous offer. Thank you, but...no."

She bobbed her head in acknowledgement and turned to leave, cheeks burning, disappointment surging through her. What would it have been like to unzip those jeans and release his cock into her hand? Was it long and thick or thinner and smaller than she imagined? Did it crook to the right or left? Was it circumcised or not? It would probably be even darker than the rest of the man's skin, a deep mahogany like the columns he carved.

"Wait!" He grabbed her arm and a warm tingle sprang from the point of contact. The pads of his fingers were thick and callused, a workingman's hands, so different from Master's kid-glove softness. "I mean, wait." He assumed a more casual tone. "Stay a while. Talk to me."

She couldn't physically leave. He was holding her arm. But inside, she hesitated. Was talking allowed? Master had said to entertain the man in any way he desired, but what if he became angry with her for chatting with this stranger?

"What's your name?" the rumbling voice continued. "Mine's Bryan Lapahie."

"My Master calls me Butterfly." Her lips shaped the words and a whisper of sound came out.

"Butterfly. That's very appropriate. You're as delicate and pretty as one."

The compliment was so unexpected she almost forgot the correct response. "Thank you."

"Actually, the woman yesterday already told me your nickname. I meant your real name."

"Butterfly is my only name."

"Okay...Butterfly."

She dared to glance at his face. His grin grew wider, as if he thought she was teasing.

"Sit down for a minute, please. It would really help me if I could study your face for a while." He gestured to a chair.

She hesitated. None of the slaves were allowed on the furniture unless given permission by Master. The prohibition was a sign of their low status, a reminder that they were no more than pets in his household. But the guest had given her an order and so she perched carefully on the very edge of the cushion, hands folded in her lap, eyes still focused diffidently on the floor.

He stood before her for a long moment then suddenly dropped to a squat in front of her. The level made it almost impossible for her not to look into his eyes, but she managed by staring just past his shoulder. He rested a hand lightly on her knee, heavy and warm.

"Can you tell me a little more about yourself, how you came to be here, how all of these women chose to...sign a contract with Gary?"

She bit her lip. So many questions. What was safe to answer? Better not to talk at all. She shook her head in answer.

"You can't tell me?"

"It's not my place to discuss Master's private business, and I don't know the journeys that led the other women to him."

"What is it 'your place' to do? What are your duties here? I mean, besides serving food, polishing mirrors, and offering men blowjobs."

"I clean Master's house and make sure his meals are ready, supervising the others' kitchen work. I keep this body prepared for him to use as he wishes, and serve him in any way he commands."

"What do *you* get from this arrangement?" Bryan sounded honestly curious. His head cocked to the side as he again tried to catch her shifting gaze. "How does it benefit you?"

"My pleasure is in giving Master pleasure. My satisfaction is in serving him and subjugating my will to his." It was more than she'd spoken in a long time. Saying it reminded her of the profound truth behind the words, something she'd forgotten and questioned recently. A surge of devotion warmed her at the thought of Master, who'd guided and sheltered her when she needed it most. He was fashioning her into the best version of herself she could possibly be, and she owed everything to him.

"It sounds..." He trailed off, and they both sat in silence for several long moments. "Are you happy?"

She didn't answer. He clearly didn't understand her life or he wouldn't ask such an inane question. How could her happiness possibly matter? All that mattered was the act of obedience.

He didn't press her. "Do you mind if I turn your face? Like this." A huge, warm hand suddenly cupped her chin and turned her face to the left and slightly up. Now there was no way she could help but see his face unless she closed her eyes. "I need to see your eyes in order to do my work. You'll really be helping me out."

She sat still as stone without blinking and stared at the harsh angles of his face, the sharp cheekbones, prominent nose, and angular jaw. Two black eyebrows were straight and heavy over his deep-set, dark eyes. She looked lower, to his mouth. It was wide, generous and smiling at her. His hand lingered on the curve of her cheek, rough fingers feeling the texture of her skin before dropping away.

"Stay just like that," he ordered, and since it was an order, she couldn't disobey.

Picking up a pad of paper and pencil, he began to sketch. "This isn't really my medium. I prefer to work with wood, but I can draw well enough and I want some sketches to reference later."

Her eyes felt dry from holding them open and still for so long. She blinked.

"Are you from San Diego originally?" He glanced back and forth between her face and the sketchbook.

"No. Connecticut."

There was a pause while he waited for her to tell him more about her past, her childhood, her life before coming here. But he couldn't know that anything she told about that girl would be unrelated to who she was now. Her former life and relationship with her parents was long gone, dead. Now she was her Master's butterfly.

"I'm from Arizona myself. Lived with my grandparents on the Rez until I was eighteen then I took off. Couldn't wait to shake off the dust." He paused to look at her. At first she thought he was simply studying her for the drawing, but her intuition, well-honed from gauging Master's moods, signaled there was more, a certain tension in his silence. Suddenly, Butterfly realized he was waiting for her reaction to his heritage. Was it possible this bold, confident man felt some inadequacy about his background? And why would he care about her opinion?

When she didn't reply, Bryan continued his narrative. "Anyway, job opportunities were kind of limited so I ended up in the Army." He laughed, a deep, rich sound that startled her. She studied his grinning face since his eyes were once more trained on his drawing. Warm. Earthy. Those were the words that described his face, voice and manner.

"Yeah, that didn't work out too well," he continued. "My temperament didn't suit Uncle Sam. I'm a little too opinionated and stubborn for that kind of discipline. The Army and I parted ways as soon as my stint was over." He chuckled again. "Almost sooner. I came close to being court-martialed, but that's a long story."

He fell silent for several moments. She was afraid he was done telling his story and she wanted to hear more. "Then?" she prodded quietly.

Glancing up, he looked into her eyes, holding her pinned for a moment. "Ah, so you are listening. I thought maybe I'd put you to sleep."

She shook her head slightly. Using every ounce of her will, she dragged her gaze from his and focused somewhere to the left of his ear again—a nice ear, well shaped and half-hidden by a curtain of long, black hair.

"A buddy of mine from the service lived in San Diego so I thought I'd check it out. We shared an apartment for a while, then...a woman happened and I moved in with her. I worked construction and met a master woodworker, Darryl Johansen, who taught me the craft. My Grandpa Butch had taught me the basics, but my apprenticeship with Darryl opened a whole new world. Suddenly I had a career instead of a string of random jobs."

Butterfly wanted to ask about the woman. The shadow of pain coloring his voice when he mentioned her suggested their relationship had not ended well. Had she hurt him, maybe left him or cheated on him?

"Now I work for myself. People pass my name along and I have almost more jobs than I can handle. But this," he gestured at a column, "is by far the best-paying gig I've ever had. Not to mention the sexiest." He grinned again, white teeth flashing against bronze skin.

Instinctively she smiled back. A little of his exuberance overflowed into her and curved her lips.

"There! That's what I was missing. Hold that smile. My God, the sun's come out!"

His joking made her laugh, and she covered her mouth, trying to hold back the light, mirthful sound.

"Don't." He took her hand, pulling it away from her face and setting it back in her lap. "You can laugh." Once more he cupped her face, and his thumb traced her lips. "It's all right to smile."

Her pussy tightened and released, throbbing with her heartbeats. Moisture wet her inner thighs. Her nipples peaked against the silky fabric of her top as his thumb lingered on her mouth and he focused there. She liked his touch too much. The urge to open her mouth and suck his thumb inside was almost too strong to resist.

He wanted to kiss her. He was poised on the edge of leaning in and doing it, she could tell. What would she do if he did? Run away or kiss him back? Kissing was much too personal and therefore forbidden by Master. She might service his guests, allowing them to use her body in any way they desired, but they never kissed her. That indulgence was reserved for Master alone, when he chose to exercise it, which wasn't often.

The moment might have spun out forever, but a woman's cough from the doorway disturbed the stillness. Their heads swiveled simultaneously toward the sound.

Jasmine, wearing black leather fetishwear, stood there with a tray in her hands and a smirk on her face. "I've brought you a snack, Sir. Would you like it now or should I come back when you've...finished."

Bryan's hand dropped from Butterfly's face. "Just set it somewhere. Thanks." His tone was curt.

Jasmine dipped her head in acknowledgement of the order and placed the tray on the desk. She turned toward them and stood there, not kneeling as she'd been taught to do in the presence of a man, her challenging eyes studying Bryan. The sleek ebony strips of her outfit served to show off her tan skin in delectable slices that fired the imagination about the parts concealed. Her pussy and tits were just barely covered, and she'd changed her regular slave collar for something a little more festive with pointed silver studs. Jasmine blatantly stared at them for a moment. "Butterfly, we need your help. There's a plumbing issue."

Butterfly's mouth tightened. "Then you should call a plumber," she snapped.

Bryan snorted.

She glanced at him. His wide mouth curved into a grin that creased his cheek. An answering mirth bubbled up inside her, a light, happy feeling filling her like helium. The sound surprised her, and it didn't last long. She turned back to Jasmine. "I'll be along in a few minutes. You may go now."

Jasmine's smirk disintegrated into a scowl, but she bowed her head. Tossing a last hot, lustful glance at Bryan to remind him she was available any time, she retreated from the room.

"That girl's trouble," he remarked after she'd gone. "Bet she's a bitch to live with."

Butterfly didn't answer, but her expression left no doubt that he'd pegged Jasmine dead-on. *You have no idea...* She should go now. Lingering here would only give Jasmine fuel for spreading gossip and innuendo. The brat could find a way to make her look bad, even though she hadn't done anything except pose for the artist and listen to him talk. Butterfly had nothing to hide from her Master. She'd merely entertained their guest as requested. If, in her heart, she'd enjoyed it too much, it was no one's business but her own. Well, maybe Master's, but she'd worry about that later.

"A house full of sex slaves," Bryan muttered. "Unbelievable." He reached out and touched the silver collar around her neck. "So, this symbolizes your, uh, status as a slave?"

She nodded. The constricting weight was always present,

reminding her of who and what she was.

"And you've worn this how long?"

"Five years."

"Wow," he breathed. "That long? Does he... Does your master treat you well?"

Her mind flashed back to her punishment for the wine stain a couple of weeks ago. Hours tied spread-eagle and upright between two posts beneath the open sky as sunlight and moonlight traded places. The cold breeze had raised goose pimples on her skin and the hot sun burned her. She suffered the complete helplessness of being exposed to the elements and to the observation of Master's friends he'd invited to witness her torment. Her tortured muscles strained from stretching for hour after hour, but worse was the humiliation of urinating because she couldn't hold it anymore and standing over the puddle. Eventually anxiety had turned to mindless exhaustion. She would have preferred being locked in a small, dark space for twenty times as long. Binding and confinement were a pleasure to her compared to the agony of open spaces.

"My Master disciplines me when he must. He knows what's best for my development."

"Oh, really?" Bryan scoffed.

She froze, fixing her gaze on the carpet, her jaw tightening.

"Sorry. I shouldn't put down your arrangement. I don't really know anything about your lifestyle, but I'm sure it gives you something you need or you wouldn't be living it."

"If you're finished with me, there are duties I must attend to. May I go now?"

For a moment, she thought he would forbid it, make her stay longer so he could ply her with more questions, but he nodded. "Sure. Wouldn't want Jasmine flooding the mansion 'cause she tried to fix that 'plumbing issue' herself."

His comment made her smile again though she fought to keep the corners of her mouth from turning up.

"Keep on smiling, Butterfly. It suits you," Bryan said as she walked from the room.

Keep on smiling. The words echoed in her head while she searched for Jasmine to check out her story. For the first time in a really long while, she actually wanted to smile. Bryan's presence in the house, her curiosity about him and his life in the outside world—these things made her feel alive. Not the panicky "I'm alive, but I'm going to die" feeling she got when faced with open spaces or a sea of anonymous faces in a crowd. No, this was an energy that made her feel like something new was almost in her grasp.

She reached the second floor with still no sign of Jasmine. Except for the faint sounds of Bryan's work, the house was silent as usual...no creaking floors as the other women padded barefoot to do their chores, no sounds of a flood or flushing toilets. Butterfly rolled her eyes at the girl's obvious attempt to lure her away from the carpenter. Master had favored Jasmine all week, as had Gary's friends the weekend before. How much cock did one girl need?

Footsteps sounded on the hall above her. Probably Jasmine on her way to see Bryan now that he was alone. A bowl of green peppers beckoned on the kitchen counter beyond. She pushed an image of Jasmine pleasing Bryan from her mind and got to work slicing the colorful vegetables into strips for tonight's stir-fry. After rinsing her hands, she poked her head into the freezer to look for some chicken. The door to the garage slammed just as she found a packet of breasts.

She closed the door and listened. The soles of her Master's expensive shoes strode across tile and wood then clicked up the stairs. She followed slowly. At the base of the third floor staircase, voices stopped Butterfly in her tracks. The conversation was distant, but she could feel the anger. She stood, listening. The cheerful clip of Jasmine's words made Butterfly want to bang her head on the nearest wall. Master's answering voice was like a whip crack. Her feet became a blur on the steps as she raced upstairs toward the sound of confrontation. Whatever trouble Jasmine had gotten herself into, her offhand manner was making it worse.

Butterfly headed for the voices and saw right away what

the trouble was. It seemed Jasmine hadn't lied about a plumbing issue after all. Water puddled around the base of the toilet from an overflow, and foolish Jasmine had called Master home instead of tending to it herself. Butterfly cringed, wishing she'd come when Jasmine asked for help instead of lingering with Bryan.

She stopped in the bathroom doorway, taking in the scene before her; water up to the rim of the toilet and Jasmine kneeling on the wet floor at Master's feet. He spun around to face Butterfly, an angry scowl twisting his features.

"Where the hell have you been?"

She glanced down. His large hands were covered in rubber cleaning gloves, *her* gloves, which were way too small for his broad palms—palms she'd probably feel across her ass and thighs any moment now if she didn't answer him. His fists clenched tighter as he waited.

She stared at the swirling toilet that had recently overflowed and threatened to do so again any minute. "The carpenter, Sir. He asked to sketch me."

Inwardly, she winced. How dare she blame someone else for neglecting a household issue? Shame burned her cheeks. Jasmine sat on her heels, the handle of a dripping plunger resting lengthways across her thighs, her usual smirk in place.

"I'm sorry, Sir." There was nothing else to say.

"Jasmine was forced to call me during an important lunch meeting because of your unwillingness to address this problem. So save the apology, Butterfly. I'll pin you for this later."

Every muscle in her body stiffened at the word "pin". Jasmine's eyes cut to the side and met hers. She even had the nerve to quirk an eyebrow.

"But your punishment will be nothing compared to what *she'll* be getting tonight." His scowl fell on Jasmine.

Jasmine's smirk faded.

Master bent toward the sitting woman and showed her what he held in each tight fist. "I believe I found the problem here."

Jasmine gave the soggy clusters of tampons a passing glance before tilting her head toward Butterfly. "They're probably hers."

Butterfly's eyes stretched so wide they hurt. To lie to Master was bad enough, but to speak without being asked would land Jasmine in more hot water. More than she may be able to handle. The tampons looked unused, and Butterfly had yet to ask for her monthly allotment from Master. Had Jasmine stolen them from the others? Butterfly wouldn't put it past her and she held her breath, waiting for the drama to play itself out.

Master ignored the girl's lack of respect and leaned in closer. "Do you think I'm a fool, that I don't know my own property? I know when you piss. Hell, I know when you breathe." He let the tampons drop to the floor beside Jasmine. "And I sure as hell know when my slaves are ready to bleed each month."

"But mine hasn't yet come," Jasmine protested. "I'm—"

"It hasn't yet come, *Sir*. Honestly, slave, your insolence is no longer amusing. Stand up."

Jasmine shifted nervously on her ankles. The plunger rolled from her legs. Master picked it up and studied the flanged end of it. "I'm tempted to make you lick it clean." He thrust it toward her face and held it there until the trembling pink of Jasmine's tongue emerged. Butterfly watched in horror as he yanked it away a split second before her tongue made contact. Master slammed the plunger into the wall above Jasmine's head, cracking drywall before it hit the Italian marble floor.

"Why the hell aren't you standing yet?"

Up Jasmine went. A delicate sheen of sweat dotted the space above her red upper lip. *Don't gloat,* Butterfly told herself. *That'll only make it worse when your next time to be disciplined comes.* But in truth she couldn't help it.

"Butterfly, bring me a pair of shears and find the others. Tell them to bring me their monthly supply of tampons." He pressed Jasmine into the damaged wall behind her. "I intend to make an example out of this liar that won't soon be forgotten."

Butterfly's feet couldn't move fast enough. She raced to the kitchen and grabbed the utility scissors, then found Sapphire and Violet polishing silver in the main dining room. She told them of Master's request before returning to the bathroom.

Butterfly wordlessly offered him the shears, her heart pounding from the run. He inspected the blunt tips with exaggerated concern. Jasmine looked faint.

As the other two women joined them, Butterfly noticed that gooseflesh pebbled Violet's arms when she passed by.

"Sir, may I speak?" she asked, head bowed, lower lip trembling.

"Are you missing something, Violet?"

"Yes, Sir. You gave me my parcel yesterday, but only three remain and I haven't started—"

Master raised his hand to silence her. Then he placed that same hand on the wall above Jasmine's head. "Turn around, slave, and brace yourself."

Jasmine did as she was told. Her thighs trembled. Butterfly trembled as well. Master never punished a slave while still angry. At least he hadn't in the time she'd known him. He always kept his distance until his temper had cooled. But not today. The look on his face told her this would be no ordinary punishment. The scissors opened. He positioned them at one of the black straps crisscrossing Jasmine's back and snipped.

Butterfly thought of her first day in this house, the embarrassment of being stripped of all her clothing, of staying naked for months until Master had thought her worthy enough of any type of garments. "You'll have to earn them," he'd told her...by servicing his friends. She'd been slow to do so, and she had the sparsest wardrobe in the house to prove it. Jasmine, however, serviced anyone and everyone. The little get-up Master was now destroying slowly had cost her probably many blowjobs. Butterfly watched as the outfit landed in strips on the glossy marble below.

"You're a liar and a thief. How unworthy you are in my eyes

today." His voice, an ominous hiss, made Butterfly's flesh prickle as Violet's had.

When Jasmine spoke, Butterfly could hear the anger. The fear. "I didn't...Sir," she said between gritted teeth, the pause before giving him respect deliberate. "It was Butterfly."

Butterfly wanted to shake her. *Don't make this worse on yourself! And don't make it worse on us.* When Master was upset with one of them, he took his anger out on them all.

"You're mine, slave. I know everything about you." The shears rose higher along her back. "So I know what a little shit-stirrer you are."

The scissors pressed on in their ascent, clipping here and there as they rose. Jasmine made the mistake of reaching back to lift her long hair.

"Did I say you could move?"

"No, Sir, I just—"

The slap of his gloved hand on Jasmine's upper thigh startled each woman. Butterfly jumped. Violet gasped, but Sapphire stayed silent. Jasmine? She broke position, the worst possible reaction of all. The women waited for the spanking to continue. Instead, he forced her against the wall, her breasts crushing into a towel bar as he kept snipping. At the straps. At her tresses. A mix of leather and hair covered the floor. Jasmine wept. Sincerely, by the sound of it.

Surely he won't cut it all off, Butterfly thought. But the metallic rasp of the shears didn't stop, not when the girl stood completely naked and sobbing. Not when she started to fight their Master.

"Hold her," he ordered.

Violet rushed forward to grasp Jasmine's shoulder. The shears reached Jasmine's scalp. Soon, white patches of skin shone through short tufts of black all over her head.

"Leave. All of you." Well, everyone but Jasmine. Master held her weeping body flat against the wall. "And Sapphire, go suck the carpenter—quickly—and tell him to take the rest of the day off."

A strange and sudden jealousy stabbed at Butterfly's heart as she followed the others out of the room. He'd refused Jasmine—and herself—but could he resist the pretty blonde and her full, pink lips? Then she wondered if he'd heard Jasmine's cries. Probably not—the study was far away from this wing of the house. But the tone of Master's words told her that he wanted the carpenter gone from the premises for a reason. For the first time since Jasmine's arrival, Butterfly felt sympathy for another girl's punishment, and in the hours that followed, she retreated to the far end of the house to tidy things that didn't need attention or polish yet another mirror. Worry nagged her thoughts with every scream echoing through the walls. When Jasmine's wails finally ceased, it was time for bed.

The three women retreated to the basement and into their pens. Each door slid shut as Jasmine's footsteps sounded across the cement in an odd-sounding gait. Butterfly settled onto her cot.

"Are you okay?"

It was Violet. Butterfly seriously doubted she had asked out of sympathy. No, Violet wanted to hear all the gory details while she listened in her stall smiling away at the new slave's plight. Especially after today's theft.

When Jasmine didn't answer, Violet changed the subject to the carpenter. "So how was he, Sapphire?"

Butterfly steeled herself for the answer. Part of her would be jealous, but another part, the disloyal part, wondered what it would've been like. How did he taste? How did he feel in Sapphire's hands as she sucked? She would hang on the woman's every word and pretend that it was her worshipping his cock, not Sapphire. Desire burned through her, warming her insides and drying her throat. Her fingers trailed down to her pussy, ready to play in the wetness growing there while Sapphire painted pictures in her mind.

"He wasn't interested," the slave replied softly.

Relief washed through Butterfly. Her fingers found a purpose without words to guide them. When the pad of one fingertip circled her clit, she lifted her hips from the mattress and relished the climb toward orgasm. At the first tingle of warning, she pulled her finger away, only for a few seconds. She savored the steady throb, the contraction of her heart and each subsequent release. Awareness of every pore flooded her senses, heightening the thrill of touching herself while thinking of *his* hands on her, the way he'd touched her face...

A quick tap of her clit sent her over the edge, pelvis grinding, muscles tightening to push her faster. Harder. Her upper body curled away from the bedding and her left hand clapped over her mouth to squelch a moan.

The crackle of Master's intercom by her head made her catch her breath. "Enjoying yourself, Butterfly?"

Just a leg cramp, she wanted to say, but she knew better than to lie. "Yes, Sir, but I've earned it."

And she had. Three white tokens on the floor beside her symbolized her freedom to choose pleasure by her own hand. She swallowed, but there was no saliva. It was as if every bit of moisture in her body had pooled between her thighs.

"I expect you to return a token first thing tomorrow morning."

"Yes, Sir. May I get some water, sir?"

"Make it quick."

When the buzzer sounded on the lock, she pressed against the heavy door. The water did little to soothe her throat, for every time she took a sip, it was Bryan she would taste—salty skin, tea on his tongue. The musky flavor of his semen. The kitchen intercom filled the room with her Master's irritated baritone.

"Are you done yet?"

She set the empty glass in the sink. "Yes, Sir."

On her way back to the stall, she hesitated at her doorway, then walked as silently as she could to Jasmine's resting place. Butterfly peeked inside the bars, but reared back almost immediately. Even in the darkness, she could see the bloody welts on Jasmine's thighs, back and ass. The girl whimpered into her bedding, a shaky hand trailing over her head, feeling for hair that wasn't there. Maybe pinning wasn't so bad after all…

Butterfly returned to her pen, slid the door in place and gathered the thick covers around her. It warmed her body but did little to comfort her, not when thoughts about today's events ran through her head again. Bryan's touch. Master's anger. She tried taking solace in the confines of the small, dark space next. A little better… After catching a fistful of her long, heavy hair, she prayed she'd never lose it, then covered her face with it like a blanket.

Chapter Three

Bryan shoved his chair back from the end of the tiny kitchen table in his even tinier dining room and resisted the urge to scream at the computer.

"Goddamn dial-up."

Wolf whimpered in sympathy, but the big mutt didn't move when Bryan carefully stepped over him to make his way through the obstacle course that was his undersized, overpriced apartment. He wasn't a slob, but there was no place to put his stuff, and being in a house like Gary's all day made it hard as hell to come back to this crappy place. His big body was forever bumping into things, like the pointy edges of countertops or the oven knobs just now when he opened the fridge door to get some orange juice. He craved space, the wide-open kind with nothing but air and sky and dirt. Ten years back when he'd said good-bye to Navajoland, he thought he'd never miss it. Miss his family, yeah. But the rest of it? No way. He'd only visited about once every three years since he left. And after he'd foolishly taken Simone with him the last time, viewing it through her critical eyes had only confirmed his belief that he came from a dump.

Compared to his grandparents' home, this one-bedroom apartment had once seemed like a step up. But when business took you into the kinds of houses Bryan had only seen in *Architectural Digest* or on TV, jealousy was only natural. He tried not to let it eat at him and funneled those emotions into work instead. They didn't call him Bust-ass Bryan on his last job for nothing.

"One day, boy, I swear. You'll get a big house. A big yard, too." He raised the glass in promise then took a gulp.

Wolf lifted an eyebrow then let it slowly sink back down. His eyes closed. The run earlier had been good for both of them. After today's frustrations—a little more envy over Gary's luxurious lifestyle and a lot of temptation—exercise was a good way to ease into evening and prepare him for what was left of the day.

When the juice was gone, Bryan picked up the phone. He had to make the call to his grandparents he'd been putting off all week. If he couldn't get around to making a visit, the least he could do was check in now and then. But lately bad news was all he ever got on the other end of the line, and it made it harder to dial the number. After several rings, his grandmother finally picked up.

"*Yá'át'ééh, shimá sání.*"

She returned the greeting but there was a weariness to her tone, more so than usual. In the background, he could hear his grandfather coughing.

"How is he?" asked Bryan.

"All the better for you calling. Let me see if he can talk."

There was a rustling of sheets and a hacking cough that echoed through the phone as Bryan pictured his grandfather trying to sit up in the small bed. Few words were spoken, but each that left Bryan's lips burdened his heart with guilt.

"After this job, I'll take a break. I'll come back," he promised.

"Your voice is enough, Grandson."

The words in Diné soothed him, their cadence matching the painful rhythm of his heart. But when his grandmother came back on the line, her words confirmed the worst.

"Soon, Bryan. Soon," she said quietly.

Bryan closed his eyes. "What happened to fifty-fifty? I liked those odds."

Grandpa Butch had liked them, too, keeping up with

treatment when most Navajo would've given up. They didn't call cancer "the sore that never heals" for nothing. Obviously this round of pneumonia had changed those numbers.

"The new wood stove is good. His breathing has seemed easier."

"I'm glad. I just wish you'd gone to propane like I—"

"Fuel's too expensive these days."

"I would've sent the money. I'm getting paid well. You wouldn't believe how well. When I come down—"

"Save the money for yourself, Bryan. Don't forget I left the Rez, too, for a while. I know how much it costs to live where you do. We're doing fine. No lie."

He gave up the battle. On the phone he only had words, but when he came back to visit again, he'd bring them things. Maybe even help them build a new house. Nothing fancy— they'd have none of that.

"Did you want to ask about anyone else?" she asked.

No. Not really. But like a dutiful grandson, he forced the question from his dust-dry throat. "How is she?"

"She's still here. Want to ask her yourself?"

"Ask her what? If she's stealing from you? Or maybe how long she's going to stay this time?" He regretted the words, the tone, as soon as he'd spoken.

"She's doing well."

"I'll believe it when it lasts longer than a month or two."

He opened his mouth to say more but his grandmother's hand covered the phone. "It's Bryan," she called.

He should have hung up, but he waited. Like he always had.

"Hello, Bryan."

Once she said it, he couldn't flip the phone shut and cut the connection. No, cutting the connection was her job, and one she'd done with apparent ease again and again throughout his growing-up years.

"Hi, Mom." He'd said it in English. To speak it in Diné

would be like paying respect to her. And that she'd have to earn back.

She switched to English, too. "I heard you found a good job in California."

"Yes."

She waited for more. He didn't want to give it, but the emptiness hung between them, awkward and pained. *What do I say now?* He couldn't ask about her job—chances were she didn't have one. And something like "Are you staying clean this time?" wasn't exactly in the best of taste.

"It pays well," he finally said. "Gives me room to be creative."

"I'm glad to hear it. I've been making jewelry again. Making a little money, too. And keeping an eye on Pop while Mom works the clay."

His mind flashed to an early memory of his mother sitting at the small kitchen table stringing polished beads of turquoise and other stones into necklaces. It had been during one of her good spells, one of those times when he thought maybe she'd actually stick around. He'd been hopeful and naïve then. He wasn't now.

"That's great," he said curtly. Before she made any more attempts to convince him she was better now, he ended the conversation. "Look, I've gotta go. Take care of yourself."

"You, too, son. See you soon."

"Yeah." *If you're there when I come.* "Say good-bye to Grandma and Grandpa for me."

She promised she would. Bryan flipped the phone down slowly, holding it in his palm until he decided to stop brooding and get something to eat. He made a sandwich, gobbled it down, and fired up the computer again. This time it hooked right up.

"Here we go."

Bryan glanced over to Wolf, who still lay in his favorite spot in the middle of the floor. He was snoring, a good sign since Bryan didn't want his beloved pet to witness whatever might happen next. His cock was already stiff as he typed.

Sex slave, sexual slavery, master...

He weeded out the hits dealing with slave trafficking. Butterfly had said she became a slave of her own free will, and he took her at her word. Next he ignored the porn and most of the fetish pay-to-view sites. Or at least he tried to. An image of a woman on her knees caught his attention, her head bowed, her arms behind her back. He slipped a hand beneath the waistband of his running shorts and eased them down. Jerking off at the computer meant he'd have to go at it left-handed, and that made it harder to come. He liked it that way. It drew things out, made him last longer.

The woman on the screen didn't look like Butterfly, but her submissive posture reminded him of that first day, with her kneeling and waiting. He played with his foreskin, worked it back and forth then over his crown. A bubble of pre-come slicked the tip quicker than normal. He clicked through a few of the freebie pics, but the graphics were too large for his crappy connection. So he gave up and closed his eyes.

They were back in Gary's study. She, on the chair, and he on the floor in front of her. The sunlight illuminated the gold rings in her nipples, and the sheer scarves pretending to cover them had only heightened his arousal. He'd sent an email to Gary before his run asking for an explanation. Clarification. A call would've been quicker, but Bryan had wanted something in writing. Could he really touch her, be "served" by her in any way he wanted? The man was a fool to let her be used like that, as if her feelings meant nothing. She'd seemed so fragile perched on the edge of the seat, so tense, making him want to hold her there, his hands on either side of her face—not too tight—and kiss her. He'd remove the scarves or maybe suck her nipples through the soft material. He'd push her back into the chair, hook her legs on either side of the armrests and just look at her open sex. Study it, like a botanist studies a rare blossom revealing itself to the sun.

He imagined he could still smell the faint scent of her pussy as he massaged his wet cockhead with two fingertips and his thumb. She hadn't been oblivious to her effect on him, offering to suck his cock like that. Once she'd sat down, the sweet tang of her mound had hung between them, making him even harder. He leaned back in the creaky dinette chair and wondered why the hell he'd refused. Next time, he would go for it. If she offered again. Maybe declining the invitation had hurt her. She'd sure seemed disappointed when he'd said no.

All this daydreaming wasn't moving his research along. He glanced at the computer screen again and clicked around. A woman who favored his ex-girlfriend, Simone, popped up, a gag in her mouth and black straps wrapping her body tight. Her breasts plumped out from the bindings, and weights dangled from the rings in her nipples. He chuckled, imagining Simone in such a predicament. That bitch didn't have a submissive bone in her body. His erection faded as he remembered the one time he'd asked to tie her up—he'd only wanted a little kink, a bit of variety. She'd shot him down, teasing him at first. *You wanna play Cowboy and Indians, Bryan?* He'd overlooked the slur and tried asking again. This time she'd called him a twisted pervert. Just further proof the two of them were never meant to be a couple.

It took several quick jerks to revive his fading erection. He closed his eyes again and pictured Butterfly in that same get-up. Minus the gag. He didn't want anything to muffle her moans when he fed his cock to her inch by inch. He wouldn't force it in; he'd let her suck it in slowly and give it worshipping licks. With both hands now on his shaft, he made them into a tunnel and lifted his hips to press his cock through. His leg muscles strained to keep the rhythm going, to force his thick head out, then back in again. He angled his right hand down toward the floor and met the crook it formed. That was the back of her throat. He made a fist to trap his cock there, as if she'd tried to swallow and held it without gagging. His flesh lost the spongy feel of an average erection and became rigid as steel. He let go. Just a thumb and a middle finger now, from base to glans. A slow, steady touch that was as light as a butterfly's wings over the contours of his penis. He grabbed his balls with his free hand and imagined her sucking those, too, pressing kisses there and rubbing her face into his sac.

The next stroke brought him off. His abdomen tensed as the spasms rocked his prick. He cupped his palm around the head to catch the gush of white before it landed on the floor.

"Jesus..." He collapsed onto the table, his head banging keys as he went down. He hadn't come this hard in months.

It took several minutes for him to pull himself together and push his chair back from the computer. He staggered to the bathroom for a cold shower; the clean-up felt good, but the freezing water did little to subdue a new erection as he sat back down at the table and noticed he had email. From Gary.

Hi Bryan,

Now you know why I said at your interview that I needed someone discreet to work on this project. Although some share my lifestyle, most people looking in from the outside don't understand it. I'm having a party next month or as soon as your work for me is finished. If you'd like to learn more about my lifestyle, please come—I'll have an official invitation waiting here for you tomorrow morning.

I think you'll like what I'm going to share with you. In fact, I think you'll find it most inspiring.

Sincerely,

G.

P.S. Yes, feel free to enjoy the girls any way you wish. There are condoms in the left-hand drawer of the desk in the study. This is a requirement, not a suggestion. I care about my sexual health.

And that of the women? Bryan seriously doubted it. He let go of the towel around his hips, turned off the computer and put his glass in the sink.

"Another run, boy?"

Wolf declined the offer with a hearty snore, so Bryan got dressed and hit the road alone, his legs pounding the asphalt faster than usual. *This is better than jacking off again,* he reasoned. *So much better.* Tomorrow morning, he'd find Butterfly. He was saving it all for her.

The next morning, he pressed the code into the keypad at the gate then followed the long, curving drive to Gary's house. He parked his rusty pickup, which looked like an abomination against the pristine landscaping, and slammed the squeaky door shut. With sweaty palms and shaking hands, he fiddled with the key in the side door lock. The images of Butterfly he'd allowed to enter his mind wouldn't leave, and he'd spent a long night thinking of sex with her in a wide variety of positions and locations.

The house was always silent, but today's quiet made the hair on his arms stand on end. His breath was short. Ragged. Just like it had been at the end of last night's run, his cock still hard in his sweats, his balls trying to crawl up into his body. Guilt entered the picture, too. What if she didn't really want this? What if she gave herself to him or sucked his cock and that was it—the fantasy ruined? He felt like a fucking predator as he walked through the hallways, looking around corners and pushing open doors that weren't completely closed.

You're acting like a goddamn stalker—just forget it. You're not getting paid to screw. He gave up the chase and headed for the study.

He should've looked here first. The key in his slick hand hit the floor. He closed the door. Locked it. Christ, the way the morning sunlight streamed into the study... She was so beautiful and lay so still, her limbs splayed on the massive desk and held in place with large red ribbons.

He just stood there watching the rise and fall of her chest. She didn't seem afraid. The bottoms of those tiny feet were nearest to him. He crossed the room slowly, looking for a reaction. Every step closer increased the tempo of her breathing, and when he reached her and touched the lightly-soiled sole of each foot, she panted as if on the edge of orgasm.

His fingers wrapped around each slim ankle. The bows

weren't anchored to anything that he could see, but she stayed in position when he gave her calves a gentle squeeze. Pale blue blood vessels spidered just beneath her creamy skin—it was that translucent. He walked to her side and let his hands trace a path to where the invitation Gary spoke of rested between her thighs. The envelope had been tied with red ribbon to the ring peeking from the fleshy hood of her clitoris.

He bent down for a better look. And to breathe in her scent. When he exhaled, a spray of goose bumps dotted the tops of her thighs, to which he held tight in order to maintain control. Another deep breath and he was ready. He released her skin. Ten almond-shaped marks in a mottled pink were left behind on her white thighs.

"Sorry," he said, rubbing them as if that would make them disappear. The texture of her body, like warm satin, made his cock throb. He wanted her off this hard table and somewhere soft.

He looked at her face. She didn't meet his gaze, but her eyes were open, fixed on the ceiling.

No, hon. None of this coy shit. If he fucked her, he wanted to see her reaction. He wanted her to want this, too.

"Sit up."

"I can't, Sir. The bows..."

So they were tied down. He walked over to where her head met the edge of the desk and felt under the curved lip of the desk's top—a small ring held the bindings in place. He pulled one end of a ribbon holding her wrist, then untied the other. In the stillness of the room, the satin rushing through the knots sounded like a roar. Her nipples thickened, and their centers grew from dusky pink to a bright red. He heard her swallow. He pressed his lips to her ear.

"How wet will you be when I pluck that pretty invitation from between your legs?" he whispered. When she shuddered, he suppressed one of his own. He liked this—the set-up, her submissiveness, his struggle to stay in control and do everything slow and right. He liked it a lot.

He willed himself to stand upright and go back to her feet.

She must have expected him to undo those ties, too; her toes gave the slightest wave. He ran a finger over the ones on the right. A rush of air left her chest. Better yet, she sat up.

Bryan put a knee on the desk between her feet and climbed up. His hands found purchase on either side of her hips and, although he stared at her eyes, she kept hers lowered. He dipped down to try to catch them, to lock with them and study the unusual green irises. Her eyes dodged his, and they made a game of it, him moving closer and crouching lower to make the connection.

She actually grinned.

He pressed his elbows to the desk, letting the weight of his body force her back down. He moved lower to place a fleeting kiss to the space above her belly; she still wore scarves there, just a twisted bundle of them hiding her abdomen. He skipped over the mass of silk, then kissed lower still, wetting his lips each time to make her wait until his feet were firmly planted back on the floor. When he reached her clean-shaven mound, he added a lick. She shivered. His nose trailed over the bare slope of her cunt and nestled against her clit. The muscles of her pussy clenched so hard, the sensitive ridge bumped him back. He inhaled. *Heaven...*

"So this is for me?" He looked up.

She nodded.

"I'm not talking about the invitation."

She nodded again. Slower this time.

He gripped the edges of the desk to hold back. To keep from unzipping. He focused on the envelope. It hid her slit well, and he kissed the thick paper, forcing it close against her concealed lips. Then, with a flick of a finger, he unveiled her secrets—the full, ruffled lips, a deeper pink than her nipples. He parted them. A trickle of juice escaped, and he gathered it on his fingertip.

He looked up again. She had propped herself on her elbows, and her eyes didn't shift away this time, not until he tasted her. Then all he got was the soft open *o* of her mouth and fluttering eyelids. He climbed back on the desk to capture her lips with his. She jumped, leaving him with only her bottom lip. He sucked it into his mouth—held it there—then pushed her back to the desktop to take the upper lip, too. She resisted and he let go.

"I want to taste all of you," he said softly.

He tilted his head to place a kiss right by her lips. She turned to him, her eyes searching his.

"What?" he asked.

"You're supposed to fuck me, Sir, not..."

"Not what?"

"Not...not love me like this."

His erection, coated in pre-come and dying for any kind of release, burned into his skin. Seared him like a fucking brand. His fingers itched to yank open his fly and find those goddamn condoms. He wouldn't last three strokes.

But he kept his head. "What do *you* want, Butterfly?"

"I'll do whatever you wish—"

"That's not what I asked."

"I take pleasure in pleasing you."

He crawled back down her body until his feet hit the floor and his lips hovered over her sex. It was wetter now, but he didn't touch it. He took a thin sliver of ribbon between his teeth and made sure she watched. Her pupils were huge, her cheeks flushed. He pulled. The bow holding the invitation came loose and dropped between her thighs. He picked up the small envelope, careful not to touch her, then tucked it into his back pocket.

After untying the bows at her ankles, he offered his hand. She took it and let him slide her to the edge. But he didn't let her get down. Instead he walked into her still-open thighs and forced them further apart. She leaned back on her hands. The bend of her legs cleared the far edges of the desk, and her eyes met his—this time in challenge.

He fingered the hoop at her clit and gave it a playful tug. "You going to be at this little party?" he asked.

She nodded.

He could barely wait.

He stepped back to let her go. She closed her eyes. In disappointment, he hoped. After what he'd just put himself through, she'd better be feeling something. When she slid off the desk, the smear of moisture she left behind was a small victory. But when she turned around on shaky legs at the door while he got his tools...that moment, the look on her face and the obvious lust there—hell, the fact that she even turned around—this was a triumph.

Chapter Four

She'd chosen this life. Over the past few weeks, she'd had to remind herself of that more often. The security she'd felt in knowing she belonged to her Master wasn't as strong as it used to be. The comfort of following his dictates to the letter, of being possessed even if it was sometimes in hurtful ways, the schedule that had given shape to her life for the past five years... Now it all felt constraining. And Bryan toying with her but refusing to follow through didn't help matters.

Butterfly felt impotent and yearning, anxious and excited. For the first time in a long time, she even felt angry. The emotion wasn't directed at anyone in particular, but percolated through her along with the stew of other emotions.

Recently she'd seen other people, men and women who liked the pain and got just as much as Master dished out. But something between these lifestylers was different. One such couple had attended Master's parties, but they didn't last long. The man...Josh? She couldn't remember his name, but a picture of how he treated his slave after all the sweet agony he'd put the woman through had stuck in her mind.

When Master and the others finished with their women and went off to enjoy cigars and Port on the patio, they'd left the slaves behind to tend to each other or recover alone. Master Josh had held his property and caressed her welts, got her the blanket he'd brought along and offered her water. Butterfly had watched, transfixed, knowing full well her own relationship was missing something.

Whether the couple stopped receiving invitations or decided this wasn't their type of party, she didn't know. But she was glad when they didn't show up again. Seeing them and the bond they shared was almost too much to bear.

She should write these feelings down in her journal, along with the information that the carpenter had kissed her—four days ago now—and she'd allowed it. The journal was kept for Master's edification as well as her own self-analysis, so he could have an intimate view of her mind and better assess what she needed in her on-going training.

Butterfly's hands flew up and down the keys. When the melodious Chopin hadn't soothed her, she'd turned to the wild, frantic, jangling chords of Rachmaninov. The energy and drive of the musical piece expressed the chained fury inside her she needed to release. All because of Bryan's kiss, the teasing touch of his hands, his mouth...God! His mouth on her pussy, the delicate flick of his tongue not nearly enough to satisfy her, only enough to drive her insane with need and bring these crashing chords pouring from her fingertips.

Bryan. His very name brought a shiver to her now that she knew what his touch felt like. How she wished he'd allowed her to do what Master had given her permission to do: explore his cock. She wanted to see it, wanted to see all of him naked. She imagined his body was beautiful underneath the worn T-shirts and ripped jeans. If he would only let her, she'd kneel at his feet, unzip his fly, and release his thick, straining cock. Oh, yes, she knew it was thick and long, had felt the bulge pushing against her through his jeans. In her hands it would be warm and vibrating with life. She'd lick the salty tip, tasting him, then slowly draw the entire length into her mouth—without ever breaking eye contact with him. Those dark brown eyes had peered deep inside her and touched her even more intimately than his hands, and now she couldn't get them out of her head, which was why she'd done everything in her power to stay away from him these past few days.

What would Master say if she really shared all she was thinking and feeling in her diary? If he could see inside her rebellious mind, what would he do?

For a moment, Butterfly stopped wondering as she reached a difficult part of the music and had to give it her complete concentration, but when she made it through the complicated passage she resumed her train of thought.

To regain her composure, she needed to remember what had brought her here, how terrible things had been before Master, and how he had saved her life. The cutting had become so pervasive for a while it was a wonder she had any blood left at all. Her already pale skin had become almost translucent as she moved about her days in a haze.

It didn't matter that she was in the top third of her class at Brown, that her GPA was stellar and her future perfectly on track just as her mother had envisioned it. None of it was ever enough. She would always be a failure, never perfect enough to please either her parents or herself.

Although she was smart enough to recognize she had emotional problems and knew cutting was symptomatic of them, she still couldn't stop the destructive behavior. Her senior year of college, only a few months before graduation, she'd met the man who would change her life and become her salvation. The Master who would take her out of the world she couldn't handle and bring her safely to harbor in his.

After another aborted relationship, this time with a self-involved athlete, she'd been drifting, feeling lonely, undesirable and unloved, when a friend took her to a very special, very private nightclub.

The things the somewhat naïve college girl had witnessed in the dungeon that evening had both repulsed and aroused her. Her delicate vulnerability had attracted a number of prospective Doms, both male and female. Politely but firmly turning down their offers to "play", she'd left the club vowing never to return to the perverted fantasyland. It absolutely wasn't her thing, she'd told her friend Cherie.

But that was a lie. It *was* her thing—in a big way—and the following weekend she was drawn back like a child who insisted on playing with matches. Wearing a mask as Cherie suggested, she could become someone else for the evening. She watched for hours, imagining it was her held tight in cuffs or stocks or intricate *shibari* knots. In her mind, flawed as it was at the time, she learned firsthand that a flogging was nearly as cathartic as cutting, and a new obsession supplanted the old one. She fell in love with the rituals, the total surrender of control and the release—no, comfort—that only subspace could bring.

On her third visit to the club, Gary had found her. Spotted her right away. Played with her for a bit then brought her to a private party. He'd given her the intensive attention she craved and promised to make her feel things deep in her dry soul such as she'd never experienced before. She'd put aside her fears that night and opened up to all he had to offer. It was more intense than what had happened at the club, like flying without a safety net. And she fell. Under his harsh, unrelenting hand, she fell and lost herself again and again until, at the end of a particularly brutal scene, she found herself. Found her purpose in life.

This great, talented man needed her. She became his outlet. His vessel. And in the humbling metamorphosis of becoming nothing and no one, she made peace with the restless, anxious part of her soul.

After a few weeks of dating, if one could even call it that, she'd sent a note to her parents telling them she was walking away from Brown and the future they'd planned for her. The college girl disappeared. Over the next few months, Master transformed her completely, and she became his butterfly.

In a way, her whole life had been a preparation for the role. She found it easy to submit, comfortable to obey. After all, she'd been doing it since she was a child. When she did, occasionally, give Master trouble, he taught her well with his creative punishments.

This was the life she'd chosen. She just had to remember that.

But Bryan's dark, searching eyes were in her mind, looking at her, telling her things she didn't want to know, awakening feelings she dare not examine too closely.

A final crash of both hands on the ivories, and she finished the Rachmaninov with a dramatic flourish. Head bowed, gazing at the keyboard, she sat for several minutes, breathing.

Then she rose and went to see Bryan as she'd known she would. She simply couldn't stay away any longer.

In the hallway leading from the kitchen she encountered Jasmine bearing a tray with a covered dish. Butterfly stopped her, not quite blocking her way, but near enough. "I'll take that."

Jasmine's eyes seemed larger and more luminous than ever with her hair shorn. They dominated her face, and coupled with her newly gaunt cheeks and pale skin, the girl reminded Butterfly of a concentration camp victim—but not one beaten down by her imprisonment. Rage shone in her dark-eyed gaze. For a moment, Butterfly thought she'd actually throw the tray at her. Instead, Jasmine silently thrust it forward.

Taking it with a nod, she turned away, practically feeling the daggers Jasmine was silently throwing at her back. The girl had always disliked her, but since the plumbing incident, she hated her. Although she'd brought that disaster on her own head by foolishly disturbing Master at work, she preferred to blame Butterfly rather than herself for the lesson she'd been forced to learn.

Butterfly shrugged off Jasmine's anger and padded toward the den on bare feet, only the tinkling of the ornaments on her ankle chain betraying her presence. She knelt in the doorway, waiting for Bryan to notice her and give his permission to enter. But she didn't bow or lower her eyes—it was too much of a pleasure watching him work, unaware of her silent presence. His big hands wielded his tools with such assurance as he carved the columns that depicted the women. No wonder he'd made her feel so good the other day on the desk. In a way, she envied his confidence and skill. To play piano well was a talent, but she hadn't created the compositions. Even in her passion for music, she was merely a vessel, a conduit for someone, something bigger than herself.

Butterfly sometimes came to the den when he wasn't there to examine his progress on the carvings. He'd caught the essence of each woman, beyond the basic shape of her body. There was the saucy tilt of Jasmine's nose, the pout of Violet's lips, Sapphire's serene oval face, and Butterfly's wide eyes. He was finishing Sapphire today—the last column in the room. After that, he'd likely be gone except for making an appearance at Master's party. If she didn't make some kind of bold offer today, her chance of touching Bryan, perhaps even experiencing another stolen kiss, might be gone forever.

Today his hair wasn't fastened by the leather tie he sometimes wore, but hung loose and straight down his back. It looked as glossy as a crow's wing, and she longed to stroke it. Tucked behind his ear, it revealed his sharp profile, the prominent nose and square jaw, thick, dark brows drawn together in a frown of concentration as he leaned toward the column.

When he licked his lips, the quick flash of pink tongue sent a bolt of fire through her. She remembered how it had felt caressing her body, pressed to her most intimate place, and, even more significant, lightly probing her mouth. Those lips, pressed to hers, had been the warmest, softest things she'd felt in a long time.

She swallowed, and the small sound, or maybe her slight movement, caught his attention. Bryan glanced over. When he saw her, he smiled, a bright, beautiful flash of teeth that lit up his face. He slowly set his tools down and turned to face her, his smile fading before he spoke.

"You're back. I thought maybe I wasn't going to see you again. Where've you been hiding?" His tone reflected a mixture of emotions: surprise, pleasure, accusation, annoyance, and...could it be hurt? Could he possibly have missed her like she did him?

Instinctively, she'd dropped her gaze when he looked at her, as she'd been so well trained to do. But suddenly she remembered her vow to make a bold move before it was too late. Rising to her feet unbidden, she looked into his eyes.

Sometimes they appeared nearly as dark as ebony. Today, with sunlight pouring through the window, they were a lighter, warmer shade of brown.

He walked toward her slowly. "I didn't mean to frighten you off. What happened? You seemed to be enjoying yourself as much as I was." The low velvet of his voice touched someplace deep inside her. Made it hurt. "In fact, I know you were enjoying it. I could taste how much."

Her stomach flipped and her sex contracted hard at the husky timbre of his whisper.

"So, did Gary forbid you to serve me or were you just pissed at me?"

She shook her head. "Neither." Walking to the desk, and putting half a room between them, she set down the tray. Unfortunately, standing near the desk, the site of their last encounter, set off a firecracker string of emotions that popped and crackled through her body. "Mr. Lapahie..."

"Please. Bryan. I think we've moved a little past 'mister', don't you?" Once more he moved toward her, crossing the room with a cat's slow, sinuous stalk.

He didn't seem to understand that titles of respect were an intrinsic part of her life here. "Mister..." She cleared her throat and tried again. "Bryan." Once she'd gotten the name out, she couldn't seem to find any other words. What had she planned to say to him—I want to have sex with you and kiss you again before you leave, please?

After waiting a beat, he prodded gently. "Yes?"

She smoothed her finger over the shiny surface of the silver chafing dish covering his plate, trying to think of small talk. "Tell me more about your family."

"*That's* what you want to talk about?" His tone was a sexual purr as his feet came into view and stopped several inches in front of her.

She nodded, staring at them.

"After what happened the other day, all you want to discuss is my family?" The heat in his voice prompted an answering warmth in her pussy.

Lifting her eyes, she looked into his once more. "Unless you'd rather do something more…intimate than talk."

Another step closer brought him to within arm's length of her. "Are you flirting with me, little butterfly?"

She smiled, a bubbly, fizzy sensation rising inside her. "Maybe."

"Very bold of you." Suddenly he took her arm, pulled her forward, and led her to a chair. "Come sit down for a moment and talk to me while I work."

Her brain reeled. After the other day and this new offer, all he wanted to do was talk and work? She didn't know whether to scream in frustration or balk in disbelief.

But per his command she perched on the edge of the cushion. She was ill at ease taking a seat in his presence, especially as he continued moving around, doing his work. "You're almost finished?" It was a question, but she already knew the answer.

"Yes. I have coats of varnish to apply, which will take some time, but I'm almost finished with the carving." He nodded at the wood beneath his hands and picked up the small chisel used for detail work. "Sapphire, right?"

She nodded, and then sat wondering what to say to him. "What you did the other day. That was… It made me feel…" *It made me feel.* That summed it up. She hadn't experienced such pleasure and excitement for a long time.

"Me, too." He paused to glance over at her. "Can you tell me something?"

"Yes, Sir."

"What's your real name? Your name before you came here?"

She shook her head. "I'm sorry. I can't tell you that."

"Why not?" Abandoning the chisel, he knelt on the floor facing her and looked up into her face. "What brought you here? Why do you live under Gary's rule? I understand his motivation. What man wouldn't want four women catering to his every whim, but what do you get from it?"

She was uncomfortable with his scrutiny and his probing questions. Her hands clenched in her lap.

He touched the side of her face lightly. "I'm not trying to be rude or nosy, but I really want to understand. Explain it to me, please."

The "please" twisted her heart. It had been a long time since she'd heard the word directed at her. She took a deep breath and opened up, praying she wouldn't regret it.

"Before I found Master, I was adrift and miserable, and with some...self-destructive behavior. But he changed all that. He gave me a home, security, and the discipline I crave. The regimen he set for me, the order was what I needed. He became my anchor."

"What kind of rules? What kind of discipline?"

"Our beliefs are based on the tenets of Gor. Perhaps you've heard of it?"

He nodded. "I've done some research."

"Then you know I learned to behave as a respectful slave, attuned to Master's every need and maintaining my proper place as one of his possessions."

"So, kneeling before you enter a room, acting as an invitation holder, no eye contact, what else?"

"No sitting on furniture." She glanced down at the chair. "We're not allowed, anymore than you'd let a pet on the couch."

He laughed. "My dog has the run of all the furniture in my apartment. Hell, I'm lucky he lets me sleep in my own bed at night."

"You have a dog?"

He nodded. "I call him Wolf. The name describes him. He's no particular breed, although he's obviously got some German Shepherd in him. He owns me like Gary owns you. If I don't run him enough, if I don't get him his meals on time or play tug-of-war until my arm's numb, he lets me know his displeasure."

Giddiness bubbled up inside her and she laughed then lifted her hand to cover her mouth. Bryan intercepted, grasping her wrist lightly. His low chuckle joined her laughter.

"Mr. Lapahie, I see you're finding my butterfly an amusing companion."

Master's voice from the doorway hit her like a blow to the stomach. She felt the blood rushing from her face as she paled.

Butterfly shot from the chair and dropped to her knees. She bowed low, her forehead nearly touching the floor.

"Yes," Bryan answered. "Very much so."

She felt movement beside her as Bryan rose to his feet. Glancing from the corners of her eyes, she could see his feet clad in stained tennis shoes. "All of your...ladies have been very generous hostesses, and the lunches have been great."

"Well, Butterfly has a lot to do with that. She supervises the kitchen. The household wouldn't run nearly as smoothly without her."

Butterfly listened carefully to the tenor of his voice, judging how angry he might be. Her heart kicked against her ribs. The floor creaked as Bryan shifted his feet then moved closer to Master. In challenge? He walked past her head, stepping around her hair, as if he meant to protect her. The gesture calmed her frantic heart, stilled her urge to fly away.

"I can imagine. A good cook is the heart of the household, my grandmother always said."

His comment made her smile. She wondered what the woman looked like. Was she tall like him? What kinds of food did she like to cook, and did he miss those things?

Master didn't respond to his words. "How is the project coming along?" His voice came closer as he examined the pillar featuring Sapphire. "I'm very impressed with your artwork, and how quickly you've accomplished the task."

"Thank you. It's been a pleasure having such a creative outlet. I'm often stuck building decks or redesigning closets. My artistic side isn't always put to use."

"Hm. Well, you can be assured I'll show my friends your work, and you can count on a flood of new commissions. As a matter of fact, before I let you go, there's another project I'd like to talk to you about. A special piece of furniture I need built to particular specifications."

"Sure. I'd love to hear about it."

Down on the floor, unable to see their faces, Butterfly read the subtext in their voices. The snide tone of Master's opening comment told her he wasn't pleased to find her sitting on a chair laughing with Bryan, but he admired the man's work so was willing to overlook the transgression—on the artisan's part, but probably not hers. She could expect a scolding later. Meanwhile, Bryan's voice was assiduously polite, but tight. He didn't like her Master, but needed the job and had to keep a courteous demeanor.

"It's a kind of vaulting horse. A playground piece, if you will. If you're interested in the extra work, I'll take you downstairs and show you my exact requirements."

Say yes. Please say yes. Butterfly dragged her fingernails against the floor and prayed. If she could spend just a little more time around Bryan, that's all she needed—a few more glimpses of him, the sound of his laughter and his rich, warm words pouring over her like honey. The blowjob she'd hoped to give him would be wonderful, too, but it took second place to her desire to spend time with him and listen to him talk.

"Sounds intriguing," he said shortly.

"Come along then. I have a few minutes right now before I have to leave for an appointment. I'll show you my playroom."

She could hear a pause, a brief hesitation on Bryan's part, as Master's footsteps walked toward the door. "Coming, Mr. Lapahie?"

"Uh, yeah, but what about..."

"Oh, yes. Butterfly, you may rise and go about your duties. I'll speak to you later."

"Yes, Master." She waited until they were nearly through the door before she lifted her face from the floor and watched them.

Master's back was rigidly erect and clothed in an elegantly tailored gray suit jacket. His build was compact, thin and sharp. Beside him, Bryan Lapahie looked huge, lumbering and powerful. His shoulders stretched his T-shirt across the back and his large hands hung, slightly clenched, by his sides. As he followed Master down the hall, he glanced back over his shoulder. His eyes met and held hers, offering an unspoken promise. He would see her again.

She would have another chance to hear that wonderful laugh, and maybe, finally, an opportunity to show him the kind of pleasure she could bring him.

Chapter Five

Following Gary downstairs to his basement, Bryan's pulse quickened. He didn't want to feel so eager and titillated, not after seeing Butterfly prostrate on the floor before her Master. That pissed him off. Everything about this controlling guy annoyed the hell out of him—except the money. But he couldn't deny excitement at the idea of seeing a real dungeon.

"I don't know how much you've figured out about our lifestyle here." Gary glanced at Bryan while leading him down a wide hallway, past a row of doors. Bars covered each one, like jail cells, and large photos filled the spaces between them. "I practice some of the tenets of Gor, a sub-culture within the BDSM community."

"I've read about it," Bryan admitted. "It's based on a world created by some fantasy writer."

"Yes, in this make-believe culture men control women, who attend and obey them. My friends and I don't go for the sci-fi, alternate world names. I call my women slaves, not *kajira*. Those who actively practice a similar lifestyle in reality are considered extremists, because most people don't want to admit the fundamental nature of a woman is to serve. She can't be truly happy unless a Master gives order to her life."

"Mm." Bryan didn't want to appear too interested, nor did he want to piss the guy off. It was a fine line, keeping the client happy while standing up for what he thought was right. His head swam with anger for the way he imagined Gary treated his women, and with lust. What had happened on the desk with

Butterfly had awakened a darker side to his personality, and he still wasn't sure how he felt about this.

They stopped in front of a sepia-tone photograph hanging on the stark, white wall. Violet's face was shown in extreme close-up, her eyes squeezed shut, the tracks of tears shining on each cheek, her mouth open in a scream. Bryan wondered what things had been done to her to produce this effect.

"Beautiful, isn't she?" Gary stared at the shot, obviously entranced by his own work. "I remember the night I took these." He gestured at the photograph, then waved his hand toward all of the others hiding in shadows. "Each image caught the exquisite moment when they could bear no more and broke. I have albums filled with memories like these."

Bryan didn't say a word. He was torn between disgust at the man's sadistic nature and a perverse fascination. He wanted to, needed to, hear more.

"I keep my women like pets. Safe, secure, well-fed and obedient to my will, while I indulge in my own particular needs."

"Causing pain," Bryan guessed.

"No." The man's silver-gray eyes were as cool and reflective as a mirror. "That's not what stimulates me. It's the moment the will is broken, and that isn't always based on physical punishment. Butterfly, for example, can resist great amounts of physical torture, and the girl truly enjoys being bound for hours. Although I sometimes indulge her, when I really need to teach a lesson, I reach her best through her weaknesses."

"Which are?" *Do I really want to know?* Hearing too many details about the life Butterfly had chosen could be unbearable. Bryan looked through the bars at the cell. There was a bed inside. That was it. No chest of drawers or closet, no washstand or any personal items. Just four walls, a cement floor and a narrow cot.

"My butterfly was a very sad and sick girl when I discovered her. Her way of coping with her problems included cutting. I rid her of that unhealthy habit and provided her with this safe haven." He chuckled. "Perhaps too safe. She became far too content with being enclosed in her pen or the confines of the house, and developed a phobia about the outdoors—"

"So she's agoraphobic?"

Gary looked annoyed at the interruption—Bryan doubted anyone dared to interrupt the man or challenge him in any way—but he had to let him know he wasn't stupid. He'd been fighting this prejudice for years. People thought just because he worked with his hands that he was ignorant. He looked Gary in the eye as if giving him permission to continue. Bryan noted the clench of Gary's jaw as he began to speak again.

"She also hates being the focus of attention. Therefore whenever I want to tear her from her cocoon, so to speak, I make her perform for an audience. Outside."

Bryan didn't respond. Was she terrorized or was there actually an element of therapy here? Butterfly spoke of Gary as if he'd saved her soul—maybe this was what she needed after all. He stared at the austere stall and tried to make sense of her world. And he had a feeling her world was changing because of him, his presence and how he tried to bring her out of her shell. He sucked in a deep breath of the cool basement air. Maybe taking on another project wasn't the right thing to do. He should keep away from Butterfly and stop trying to influence her.

Gary beckoned him toward another photograph. Taken from a distance, it showed Butterfly sitting nude at a piano atop a makeshift platform built on the lawn. The blurry backs of heads at the lower edge of the picture indicated an audience, but the focus was on the rigid nude female figure. As Violet's pain had been evident in the details of her face, Butterfly's fear was clear in her posture. The set of her shoulders and her slightly bowed head indicated her intense humiliation under scrutiny. The camera caught the look of terror in her eyes that said she'd fly away at any second if she wasn't pinned to the spot by her Master's command.

For an agoraphobic, such a situation would be pure hell. No extreme flogging, burning, or piercing, just a naked piano concert under a sunny sky. No wonder Gary had chosen this shot for her "breaking" point.

"This simple act is enough to put Butterfly back in line when she misbehaves."

The guy spoke of helping her with her issues, then of punishment using her weaknesses. Bryan looked at the Dom or whatever the hell he was. *Sick fuck.*

"What constitutes misbehavior?" He was afraid to ask, but he had to know, especially after he'd made her break the ridiculous no-sitting-on-the-furniture rule.

"Any infraction of rules or willfulness. Come along. I'll show you the dungeon." Gary's voice was light, his manner as excited as a child eager to show off his toys to a new friend.

Bryan's heart felt like a stone. He glanced in the cell beside Butterfly's picture. He imagined her lying on the bed in that dark, enclosed place every night, locked into the dismal cage until Gary chose to set her free again. He shivered. Simply being in this windowless corridor made him nervous and a little short of breath. He wasn't claustrophobic, but hated being cooped up anywhere for long. He'd grown up beneath wide-open skies, and camped out more often than he'd slept in his bed at his grandparents' home. God, Butterfly would hate that.

"What you have to understand about women," Gary continued, "is that on a very deep level all of them want to be controlled. Their sex craves it. I've carefully selected my women for particular attributes of their personalities, but also for a strong streak of that elemental craving. Some are more willful, like Jasmine, and require heavy-handed methods to break them, but others, like Butterfly, are perfect specimens of womanly subservience."

"Oh." What else could he say? If he expressed his aversion to Gary's beliefs, he'd lose any chance at other jobs from him, as well as access to new clients. He had to maintain a calm front even though the idea of this twisted creep hurting sweet, gentle Butterfly made him want to rip out the man's throat. Gary's culture and sophistication hid a dangerous, cruel devil. He could probably be arrested for some of what he did here, whether the women gave their consent to be treated this way or not. Weren't there laws against abusing people even if they believed they deserved it?

"And here we are." Gary smiled as he opened a heavy oak door that looked like a set piece in some medieval historical movie. "My own private playground."

The room was huge, the walls removed and only bearing supports set at intervals. Why did the man need new stuff made? He had all the expensive equipment Bryan had seen on the web and more—stocks, harnesses, electronic fucking machines and a wall hung with neatly coiled whips, floggers and other implements.

Shiny metal shackles hung from hooks embedded in the ceiling or walls. A St. Andrew's cross dominated one corner and cages stood along one wall, doors open and waiting for an occupant.

"Pretty impressive, eh?"

Bryan nodded, although the words "egotistical ass" wanted to tumble from his lips. No, what was impressive was the erection pressing against his fly. He'd been hard with Butterfly stretched out on the library desk, but this was worse, mainly because he was imagining her in here with him—no Gary, no other women. Just her and his own inner devil controlling her body. A chill ran through him. Where did one draw the line between pleasure and abuse? Who made the call? In his mind, Butterfly would.

Gary continued to gloat as they walked through the room, and Bryan knew on a fundamental level they were different kinds of men. But how different?

Picking up a thin black rod from a table full of implements, Gary snapped the flexible strip against his thigh. It sliced through the air and made contact with the fabric of his gray pants. The sight of him in his conservative suit and tie in this medieval dungeon was surreal.

Hell, just being here was surreal. Bryan studied the equipment, horrified yet fascinated, as he had been as a child the first time he visited a zoo. He'd been stricken with a physical pain in his stomach after looking into a pacing tiger's frustrated eyes. Could these human women, kept as pets but treated with cruelty, actually be content?

But maybe Bryan's level of interest in BDSM wasn't enough for someone like Butterfly, who apparently thrived on hardcore. What was the phrase? *Weekend warrior.* Yeah, that was more his style. This 24/7 stuff would overwhelm him—kinky sex seemed good, damn good—but to live it with four women every second of the day? Who had the time? Apparently a rich fucker like Gary.

"I want to show you something, and then we'll move on to the specifics of what I want you to build." Gary flipped a switch in the wall, illuminating a shadowy alcove. "What do you think of her?"

Byran sucked in his breath. In the corner was an enormous spider web of entwined white ropes, like the kind sometimes found on children's playgrounds. But this web, drawn tight between metal eyes anchored in the walls, floor and ceiling, featured a unique spider at its center: Sapphire.

She was sprawled against the mesh—upside down. Her blonde hair cascaded from her head and her face was a blotchy red from the blood rushing to it. Ropes stretched her limbs and suspended her body. White strands tied around her body divided her flesh into intriguing slices. Her pussy was open wide with a spotlight trained on the glistening folds.

Bryan's already stiff cock hardened to steel at the unexpected sight of the bound and blindfolded woman, caught like an insect in the spider's web. He suddenly realized she didn't represent the spider, but its prey.

Snap. The sound of Gary's crop hitting flesh startled Bryan from his gape-mouthed stare. He shot a glance at his employer in time to see the red mark the crop had left on his palm. *Snap.* Gary brought the crop down against his hand again as he gazed at his creation. "She's exquisite," he murmured.

"Um, how long can she hang upside down like that?"

Gary grinned. "As long as I want her to."

No, but seriously, Bryan wanted to say. *Wouldn't all that blood rushing to her head cause brain damage or something?*

72

As though he'd spoken the thought out loud, Gary said, "Trust me, I never injure my property. I would never do anything to leave lasting damage or scars—unless I want scars."

"Unless you *want* scars?" Bryan couldn't stop himself from speaking up. "But the whole thing with Butterfly's cutting. You said you were helping her get over that."

The crop snapped against Gary's hand again. His eyes narrowed. "Bryan, it's a good thing I like you. I knew inviting you into the house was a risk. You're here to do a job, not question the choices I make. But rest assured, I don't leave scars on Butterfly. I save that type of thing for Sapphire here."

Gary moved close to the web to trail the crop over Sapphire's body. Thin ribbons of raised flesh were etched into her skin. Sapphire shivered as the crop neared her sex, setting the ropes swaying and her body with them. Was it anticipation or fear that made her tremble?

"Don't..." Bryan bit off the words.

Gary raised the black crop and brought it down at the junction of Sapphire's legs, right across her exposed sex. *Snap!* She jerked and whined. The ropes moved and Sapphire's body floated in space, tangled in the manmade web and pulled in all directions.

Gary turned to Bryan and extended the crop. "Would you like to try it?"

Bryan's fingers itched to take the smooth leather grip in hand. His cock ached and blood rushed through his veins. Yes, he wanted to wield that implement, but under a completely different set of circumstances. With a partner he had a connection to, not one helpless to choose who hit her.

"I know what you're thinking."

No, you don't, Bryan wanted to protest, but Gary kept talking. "You're repulsed, but turned on. You're probably thinking about negotiations and safe words." Gary clapped Bryan on the back. Hard. For a small man, he was powerful. "We left those quaint concepts at the door. In my world, a man can fulfill his darkest desires."

The door was only about forty feet away, but it felt like miles to Bryan. He'd left a few things back at the door as well. Like his sense of right and wrong. He stiffened and the hand lifted from his shoulder.

"I could look at her for hours, but I still have that appointment to get to." He tossed the crop to the floor, making Sapphire quiver once more. "Let me show you what I want done."

He hit the switch, plunging Sapphire and her web back into darkness. The muffled sound of a quiet whimper followed them as he led Bryan to another part of the dungeon.

"Here's what I want built. You see this spanking horse?" He indicated a contraption something like a gymnast's vaulting horse. "It was one of the first pieces of furniture I bought, about a dozen years ago now. But it's outdated and worn. I want a new one built to certain specifications."

As Gary described the height, length and other requirements, Bryan floated in and out of listening to him. *Snap!* The sound of that crop coming down on Sapphire's vulnerable pussy rang over and over in his head. Her cry and the soft sobs that followed haunted him. And he was turned on by it—Gary had nailed that pretty quickly—was he that transparent? He couldn't help it or deny it. His cock dripped come from its tip and strained against the fly of his jeans. Clenching his fists at his sides, he refused to reach for the bulge and reposition himself. He didn't want Gary to know he'd been nearly goaded into coming in his pants from the display.

"Did you get all that?" Gary's voice interrupted his train of thought. "Never mind. I'll write it down. I can see you're a little overwhelmed by all this. How I'd love to be in your place again, everything fresh and new." He shrugged. "But, that's what new slaves are for, to experience the sense of wonder as they learn their place all over again." He glanced at his watch. "Okay, I have to keep moving or I'll be late."

Still thinking of Sapphire hanging upside down in the dark, Bryan followed Gary from the dungeon and down the hall.

"One issue I need to address," Gary said. "I'm happy to

have my girls service you while you're working here. You can have all the blowjobs you want on your breaks, although I understand you haven't asked for any yet. But I don't want to see what I walked in on today."

Gary's silver eyes pierced him, and Bryan imagined that cruel little crop coming down on his dick and balls. His erection wilted.

"My girls aren't available for idle chatting. And they're not allowed up on the furniture, which Butterfly knows and should have told you. I'll just have to remind her of her place."

The idea of Gary doing horrible things to Butterfly made his stomach clench.

"I told her to sit on the chair, and she has to follow my orders, right?" Bryan said calmly, reasonably. Firmly.

"My rules supersede those of a guest. No slaves on the furniture, period. It undoes my training. But, like a little dog that piddles on the floor, I'll rub her nose in it, hit her with a proverbial rolled up newspaper and toss her outside." He laughed at his analogy.

He probably *would* toss her outside, the worst punishment of all for Butterfly. Bryan tasted bile.

"Actually, dogs respond better to positive reinforcement." Bryan bit back his rising anger before continuing. "Please, don't punish Butterfly for my mistake."

"Are you offering yourself in her place? I have a friend who'd love to bring a big man like you to your knees." Gary's chuckle was back. Bryan wanted to punch the grin from his face.

"I don't want you to hurt Butterfly for sitting on the chair or talking to me," he persisted.

Gary's gunmetal gaze swung to him again, and his grin vanished. "You're taken with the girl. I thought so. Well, for God's sake, why haven't you used her then? I had her practically gift-wrapped for you on my desk and she said nothing happened."

So, she'd talked about him and what had happened that

day to her master? Well, of course she had. He should have known it, but somehow Bryan was hurt, as if she'd betrayed a confidence by telling about their intimacy. Had she also told Gary about the stolen kiss? Not likely or there would have been repercussions.

"I do find Butterfly very attractive. I'm simply taking my time."

"Savoring the foreplay, understandable, but believe me there's no need to woo her. Use her any way you like. And while you're working down here you can use any of the equipment you want on her."

Oh God, the hard-on was back full force. He thought of the St. Andrew's cross and wondered if he could secure her wrists and ankles to it before exploding in his pants. No, he needed to do more research, maybe even some of the hands-on variety. If he took her down here, he wanted to do it right—when Gary would be gone for hours. That way he could hold her in his arms afterwards, show her there was a better way to do this.

"Maybe one day," Bryan said.

"I believe you have a crush on my little butterfly. And I think she has a big one on you." Gary paused at the foot of the stairs. "She's been acting different lately. Even more quiet and introverted than usual, if that's possible, and slow to comply with my demands sometimes. And now sitting on a chair..."

As though finally catching the current of Bryan's anger floating in the air, the depth of it, Gary looked at him.

"But don't worry. It won't be anything too harsh. I think a simple pinning will help her remember her place."

Pinning? Bryan wouldn't ask, and then Gary moved on, changing the subject abruptly.

"So you'll build the spanking horse?"

"Yes." If only to stay close to Butterfly for as long as he could.

"I'll pay extra if you can have it finished by the date of my party." Gary threw out a dollar figure that nearly made Bryan gasp aloud. "Will that do?"

Bryan cleared his throat. "Yes. I think I'll manage to get it done in time." *If I have to work round the clock, I'll finish it.* His grandparents needed the money. He could get his grandfather's truck fixed, maybe even use it toward a new, better house for them.

They climbed the stairs leaving the gloomy dungeon behind, but not the sense of darkness that had invaded Bryan's heart. Maybe because he was going to leave Butterfly to her master's discipline rather than cross Gary and chance losing all that money.

"You know," Gary said, "with the connections you're going to make at this party, you may want to think big. Pick a company name that reflects the nature of your new line of work. I have a marketing friend who can hook you up with business cards before the get-together. Choose a name and I'll take care of it all."

By the time they reached the top of the stairs, Bryan had gone back more than a decade to a time before he wanted to leave the Rez and made the mistake of joining the Army. As a young, idealistic boy, he'd wanted to become a medicine man. This wasn't the way a *hataałii* behaved, closing his eyes to mistreatment.

Following Gary to the living room, he watched him pick up a large portfolio and his BlackBerry.

"I have a name already," he said softly.

"Jot it down on this." Gary handed him a scrap of paper and a sleek gold pen.

The pen felt like a thin, slippery fish between Bryan's callused fingers. His soul felt slippery, too, as if it slid back and forth between wrong and right. He pressed hard and printed the letters clearly before handing it back to Gary.

"Hm. Interesting name."

Their gazes locked. Bryan didn't say a word.

"You sure about this? I mean, we're talking about branding a new company here. The connotations..."

Bryan simply nodded.

"Okay, Judas & Company it is." Gary extended his hand.

Bryan didn't want to shake, but what else could he do when making a deal with the devil?

Chapter Six

"I've been thinking a lot lately."

When Master shared his thoughts, this was rarely a good thing. Butterfly shuddered in her restraints, the metal around her wrists clanging against the cold metal table she rested on. He placed her feet in the adjustable stirrups and spread her wide. She waited for the gag. Master had an order to everything, and pinning her to the butterfly board was no different than any of his other rituals. Was he preoccupied with whatever thoughts filled his mind? Or did he expect this to be a dialogue of sorts? Baffled, she clenched her hands into tight fists. This particular scene, as painful as it was, became her release. She didn't want to talk or share her feelings. At least not with words. No, she only wanted to express her agony, her beautiful agony, through her body. The squirming. The tensing of muscles and whatever sounds he'd allow her. She let out a sigh of disappointment.

"Do you have any idea what I've been thinking about?" he asked.

"No, Master."

He lifted the thin balsawood board from her stomach and placed it over her sex, moving it slightly up and down to let her lips peek out from the hole in the wood's center. Butterfly stretched her legs farther apart. About five inches in width, the board barely fit between her thighs, and he repositioned the stirrups to help her adjust or perhaps provide himself a better view.

Like his other toys, the board was custom made, her folds fitting perfectly through the opening. Once Master was satisfied with its placement, he knotted ribbons through the small holes at the four corners of the wood then tied the streams of blue silk to her thighs. When he was finished, the wood pressed into her pubic bone and covered the entrance to her ass.

"I'm thinking about the same thing you are, Butterfly."

She looked up. Locked eyes with him. Quickly, she glanced away. She hadn't made that mistake in years... He laughed. Not an evil, "You'll pay for this" laugh, but something more telling.

"See, you're changing, Butterfly. Emerging from your cocoon, as it were. We both know why."

The reason was Bryan, but she wouldn't say his name. Not first.

Master pulled up a rolling stool and sat then pressed a button on the exam table. The hydraulics lowered her as a soft hum filled the room. When her pussy reached Master's eye level, she heard him open a drawer below her lower body.

And so it begins. She forced her breathing to settle down and her fists to relax. He pinched the right lip of her cunt with a clamp and stretched it taut before fixing it in place with a dressmaker's pin. She gasped as it pierced her sensitive flesh, the pain spiraling through her, making her dizzy with the kind of conflicted rapture she so often felt under his skilled hands.

At first, her thoughts were cerebral, as they usually were at the start of a scene. She'd try to figure out something more about herself in these early moments and wonder why she needed the pain to feel worthy of pleasure. Another pin went in, then another, each puncture sending a flash of sweet hurt through her cunt and into her stomach. Endorphins coursed through her, flooding her pulsating lips with a meager defense to the next assault. But her body's safety net would build, and soon only bliss would remain in the wake of each sturdy pin.

"So what is it about him?"

If only Master would stop talking...

"I don't know, Sir."

"You don't know?" He ran the tip of a pin along the innermost part of her exposed lip. She shivered.

"Truly, Sir. He's just..."

His next pin pierced her quickly. Too quickly. When he rushed it, her pain—and the paradoxical pleasure the pain brought—bottomed out. Then again, he knew this.

"Jasmine says you favor him. That you've taken him lunch when it was her turn."

"He's kind, Sir."

"Is he?"

"Yes, Sir."

"Kinder than me?"

She paused a beat too long. Master stood. Leaned over her torso and yanked the scarf from her stomach, exposing her old scars. Sometimes her cutting days seemed so distant—light-years away—except when Master reminded her, which he did more often of late.

"Did he help you stop that?"

"No, Sir, but—"

"But what?"

She bit her tongue. This wasn't the right time to tell him about everything that had been building up inside her, threatening to burst free at any given moment during the day.

Or was it?

"Sir, how is what you do to me any different than what I used to do to myself?"

There. She'd said it. At least part of what she'd been thinking lately. Now she had only to wait for the repercussions.

"I took you in when no one else understood you. I give you the pain you need, the release, in a positive way." His slim fingers trailed over her scarred abdomen, each mark a notch in her fragile psyche. "I keep you from doing this."

"Only because you don't allow it. If this were a real relationship—"

"This *is* real, Butterfly. I take care of you. How dare you bite the hand that feeds you. You think Bryan could do better?"

"I didn't say that, Sir."

"But you've thought about it." He took a deep breath, as if determined not to show his temper like he had with Jasmine, then sat down again and continued the pinning.

"With all due respect, I haven't known much of the world. Of people." She hesitated, unsure of how to proceed. "He cares about people...in a different way than you do."

"The question is, are you a person, Butterfly?"

Yes, she wanted to say. She *was* more than this, more than a slave. And she deserved a decent life. God knows her parents and their impossible expectations hadn't given her one.

"Sir...I've been thinking of leaving."

A pin tumbled to the floor, a small sound. The calm before the storm. He'd never dropped a pin before. She braced herself for his temper or maybe some sarcastic remark; he knew how easily words could hurt her. Then he pulled a pin from her lip. Her nerves felt alive at the site of the puncture, as if her heart was nestled low in her groin, her lips there ready to flutter and fly away like her namesake. This was the good part—her reward. But he hadn't made her wait for it, and giving her relief too soon made her earlier agony worthless. She should've waited to mention leaving until after their session...

With no further warning, his wrath came to the surface, and he plucked the pins from the soft wood too quickly, too roughly. They pinged into the open metal drawer, and he untied the ribbon with jerky movements before yanking the pinning board away from her pussy. It clattered to the floor. Next, he unfastened her wrists. Anger blazed in his eyes. He leaned down inches from her face. She thought of Bryan's stolen kisses. Should she speak of these as well? Her recent transgressions were mounting up in a big way—no, telling him about the kisses would only make things worse.

She covered her chest with her arms and waited for his fury.

"You barely know the man and you're thinking of leaving

with him? What the hell did he say to you?"

"Nothing, Sir. And I didn't mean leaving with him necessarily."

Master laughed. "How else would you survive? I hate to break this to you, but pianists, no matter how good they are, don't exactly make a living if they can't get up on stage."

His words stung her to the core. He had to know that she knew this. There would always be obstacles to overcome when a person was...damaged. Suddenly his expensive cologne seemed cloying. She turned her head away, and for once in a very, very long time spoke without being addressed.

"I remember the first day you brought me here. You said you would make me into someone else."

He didn't reply.

"You said you could help me. Really help me," she whispered.

She rolled from the table, no *Sir* in that sentence. And no hope for the future as things stood now. The rage coursing through her was the only thing keeping her feet warm on the cold dungeon floor as she headed for the door.

"And you lied."

Bryan carefully pushed the final plank for Gary's spanking horse against the band-saw blade then turned the machine off. "She's sweet, Darryl. Real fucking sweet."

Darryl's deep laugh echoed off the workshop walls. "The saw or the girl?"

Bryan laughed, too, and glanced around the place. "Both, I think. Congrats on the small business loan. The new shop is amazing. I'd give anything for this kind of space."

"Thanks." The older man beamed with pride as he pulled a business card from the box Bryan had left on the worktable. "These are pretty sweet, too."

"Man, don't get me started..."

"What? Some wealthy fucker sets you up and you're pissed?"

Bryan checked the cut on the board with a level and, once satisfied, set it on a worktable. Then he looked over his friend's shoulder at the bright white cards. "For starters, Gary changed the name on me. I told his rich ass 'Judas & Company'."

"I kinda like 'Judas Tree' better. Hey, they didn't charge you for any of it. Just smile and thank 'em. That's what I'd do."

Bryan had to admit the graphic was sharp—in the center of his card, twisting branches of a tree's silhouette held the red letters J and T. Below, in a strong, simple font, was the company name, a website address and his cell phone number. Oh, and his new "tagline", whatever the fuck that was... *Uncompromising craftsmanship for discreet Masters.*

"They wouldn't even let me pick my own goddamn slogan. These dominant types are a breed apart."

Darryl slapped him on the shoulder. "Yep, we're all a bunch of assholes," he said with a chuckle.

"I didn't mean you, and you know it."

"I'm only messing with you. Lighten up. Besides," Darryl looked him dead in the eye, "if what you told me is true, you got quite a bit of Top in you."

"But I'm different—"

"Bryan, we're all different. Every last one of us. We all have different 'real lives' and tastes and ways of playing. That's the cool thing about the kink world—there's something for everyone."

"I get it, Dar. I get it."

"Then come out with me tonight. See what all's out there and where you fit in. It'll be a blast."

A blast? Not when the only thing he'd think about was Butterfly the whole time. No, he'd be miserable.

"I'll think about it," he lied.

"You better." Darryl slapped him on the back again and headed outside toward the house. "The horse is gonna be a beaut. You have a real gift."

"Thanks," Bryan mumbled.

When his friend's boots hit the gravel outside the small

garage, Bryan tucked the once pristine card now marked with a dirty thumbprint back in the box. A box that was no longer full. Gary and his designer friend had helped themselves, giving them out to whomever they pleased. Hell, he'd already gotten two calls, one for some stocks and another for a St. Andrew's cross covered in spikes. He told them he had a waiting list. He needed time to sort through this, to come up with a plan.

But other than making furniture without much more than a few sketches, what the hell did he know about plans? Gift or curse, his lack of planning was what took him away from his grandparents and nearly got his ass court-martialed all those years ago. Like the wind, he simply blew in one direction or another, along for the ride with the hope that luck would work in his favor no matter how fierce the once-tame breeze became.

A vision of Butterfly in her signature scarves filled his mind. A strong wind would blow those little scraps of fabric right off and reveal every inch of her beautiful body. Gary had spoken of cutting, but Bryan hadn't seen it, not yet. Maybe she'd healed up okay, like his mom had after she'd kicked meth that last time. Jesus, the night he'd found her scratching out the crank bugs in her arms... He thought the wounds would never get better, but they did.

Bryan stared at the freshly sawed-off plank, searching for flaws, running his fingers over the surface of it with eyes now shut. He didn't want to revisit that nightmare, not today. His finger caught a splinter from the sturdy oak, but when he reached over to pull it out, he opened his eyes and stopped short. In between the measuring and sawing today, he'd opened up to Darryl, told him about Butterfly. And good ol' Dar had reserved judgment and kept an open mind throughout the conversation.

"She must like it," he'd said. But he hadn't heard of Gary. Gor? Yeah. Extreme lifestylers, too.

In the end, Dar came close to showing a bias or two. After tilting his head toward the house, where his girlfriend Melanie cooked dinner, Darryl told him to watch out for submissives who couldn't do anything for themselves. "That 24/7 stuff is great for rich folks, but Doms like me," he'd said, "we have jobs, kids, regular lives."

Bryan didn't bring up the fact that Butterfly could barely leave the house.

His finger began to throb, and he sat and closed his eyes once more. Soon the endorphins would rush to the rescue and bring some relief. He pushed on the place where the splinter had entered. Pushed it hard. With his eyes shut, he could almost imagine what it felt like to get off on the pain. He blinked. Melanie was crunching down the driveway, a plate of food in hand. She looked good. Damn good, but although Dar had made it clear that he could join in their play at any time, Bryan still kept his distance.

"Hi, Bryan."

"Hey, Melanie. You didn't need to do that."

The chicken smelled like Sundays at his grandmother's table. She placed a fork and knife on the worktable then studied his outstretched finger.

"Want me to pull it out for you?"

He raised his hand and watched her work the offending sliver of wood out of his sore flesh.

"There," she whispered. "All better."

She didn't let go of his hand. The way her long hair hung down around her face, the size of her body... He thought of Butterfly, and his cock grew stiff.

Melanie licked her lips, not in a sexual way. More like nervous. Her black boots shifted on the cement floor. "Darryl and I are going out tonight. Would you like to come?"

"He mentioned it. I don't know, Mel."

"Okay. It's just..." She let go of his hand. "Darryl thought if an invitation came from me, then maybe you'd feel better about it."

"An invitation for what exactly?"

"To observe. Maybe play a little. He said you were curious." She grinned. "You've got it in you, ya know."

Yeah, I know. The things he'd thought of doing to Butterfly last night. Oh hell, every night since he met her. Bryan nodded then glanced down at the horse waiting for the final plank still in his hands. He'd need to sand the edges again, but other than that, the bulk of the work was done. As soon as the special order of red leather arrived, he'd try his hand at the upholstery. Until then, he'd stay away from Butterfly and try to sort out where all this was heading. If anywhere.

"What time?" he asked.

Her grin widened. "Seven."

He'd have to eat fast, then go home and take care of Wolf. And dress. What the heck did a guy wear to this kind of thing?

"Any tips on the dress code?"

"We're a pretty relaxed bunch. Jeans and a T-shirt will do."

She left him alone to eat, which he did in record time. His apartment was only minutes away, so after a quick walk around the block with Wolf and a shower, he was ready.

For what, though, he wasn't quite sure.

Dar drove them to a plain looking ranch on the outskirts of town. Nothing fancy like Gary's place. No Jags in the drive or gates to keep the riffraff out. Bryan took a deep breath and followed his friends inside. They were the last to arrive, and the four couples—well, one trio—greeted him warmly. He grabbed a Pepsi and some chips before settling into a chair by the kitchen.

The host, a thick man whom everyone addressed as Master Thomas, claimed the seat next to him. "So, Bryan, what's your pleasure?"

"Oh, the soda's fine."

A gentle rumble of laughter made the rounds. "What I meant was, what kind of play do you enjoy?"

"Ah. Gotcha. Um... Well, I guess I'm here to start exploring that."

"Fair enough." Thomas offered him a wide, earnest smile, then stood and waved a hand toward the hallway. "Shall we begin?"

Everyone headed for whatever lay beyond the modest living

room. Thomas led the way and ushered his guests down the stairs to a finished basement. Downstairs was dark, but not so dark he couldn't see the equipment. Decent stuff, most of it homemade or ordered online, though it paled in comparison to what Gary's dungeon offered. A table held several bottles of water, blankets and black cases personalized by their owners. Dar added his to the bunch while Bryan tugged on a circle of steel bolted to the brick wall. It didn't budge.

"This is Melanie's favorite spot." Darryl grabbed the other ring then led him to where the rest of the men were busy setting up metal folding chairs.

Bryan glanced around the room, checking things out. Melanie—along with all the other subs—had disappeared. "Where is she?"

"Getting ready," answered Darryl. "Why don't you have a seat, get comfy?" Bryan sat, his friend taking the chair beside him. "Feel free to ask all the questions you want afterwards—"

"I know the etiquette. No talking during a scene. No touching anything that isn't yours, bodies included."

Dar nodded. "Done your homework, I see."

"In theory only. Now I need some hands-on experience." He chuckled and Darryl joined in. But just for a few seconds.

"Shhh. Here they come."

Three women and two men had left their street clothes behind. Bryan admired Melanie's lithe body, firm yet soft in all the right places. Her bare breasts sported nipple rings slightly larger than Butterfly's, and she wore a slim circle of steel around her neck. Other than the neatly trimmed hair on her mound, the rest of her was all tan skin and long legs. Other subs knelt by their Tops or sat on their laps.

A woman in stilettos came last, her Dom walking her slowly to the wall in front of the small audience. He placed her hands on the bricks and made sure she wasn't too close to it; her ass, covered in fishnet like the rest of her, tilted up prettily as the man spread her legs farther apart. Bryan watched her inhale deeply, as if preparing for whatever would happen next. The man admired the generous curves of her body with a light, unrushed touch, and she shivered with every sweeping caress.

The Dom opened his case and pulled out a small piece of something white from inside—chalk, it appeared—then traced the blonde's splayed fingers with it. He bent next, predictably drawing a line on the floor at the tip of each pointy-toed shoe. Bryan was impressed by the ingenuity of it—no ropes, no handcuffs—only white dust to keep her in place. He leaned back against his chair and waited to see how successful she'd be in obeying.

When the Dom placed a finger on the base of her spine, she raised her ass higher. The man cupped her round bottom, worshipping it for all to see, then gave each globe of pale flesh a healthy pop. The blonde stiffened, but held position, even as the warm-up that brought a blush to her ass grew in intensity. Pink skin peeking out from the netted fabric turned to red. Bryan scarcely breathed as the spanking progressed, and he had to force himself to relax against the uncomfortable chair. Could he do that to Butterfly? He swallowed and considered what it must feel like for the woman—and for the Dominant. The heat rolling off her bottom would warm his tingling palm. His muscles would ache, and his awareness of the woman's condition would become sharp and meld with his own arousal. At least it would in Bryan's head. He pictured Butterfly looking up at him, the desire in her eyes turning into something less focused, less aware.

The man stepped away. Took a drink of water from the nearby table. Sweat slicked his chest and arms, and Bryan wondered if the man's heart was pumping as furiously as his. The tension in the air, palpable and taut, increased when the Top selected a black leather paddle from the guts of his case and slapped it against his hand. Bryan noted the clenching of the woman's ass muscles. She took a deep breath, steeling herself for the first smack. When it came, she held firm to her stance. Bryan admired the little lift of her spiked heels, and that of her lush ass as if asking for more, one more. Harder.

And the man gave it to her, his appreciative gaze ever watchful to her body's reactions. If she trembled, he teased her, placing the paddle between the split of her legs or trailing it over the crevice higher above. Sometimes he'd whip the tool through the air, then stop short or give her only a light tap. The woman's chest was heaving now and tiny whimpers filled the air. Her red-tipped fingers slid from the chalk outline. The man leaned in with whispers of encouragement, or maybe dirty talk.

One thing Bryan knew for sure was that he enjoyed talking. That day in the library with Butterfly tied to the desk...saying those things to her had made him more connected to her. They hadn't talked much since meeting, and talking also gave him the feeling of control, although he was surely on the brink of losing it. Walking away from her, away from her invitation of splayed legs and sweet-smelling pussy, had been next to impossible.

The Dom turned back to his toys and selected a flogger, deerskin tails by the looks of it. He ran the red and black tips over the woman's back, a warning of what was to come. The supple tails would be a good way to start the flogging, and Bryan studied how the man used it, the motion of his wrist and the strength of the toy's impact against jiggling flesh. An earthy scent of deer hide rode on the charged air. He sucked it into his lungs, memories of hunting deer with his grandfather streaming into his brain. Butterfly reminded him of a deer—those wide, wary eyes, the color of her hair. He closed his eyes and wondered when his fascination with this woman had turned into a full-blown obsession. He was here to learn more about his desires, not torture himself with thoughts of what he'd do to her if he ever got the chance. Sure, Gary had okayed a blowjob or a quick fuck, but that made him still in control of things. He allowed whatever happened to happen, and Bryan didn't care to be a pawn in his game.

No, if he was going to enjoy Butterfly, it would be on his own terms.

The panting man before him switched to a sleek flogger with tapered tips. His submissive was shaking now, her hands barely lying flat against the wall. The man lifted her away from it then helped her to lie on the floor. Her back must've been cold against the cement, but Bryan doubted she noticed. The man spread her legs wide, and she managed to find the strength to hold them in place as he returned to the toys. Blunt-tipped scissors shone in the muted basement light. He cut the fishnet away from her hairless pussy with care, the heel of his palm pressing into her clit while he clipped lower. She writhed.

"Don't come," he whispered. "Not yet."

She didn't nod, but her glazed eyes met his in unspoken acquiescence. After opening up the netting to expose her from clit to ass, he cut larger chunks of fabric away from the sides then went back for two more floggers. The horsehair one had long tails that broke the silence of the room with a *swish* as the tips danced against the dark pink of her cunt. The Dom stood for the dozen or so strokes with this flogger before switching to a short one with tiny knots at the end of its tails. Lowering himself to his knees, the man took aim and expertly lashed at the moist sliver of flesh until the woman began to shake.

"Do you want to come?" he asked.

She was too far gone to answer. From his seat, Bryan could see the man smile, probably granting her permission to climax while the knots pummeled her clit. Her lower half lifted from the floor to meet each rhythmic thrash until she cried out her release.

When she grew still, her Dom gathered her into his arms and kissed her gently. Bryan had the strange urge to clap. The depth of their relationship was obvious to all who watched. The man grabbed a blanket, wrapped it around his sub, and carried her to the back of the basement for privacy as soft murmurs of conversation hummed through the room. Dar kissed Melanie then glanced his way.

"Well, what'd ya think?" Dar asked.

"I'm not sure." *Not sure I'm the type to do this in front of people,* he wanted to say. And the hurting part... Knowing what he did about Butterfly, could he ever do that to her?

"If you want to leave—"

"No. That'd be rude, especially after Master Thomas invited me into his home and all. I'll stay. And keep an open mind."

Melanie smiled from her perch on Darryl's lap. "The wonderful thing about BDSM is there's no one true way to do things."

Dar chuckled. "Some people 'scene' in public, others keep it in the bedroom. Some, like this next bunch, love to draw blood." He tilted his head in the direction of three people unfolding a tarp for the floor. "As long as it's safe, sane and consensual, it's all good."

Bryan smiled tightly at his friend's last comment then watched as a man and his two subs—one male, one female—found their positions. Their play was much more brutal than the sensual flogging before. The male bottom was a real pain slut who seemed to relish the snap of a thorny flogger against thighs, ass and back.

It made him think of the cutting... How damaged was Butterfly when Gary had found her? And if an emotionally fragile person gave consent, was it still "all good"? Gary was merely a predator in Bryan's eyes, like the sly coyote of Navajo mythology taking what he wanted and leaving nothing in return.

Halfway through the scene, everything faded to a blur as Bryan's mind focused on another order Gary had tossed his way: stocks for each of his slaves, due in time for the party. This project, like the spanking horse, would keep him away from the house, at least for a while, and put some distance between him and Butterfly—he'd need to use Darryl's tools to get the job done. He had a hunch Gary had wanted him out of the way, had sensed a growing attraction to the woman whose silly slave name seemed more like a nickname you'd give a kid or a pet than a real name.

He wanted to know her real name, and hoped to hear it from her lips before he had to leave her behind for good. The sudden realization that this was only temporary, that he had but little glimpses into her strange world, stabbed at his heart and gut. Not seeing her again would make him feel...empty? No, that couldn't be it. Not this soon anyway. Christ, they'd hardly talked at all—he barely knew her. Yet somehow he knew he didn't want to leave, and for a split second, she was in his truck, shaking with fear, and relief, as he sped off toward the Arizona state line.

He blinked, wondering where the hell that last image had come from. Surely he couldn't take care of her, not like Gary or some other Master could.

Or could he?

When the play party ended—and his erection, which was painfully hard after watching Darryl play with Mel, finally faded enough for him to stand—Bryan thanked everyone for allowing him to come and even asked to handle some of the toys that interested him. The deerskin flogger, his favorite, looked easy to make, and it felt good in his hand. He snapped it at the air, observing how the tips reacted as he changed up the action in his wrist or the strength of his swat. This he could do to her. And he'd enjoy bringing a bright blush to various parts of her body as he worked her over. He'd let her come, repeatedly, then hold her tight before fucking her senseless. He had a feeling none of that would happen at Gary's party.

He said his goodbyes and headed for Dar's truck. Suddenly he felt drained. Alone. He looked westward, in the direction of Gary's estate, and hoped she was doing well tonight on her sparse cot with no warm body to cuddle with after God knew what Gary had put her through.

Dar and Melanie's voices weren't far behind. A good thing, because he was more than ready to go home.

Chapter Seven

Bryan hadn't meant to finish up the spanking horse at Gary's, but he couldn't stay away from Butterfly any longer. He'd put the finishing touches on the library pillars then turned his attention to the horse and stocks down in the dungeon.

His fingers traced a vigilant path over the thick red leather to find any lumps in the upholstery or scratches on the crimson surface that glinted in the dim lights. As expected, he found none. A perfectionist at heart, he'd been very careful to create this piece of furniture with the same attention to detail that Gary gave his own art—and slaves. His hands ran along the long line of steel tacks holding the padding in place and met the sleek oak beyond.

The padding had been a major concession on Gary's part; he'd wanted the women's bodies to rest on bare wood at the apex of the piece, but Bryan managed to convince him that, should he ever miss his mark, the wood would scar. A cushion, he suggested, could be easily replaced if damaged. At first Gary scoffed at the idea of making such an error in judgment while punishing a slave, but he gave in once Bryan mentioned that the extra bit of comfort would allow the girls to be strapped to the apparatus for longer periods of time. He'd regretted the words as soon as they'd left his lips.

His hands kept moving. The varnish gleaming on the wood was no longer sticky to the touch. He'd worried about the humidity down here in the basement but the fans he'd brought had done the trick. Satisfied with the glossy finish, he knelt and checked the piece for splinters. Bryan didn't want to cause the girls any pain—well, any more pain than they'd get while tied up on the spanking horse. They'd have enough to endure when bound there hand and foot, and a stray sliver of wood would only add to the unrelenting punishment their master most likely dished out on a regular basis.

Bryan stood. His left knee pressed into the padding, sank deep into it and tempted him to lift his right. *This is silly,* he thought, but couldn't resist. Besides, he was alone in the basement; the women had gone outside with Gary, except for Butterfly. So he straddled the horse, checking it for stability and comfort, making sure Butterfly's petite frame would be okay up here. It reminded him of his childhood dreams of being a rodeo star, like almost every boy on the Rez had aspired to be. That made him feel silly, too. He remembered sharing that blast from the past with Simone and how she'd laughed. He wondered if Butterfly would laugh, too.

He then felt between his legs to measure the distance from his crotch to the top of the arch. There was plenty of room— she'd be all right. Next, he lowered himself onto the padded length of the horse, stretched out his arms and relaxed his legs. His cheek rested against the cool cushion. He closed his eyes, imagining her agony there, or perhaps her bliss.

When his groin made contact, the erection he'd been ignoring grew. He pushed into the horse, willing it to subside. It refused to wane. What would she look like spread open on his creation? He pictured her ass angled up, her small breasts on each side of the horse swaying with every smack of Gary's paddle against her bottom.

A small laugh by the stairs forced his eyes open. It was Butterfly. He hopped off the horse, dying to get closer to her, but forcing himself to maintain control.

"Hey," he said, his eyes never leaving hers. Surprisingly she didn't look away.

She took a step down. "Are you exploring your submissive side?" she asked with a grin.

He grinned back. "Just checking it out, making sure it was

sturdy, that kind of thing." *Checking it out for you.* His cock strained against the zipper of his Levi's.

As she approached the horse, the track lighting above highlighted the sheen of sweat on her chest and shoulders. She must've seen the curiosity in his eyes about how someone who never left the house could work up a sweat.

"I have a treadmill. When the others go outside to exercise, I do the same indoors." She stared at the horse. "It's beautiful. May I touch it?"

He leaned into her. Big mistake... Her workout had made the air around her body hotter, her scent stronger.

"Yes, you can touch."

But she didn't just touch. She mounted the horse and laid her cheek where his had been. The fans lifted her long hair, then blew against the tiny, sheer scarves pretending to cover her body. They rose away from her thighs and bared her bottom for a few seconds, then hid it again. Her hands reached for the front of the horse. Green eyes stared up at him in a silent invitation.

Today he was too weak to decline it. He walked over to her. Grabbed her hips and inched her bottom closer to his groin. She was at the perfect height for fucking, and he brought her pussy flush against him. Her breath caught. He swayed to one side to see her face, the invitation still there, her small nipple tight and darker against the red padding. He pushed his pelvis against her then bent to kiss her soft bottom.

"Tie me," she whispered.

It wasn't a request, but a command spoken in a husky voice. His hands shot to the scarves knotted at her waist. She flinched.

"Not with those."

He didn't miss the panic in her voice. "Yes, with those. I want to see all of you."

Her stiffened body took its time in relaxing and, when he undid the scarves, he saw why.

"What the hell?"

Jesus, had she been cutting again? If so, this was proof absolute that Gary's so-called help had failed. The urge to hold her became unbearable and he followed his whim, pulling her up and back to cradle her in his arms.

"It's not what you think—"

"Did Gary do this to you?" He turned her around and lifted her face to his, seeking the truth in her features. "Or did you?"

"Neither, actually. Jasmine…"

"Jasmine?"

She nodded. "She's been a little out of control. Something happened a while back and, well, she blames me." Butterfly glanced away. "Perhaps rightfully so."

He turned his attention back to the angry red gash that marked her pale skin just above her hip. It wasn't deep, but ran a jagged four inches long. "How?" he asked, touching it lightly as if to soothe it away.

"A broken wine glass." She took his hand from her hip and smiled. "Don't worry. It could've been much worse."

"And here I thought Gary was the one to watch out for."

She gave a little chuckle and turned to mount the horse again. He held her still. Kept her tight in his arms. "You should leave."

There. He'd said it. Now the ball was in her court. And he knew without a doubt she'd knock it back over the net with a "No way" or a timid shake of her head. Instead she offered a quiet, "Maybe." Then she slid from his stunned embrace to resume her position.

She even handed him the scarves.

Her pulse thundered as she shifted against the cool, supple leather. It was as soft as velvet against her flesh and with her cheek pressed into it she couldn't help but inhale the powerful, masculine scent. The smell of leather was synonymous with sex to her. She couldn't catch a whiff of a handbag or pair of shoes—not that she'd had much access to either of those in years except on rare occasions when Master had her dress up—

without going soft and buttery between her legs.

The anticipation of what Bryan would do ratcheted her sexual tension to an almost painful degree. Moisture pooled at her pussy and wet the leather beneath her. Any second she expected a sharp smack of his hand on her ass. Her eyes closed and she licked her lips. She couldn't remember the last time she'd been so excited about a spanking, or any kind of sex play for that matter. Probably not since her early days with Master.

But, no. That wasn't true. She'd been just as excited when she'd been tied on the desk with Bryan's invitation nestled between her thighs.

The wait was so long, Butterfly began to wonder if he would walk away, leaving her sprawled across the delicious-smelling horse, aching and unfulfilled. Didn't the sight of her please him? Didn't he want to slap her bottom bright red then fuck her until she couldn't stand?

At last his touch descended on her, but it wasn't the hard spank she'd expected. Like a light breeze blowing over her back, the very tips of his fingers brushed the length of her spine and danced over the globes of her ass. She squirmed and smiled at his tickling touch.

Bryan's fingers drifted between her legs, sampling her wetness, probing into her slick entrance before withdrawing again. Heavy hands cupped her buttocks, squeezing and kneading lightly, then pulling them apart to expose the entrance to her ass. It clenched tightly, and she imagined how the tiny opening must look to him. A new thrill of lust coursed through her. Oh, how she longed for him to plunge roughly into the taut hole...or into her pussy or mouth. Any place, just so long as he was inside her. She was desperate for him to fill her.

He gave a soft groan that made the hair rise on her nape. "My God, you don't know how hot you look like this. Lift your ass higher."

She responded instantly to his commanding tone, such a contrast to his usual relaxed voice, raising her rear to offer every bit of herself to his inspection.

Still Bryan didn't spank the rounded flesh she displayed.

Instead, he returned to trailing his fingers up and down her back and over her cheeks and upper thighs. His touch was like feathers or the trailing ends of ribbons, an endless teasing torture that had her squirming.

"Aren't you going to tie me?" she dared to ask. Over the past few weeks, she seemed to have forgotten every bit of Master's training about not speaking unless spoken to.

"Do you like to be tied?" The disembodied voice coming from above and just behind her was deep and quiet with a soothing quality that made her feel nearly as safe and secure as bondage.

"Yes." She flexed her fingers. Her wrists felt naked and vulnerable without something encircling them, and her body might fly away with nothing holding it down.

"Tell me why," the calm voice continued. "What is it about being tied up that excites you?"

"It's not as much about excitement as it is security. I like small spaces and being contained. And I like being held in place." It felt odd confessing this to a near-stranger, yet at the same time she was completely comfortable telling Bryan. What a relief not to have to weigh and second-guess everything she said to him, afraid a wrongly chosen word might ignite his temper. Master's volatility, which had once seemed thrilling, was now exhausting to her.

The brushing fingers abandoned her body and his hand settled on her head, stroking her hair back from her face. "I went to my first play party the other night. There was a woman who was held in place entirely by her own will. That was her Dom's challenge, to keep her position no matter what he did. A chalk line drawn at her hands and feet were all that bound her. What do you think of that?"

It took her a moment to realize he was asking her opinion. She wasn't accustomed to it. *What does he want to hear,* would be her first consideration if Master had asked her such a question, but with Bryan, she realized she could give an honest opinion. She could *have* an opinion that might contradict his and he wouldn't get angry.

"I think that's an interesting challenge, but I really like being tied." Her wrists were nearly aching for restraints as she said it.

The warmth and weight of his hand lifted from her hair. "I'd love to give you what you want, but I think what you need is something different."

She heard him move and wondered what he was doing, then she felt the scarves wrap around her wrists, first one then the other—much looser than Master would have tied them. Bryan's hands molded around hers, pressing them to the sides of the horse.

"You aren't tied. The scarves are just there to give you the illusion, but you must keep your position and your hands where I've placed them."

A smile curved her lips. Bryan had managed to accommodate her and set her a new challenge all at the same time. This was a game, something amusing and light, which she'd never realized bondage play could be.

Bryan bent low and whispered near her ear. "Now the fun begins."

The first slap was as light as though he were swatting a fly. It barely stung, but his hand remained on her after it hit, squeezing her flesh lightly, replacing the little hurt with comfort.

Butterfly didn't have any trouble remembering to keep her ass lifted. It naturally curved up into his hand like a cat arching its back for more petting.

His hand rose and fell with a more solid smack across both cheeks. Another two swats and her rear burned nicely, a warm, toasty feeling that sent waves of pleasure through her and made her pussy contract and release wildly as if gulping for air.

She checked her hand placement and thought they were where he'd put them, although it was hard to tell on the smooth wood. They might have slid forward a little. With Master she would begin to worry about that fraction of an inch, blowing it up in her mind until it was a mile and fearing what his punishment for disobedience might be. But with Bryan she could relax and enjoy her spanking without fear of something far more painful or humiliating to follow. She gripped the slippery wood as best she could and held on through a short series of spanks, keeping her ass tilted up and trying not to jerk at the sting of each blow.

Bryan paused and again massaged her flesh, rubbing and stroking each cheek lovingly before running a finger down her cleft to her opening. She nearly sighed in contentment as he slipped several fingers inside her, filling her yearning emptiness. Her muscles clutched at his fingers when he pulled them back out. The lips of her pussy were still tender from Master's pinning, and that ache only added to her pleasure. She wondered what this man would think of her special punishment, which had inspired Master to name her Butterfly. Would Bryan stare entranced at her wide-open pussy pinned to the board? Would he be horrified yet incredibly aroused and push his fingers inside her as he was doing now, perhaps knocking the pins askew as he entered her?

Immersed in a fantasy of him tearing her free of the pins and burying his cock deep inside her, Butterfly was so stimulated that when he touched her clit with his finger and circled it lightly she abruptly came with a shudder and a soft moan. It was completely unexpected. She'd learned to control her reactions and time every orgasm to Master's will. Spontaneously letting loose like that, even though the climax had been small, was not allowed. Instantly she froze, all her muscles tightening as she waited for Bryan's reaction. "I'm sorry," she whispered. "I didn't mean for that to happen."

His finger stopped moving. "Why not? I meant to give you pleasure."

"But I came without your permission."

He rubbed her heated buttocks with his other hand. "You're allowed to come as many times as you like, as often as I can make you. That's what I want. Sound good?" And with that he resumed playing with her pussy, backing off from her clit and giving her a moment to recover sensitivity while he plunged his fingers in and out. He trailed the gathered moisture up the crack between her cheeks and inserted a wet finger into her anus, stretching it slowly until he could push two digits inside.

When she pushed back onto his exploring fingers, he asked, "You like that?"

"Yes." She loved to be taken there. Something about the impossibly tight fit of a penis in that channel, the dull burn as she stretched to accommodate it, thrilled her. But Gary...Master didn't fuck her ass very often. Actually, he rarely fucked her at all anymore, seeming more content to inflict physical or psychological tortures. He was, however, still fond of impaling her mouth with his cock hard, fast and deep enough to make her gag. He took pleasure in her struggle to breathe as he held her face between viselike hands and filled her throat. When she choked, he'd pull out long enough for her to gasp for breath then resume pumping.

Butterfly shook off the memory and concentrated on what Bryan's hands were doing to her now. While he continued to play with her ass, the long fingers of his other hand probed her sex while his thumb massaged her clit. The little bud was already simmering with sensations from her first climax, and he quickly nudged her to a second one with a few deft circles. She gasped as another surge of ecstasy overcame her and clung tight to the spanking horse, bracing her knees on either side of it.

He removed all his invading fingers from her body as she trembled and shook. The waves of delight hadn't subsided when an unexpected smack to her rear pulled her back to earth. Bryan's slaps were harder this time and aimed low on her bottom where cheeks met thighs, right near her still pulsing vagina. The stinging enhanced the pleasure throbbing through her, making it grow again. Then she felt something she'd never expected—his mouth on her ass kissing away the pain even as he created it. Each hit was followed by a soft nibble of lips and a slow stroke of his tongue on the globes of her ass and in the cleft between. The contrast of the harsh and gentle treatment was incredible.

Butterfly moaned and wiggled, thrusting her bottom toward

him, her leg muscles cramping from the effort of keeping her position and her damp palms still pressed to the smooth leather. His touch felt so good, so deliciously perverse in its juxtaposition of hard and soft, that the lingering pulses from her climax swelled. Another burst of pleasure shook her, the intensity even stronger this time, and she cried out, her eyes squeezing shut as rapture swept through her. *Oh, this is what sex should be!* She felt as though a puzzle piece had snapped into place and she was finally presented with a complete picture. *This is what I've been missing.*

Bryan's mouth and hands were on her back now, kissing and touching her all over. He nibbled on her shoulder and said words she couldn't understand. The sound of his native language spoken in a husky murmur sent a thrill through her, and the ends of his long hair brushing over her skin made her shiver. *Yes. This is what I want.* The knowledge was crystal clear and undeniable...but impossible. She couldn't imagine Gary allowing her to break her contract and go off with this man.

Besides, Bryan might not want her.

She brought her ragged breathing under control as the last waves of her climax died away. His mouth was still pressed to her shoulder, one arm slung across her back as he half-covered her. Why he didn't mount and fuck her, she didn't know, but for some reason he held back as he had the other day in the den. What was he waiting for? Their time together was so short.

Impatiently, she wiggled beneath him. His weight lifted off her and he raised her upper body, helping her to sit facing him, still astride the horse. His eyes were deep walnut today and so piercing it felt as if he could read her every thought. But clearly he couldn't since his next words were, "What's the matter?"

"I know it's not my place to do more than offer myself to you, but..." She trailed off, her cheeks burning in anticipation of the request she wanted to make.

"Go on." His eyes searched hers.

"I wondered why you haven't..." Again her words faded. She was making a mess of it, unable to express her simple request like a normal person. Instinctively, her arm crossed over her abdomen to hide the faint scars.

He noticed and pulled her hand away. When he took in the faded marks, he didn't flinch. In fact, his quiet presence remained as solid as a rock and as uncompromising. When he spoke again, his voice held the firm command of a Master. "Say it. Tell me what you want."

When he stressed the word "you", Butterfly finally understood why he'd held back for so long. He wanted her to give herself freely to him, not because her Master had bid her offer herself to a guest. Her offer must come from the heart. Bryan couldn't see that true desire for him had been growing in her since the moment she'd seen him.

Drawing a deep breath, she licked her lips. "I want to give you the same pleasure you've already given me. Will you let me service you?"

A quick smile curved his mouth. "Service? Sounds like a motel maid."

"What expression do you prefer?" She was amazed at the teasing lilt in her voice, which sounded so light she barely recognized it. "Go down, give a blowjob, suck off, or the more formal, fellate?" Her lips trembled with amusement.

He caressed the side of her face, tracing his thumb over her lower lip. "I'll take any term you want to throw at me, and the answer is yes."

Leaning in, he kissed her, a soft press of the lips from which she didn't pull away. She no longer cared that her kisses were supposed to be reserved for Master. Beliefs she'd held as the truth of her life for the past several years had evaporated in the course of a few weeks. What did that say about the depth of her commitment to her lifestyle, not to mention her integrity? But she didn't care, because Bryan's mouth was warm and his tongue wet and searching and she wanted him to go on kissing her forever. Master's well-trained slave was gone and a yearning, passionate woman had taken her place.

He lifted her from the horse, gathering her into his arms and against his broad chest. She wrapped her legs around his hips, her arms around his neck, her fingers snarling in strands of his long hair as she pulled him to her for another kiss. She opened her mouth wide for his plunging tongue and coiled her own around it. The bulge of his erection pressed rough denim into her pelvis. The delicious scrape on her over-stimulated clit made her squirm. Heat shot through her from the contact and she thought she might come again.

"Mm," she pulled away from his mouth. "Put me down now, please."

Reluctantly, he let her slide down his body until her feet rested on the floor. She reached for his fly, pushing up the material of his T-shirt so she could unfasten his jeans. Her fingers fumbled at the task—she was so eager to see what she'd only glimpsed the shape of, and when she pulled the zipper down, his cock was covered by neither shorts nor briefs and sprang free.

She exhaled raggedly, her eyes feasting on the length and girth thrusting at an angle from his groin. A thatch of black hair curled wildly at its base and a heavy sac swayed below. The shaft was an even deeper mahogany than Bryan's dark skin, nearly purple at the head and uncircumcised, although the round crown was already peeking from its hood. Pearls of pre-come dripped from the slit in the swollen tip, and Butterfly licked her lips in anticipation of tasting his essence. She should find a condom. There were plenty secreted in unobtrusive spots around the dungeon for guests to use. But she wanted to taste *him*, feel his skin on her tongue. Master need never know.

Bryan groaned. "Hurry. Do it before I embarrass myself and come just from you looking at me!"

She smiled as she knelt before him, pleased that her mere gaze aroused him so much. Her hand slipped around the base of his shaft, gripping hard, cutting off the blood flow to help delay his orgasm. With a long look into his eyes, she leaned forward and licked the white drops glistening on the smooth head. He groaned again, a low rumbling that vibrated right through her. His lips parted, revealing a flash of white teeth, and his tongue darted out to lick them. His eyes closed then opened again to fix on her once more, as though he didn't want to miss a single moment of the experience.

So she put on a bit of a show for him, tracing her tongue around the head then starting at the base and giving a long, slow lick all the way up the side. The musky flavor of come and salty skin combined in a flavor that was like Master's yet completely different. Maybe it was because she'd chosen to savor it, had invited Bryan's cock into her mouth instead of being commanded to swallow deep. All she knew was that a sense of power flowed through her when he moaned in pleasure and thrust slightly toward her. It was a feeling she'd never experienced when performing this service for her Master. She was in control of Bryan's reactions and the strength that gave her was heady.

Wrapping her lips around the soft head, she slowly engulfed him, inch by inch, until she could hold no more. The soft hiss of his intake of breath and a murmured "Baby, that feels so good" were her reward.

Equally slowly, she released him from her mouth in increments until she could view his entire gleaming length. She scratched it lightly with her fingernails then reached beneath to fondle his balls, their warm weight nestling comfortably into her palm.

Bryan rested his hand on the side of her head, but not to force her back onto him. He stroked her hair and encouraged her gently. "More. Please."

Once more she glanced up at him, towering above her so big, broad and tall, yet helplessly under the sway of the cock in her hands. She smiled and bent to her task with a sense of purpose, no longer exploring him, instead concentrating on giving the most thorough blowjob of her life.

The hand she'd been using as a makeshift cock ring loosened to slide up and down his shaft. With the other she rolled his balls between her fingers and traced the sensitive path toward his anus. Again she drew his cock into her mouth, smoothing her tongue over it as she sucked. She imagined what that hard suction must feel like for him—as though she was going to pull the very life out of him and into herself.

Bryan groaned and thrust, his hips pumping with every stroke of her hand. He muttered, "Baby," again followed by something in his language that might have been an endearment or a curse.

Taking it as encouragement, she increased her efforts. Then, when she thought he was on the edge of coming, she broke off, released his length and clamped her fingers in a tight circle around the base again. He made a soft sound of protest in his throat.

Lowering her head and nudging between his thighs, she guided his balls to her mouth and engulfed the soft sac, rolling her tongue over and around each hard orb. His inner thighs were so hot against her cheeks, and his taste and scent were pure male musk. She inhaled deeply, feeling like she was breathing in his very essence.

She wet her fingers with saliva then explored further between his cheeks, locating his anus and slipping a finger inside, teasing the tight ring of muscle to open just as he had done to her. She probed in and out with one then two fingers, searching for the sweet spot. Master didn't enjoy ass play, but some of his guests did. Butterfly had read a library's worth of information and learned every technique that could possibly please a partner. She knew what she was looking for and could tell when she'd found it, because Bryan gave another long, low groan and his hole squeezed tighter around her fingers.

She worked them in and out, wishing she had more than saliva to lubricate the passage, but Bryan didn't seem to mind. He pressed back onto her probing fingers, his legs trembling a little from the effort to stand upright. "Oh, Jesus!"

Leaving his balls, Butterfly returned to sucking his cock and released the constraining ring of fingers around the base once more. She felt the pulse of life vibrating through him as she drew him closer and closer to the edge. His thrusts became more erratic and he gripped either side of her head, holding it steady, but still allowing her to control the depth of his entry. She rammed her fingers harder and deeper into his ass, enjoying the idea of giving as well as accepting penetration.

Suddenly he drove into her and froze. His cock swelled and his body shivered. He gave a wordless cry as his orgasm exploded through him and he released in the back of her throat. She swallowed while continuing to stroke her hand up and down his shaft.

When she felt she'd milked it of every last drop of come, she let it slip from her mouth and hand. She drew her fingers from his ass and brought her hand back between his legs. Still kneeling before him, she sat back on her heels and gazed up at his face, his mouth open and panting, his brows knitted in a frown. He opened his eyes to look down at her. He smiled and stroked back her hair.

She loved the weight and warmth of his hand cradling her head and leaned into it.

"That was..." He shook his head. "'Great', 'wonderful' and 'amazing' are too ordinary. It was beyond that. Phenomenal?"

Butterfly didn't answer, but returned his smile. She couldn't remember receiving a compliment or an expression of appreciation since her earliest days with Master, before he brought her home and transformed her into Butterfly.

Bryan took her hand, pulling her to her feet and into his strong arms. He was so tall she had to tilt her head back to see his face. His dark eyes gazed at her with warm approval that made her glow inside. "I could get used to that."

Me, too, and to being held like this afterward.

Their eyes locked for a moment and then his gaze moved to her lips. He inclined his head slightly, and she rose up on her toes.

A loud, deliberate clapping near the doorway broke the stillness. Butterfly jerked from Bryan's embrace and swiveled toward her Master, who was slowly strolling toward them, bringing his palms together in sarcastic approval. "It's about time you took advantage of my hospitality, Bryan. I was beginning to think you didn't like any of my slaves—or that you had romantic notions of wooing a particular one."

Butterfly dropped to her knees and bowed her head as he approached. His hand settled heavily on the crown of her head, pushing it lower. "I know you've taken a special liking to my little butterfly. But what you don't realize is that these girls are all here merely to provide service, one slut the same as the next with no more value than as an object of pleasure. And didn't my pet blow you well? I could tell from your shout that she did." He laughed without any real mirth.

Butterfly suddenly realized she no longer took pride in being one of Master's possessions. The past few years of her life flashed through her mind in a blur and it was as if a spotlight illuminated every tawdry detail. She could see her subjugation for what it was, not a transcendent offering of self, but a sad woman surrendering to a cruel man's perverse pleasure.

Bryan remained silent. What was he thinking? Did he agree that her worth was only equal to the pleasure she gave him or did he feel something different for her?

Master grabbed a fistful of her hair and tugged her to her feet. "Go to your room." His voice was level, but she recognized the tightness of anger in it. He knew he'd walked in on more than the aftermath of a blowjob. He'd seen them gazing into each other's eyes, leaning in for a kiss.

Butterfly had no doubt there would be severe punishment in store for a slave who imagined herself as something more than her Master's possession. But did she belong to him any longer when she didn't feel it in her heart?

This new insight didn't stop her from obeying. Her training was too ingrained for her to defy the power of her Master's voice. Silently, she padded from the room without a backward glance at Bryan.

Chapter Eight

As he watched Butterfly walk away, naked but for the scarves still fluttering from her wrists and the silver slave collar around her neck, Bryan felt a surge of intense rage so white-hot it literally clouded his vision. His gut churned and he drew in a slow breath, trying to calm himself as his hands became tight fists at his sides. He couldn't attack this guy and pound the shit out of him. Any move he made at this point was bound to get her in big trouble. He remembered seeing Jasmine on her way outside earlier. What the hell had she done to get her hair whacked off like that? The woman's whole attitude had changed, the temptress now replaced by a mere shadow. Not that money mattered when a person's well-being was at stake, but his financial future hung in the balance, too. This was what happened when you made a deal with the fucking devil.

Anger never wins the goal. Be sly like the coyote to get the best of an enemy, his grandfather used to say. Maybe he could find a way to free Butterfly, or at the very least protect her from whatever punishment he may have inadvertently brought down on her head.

"So what's the going rate for..." He could barely bring himself to say the word, especially after the gift Butterfly had just given him. "...for sluts these days?" He pulled up his jeans and zipped them as he spoke, struggling to keep his voice calm.

Gary's eyebrows lifted and an amused smile played on his lips. "So you're making me an offer for her? How much do you think she's worth?"

Fuck! He wanted him to name a price? The man had to know he had nothing. A little savings, not much, but he'd give it all to get her out of here. "Eight hundred." He stared into cold gray eyes, hoping his own weren't burning like black coals with suppressed anger.

The bastard laughed, and Bryan wasn't sure if it was because he thought it was too much or too little.

If Gary guessed how much he cared, it would destroy any chance he had of winning her. Guys like this loved games of control. The value of a possession rose in direct proportion to how much someone else wanted it, and Gary would delight in dangling over his head what Bryan desired but could never afford.

"Like you say, she's good. I'd like more of that, but you know I'm not rich."

Still smiling, Gary stroked his hand over the supple red leather of the horse then reached down and tugged on one of the metal hoops in front. "I'll have to sleep on it. Maybe fuck her a few times to see if her cunt's still tight enough to hold my interest." His gaze shot up to check Bryan's reaction.

Although his neck and jaw tightened, he continued to reign in his anger, quieted his breath to help calm his temper. Gary's taunting showed he wanted to snap Bryan's control. This was just a game to him, the kind of power play he thrived on. Bryan had to act cool, even though the idea of this fucker touching Butterfly in any way killed him.

"You want the stocks you've commissioned done in time for your party?"

"Yes." Gary's eyes narrowed, and Bryan could almost see him trying to figure out where he was going with the question.

"Plus I still have a little finishing work to be done on the pillars before you show them off to your guests. It's a lot of work and very little time to complete it." He pursed his lips as though considering. "I have a proposition for you—the rest of my work for free if you sell me the girl without a fresh mark on her. I want her body unblemished...a fresh sheet for me to write on, so to speak."

Gary's little smile returned, and Bryan wanted to punch the smirk off his face. "For someone like you that's almost a fortune, isn't it, probably your rent money for a few months? What will you live on? Love?" His laughter was dry and humorless. "Do you think a woman like Butterfly is capable of love? How can someone with no self-respect, someone who's not even a person, really, offer that? Gratitude and neediness perhaps, but without a firm hand to keep her in line, she'll soon fall apart. She can't survive outside of the environment I've created for her."

Bryan despised this assessment, but the last statement caught his attention. Perhaps there was a kernel of truth here. Could he take Butterfly from her proverbial cocoon and expect her to thrive? He couldn't provide her with the things she was used to. All he had was a crappy apartment and a gut feeling that she needed more in her life than torture and demeaning treatment. What if he was wrong? What if her psyche was too fragile to survive in the real world? For that matter, what if she didn't want to leave with him?

"Are you willing to take my deal?" *What if I can't handle her? This is a huge commitment. I'd be taking on a human life!* He brushed his worries aside. "In fact, let's turn it into a bet."

Gary gave another sharp bark of laughter and folded his arms over his chest. "I can't wait to hear this. Go ahead."

"The money plus my work on the dungeon equipment, and..." Bryan took a deep breath and the biggest gamble of his life. "...we'll leave the decision to Butterfly. She can choose to remain here with you or leave with me."

"Interesting." Again caressing the leather of the horse as if it were a woman's skin, Gary contemplated the offer. "I like a gamble, especially when I know the odds are in my favor. All right. We'll present the choice the night of the party and ask her what she wants to do." He held up a finger. "But with one stipulation. You can't have any contact with her between now and then. I don't want your influence clouding her judgment—such as it is."

Bryan's mind raced. Without a chance to talk to Butterfly

and present his case he was taking a huge risk. The devil she knew was familiar, safe. What if she refused to take a chance? He'd lose the girl *and* everything he'd worked so hard to save. He finally nodded. "Agreed, but with a condition of my own. Leave her completely alone, don't threaten or hurt her in any way." He gave a tight smile. "I wouldn't want you influencing her decision either."

"Done! A gentleman's agreement that neither of us will interfere." Gary held out his hand. It took Bryan a few seconds to get past his repulsion enough to take it. All he could think of during the brief clasp was that this hand did horrible things to Butterfly all the time.

"Trust me, I don't need to threaten. The bitch is completely under my control." The man's smug smile expressed his utter confidence that he'd reduced Butterfly to a mindless drone who would respond exactly as he predicted.

God, what if he was right? Bryan pulled his callused hand from Gary's smooth grip. He pictured Butterfly's wide, vulnerable eyes gazing into his and her sweet smile, so hopeful and trusting when she gave it to him.

He focused all his thoughts on her and willed her to hear him. *Please, baby, listen to your heart. You know what's best for you. When the time comes, choose me.*

Chapter Nine

He'd agonized over his wardrobe like a high school kid getting ready for a dance for far too long. How the hell was he supposed to know what people wore to an event like this? Formal wear, fetish gear, nothing at all? Somehow he knew Gary's friends would be different from the people at the party Darryl and Melanie had taken him to. In the end he'd chosen a "fuck you" ensemble consisting of a faded T-shirt and ripped jeans, because who the hell were these people that he needed to impress them?

Besides, when Butterfly made her choice later that evening, he wanted her to be in no doubt that he was a poor carpenter, not some rich guy in a fancy suit. With him, what she saw was what she'd get, and hopefully she'd think it was enough.

Now, wandering the periphery of the well-dressed crowd in Gary's living room, Bryan wished he'd at least put on a dress shirt and trousers. These were potential clients, after all, men who could turn his business cards into jobs. No matter who Butterfly chose tonight, his life was about to change. He might very well leave here with a woman so damaged he'd have to take care of her for God knew how long. His savings account would be empty, so he'd really need whatever work he could line up with these rich bastards.

"Beautiful work." A man in black leather pants and a designer shirt stopped Bryan as he walked past. "Those pillars in the study are real works of art. Who taught you?"

"I apprenticed under a master craftsman, Darryl Johansen,

and my grandfather taught me woodworking prior to that." Bryan pinned a smile on his stiff lips, trying to concentrate solely on this business contact for the moment, but Butterfly's eyes haunted his mind.

She was all he could think about, and he hadn't seen her in over a week. Did she think he was finished with her once she'd given him a blowjob? Did she know why he was staying away? She was supposed to remain ignorant of the bet until the night of the party, but maybe Gary was fucking with her mind on a daily basis, perhaps punishing her in some way to break her spirit and mold her to his will.

Or maybe she'd received instructions to refuse Bryan without a flicker of dismay. *Yes, Master. Whatever you say, Master.* Maybe he'd deluded himself into thinking she cared for him when she was merely doing the task assigned to her. What did he really know about the woman and the way her mind worked?

"Here." The man in the tight leather pants handed him a business card. Bryan studied the shiny black card with the gilt edge that proclaimed in flowing, gold-metallic script "Specialty leathers for the discerning Dom". Underneath in plainer text was "Chase Roberts" and a phone number. Bryan had been so distracted he hadn't registered that this guy was a craftsman like himself.

Chase lowered his voice. "These people don't buy anything that isn't designed and custom made just for them. It's all about pride and one upping each other. Trust me, you can make a fortune doing nothing but work for the group in this room. They're elite and rich as fuck. And doing this kind of work—with the free pussy, the free shows and no limits—man, that's really hot!"

"No limits?"

"Yeah, extreme stuff. I'm sure you've noticed."

Bryan nodded as he hooked a glass off a tray held by a passing caterer and sipped the champagne just for show. He was surprised that none of the servers were clad in fetish wear or fishnet. They wore classic wait staff black and white, and most of the party guests were dressed in formal attire. This could be any high society party, but he knew other festivities awaited them later in the dungeon. He wondered what Gary had planned.

Chase seemed to have decided Bryan was a peer and a confidante. He leaned close and dropped his voice to a whisper. "This scene isn't like your suburban couples who decide to playact. These people are beyond hard core. No negotiations or safe words. Their masters do whatever the hell they want with them, whenever, however and for as long as they want, and damn, that's hot!"

"Mm." Bryan grunted.

"The shit I've seen, you wouldn't believe. Girls kept in cages, sleeping in their own waste for a couple of days for punishment. Tortures that skate right on the edge of snuffing." He shook his head. "Kinda scary, but also so fucking—"

"Hot. Yeah, I got that." He'd had enough of the guy. The images Chase's words evoked made Bryan's resolve to free Butterfly firm. He had to rescue her from that crazy bastard, Gary, before something really bad happened.

"Gary's a pussycat compared to some of them," Chase continued.

The man seemed to have the inside scoop, so Bryan decided to pick his brain. "Do you ever hear about a slave choosing to leave and going back to regular life?"

"Most of these chicks are so fucked up they take a beating and beg for more. These guys can talk their slaves into anything and convince them it's for their own good. And they trade the sluts like baseball cards. They get bored or want fresh meat to play with and convince little Betty Lou it's for her emotional growth that she be passed on to Master Whoever-the-fuck."

"Are they ever kidnapped and kept?" He almost hoped for an affirmation so he could give some of these peoples' names to the police.

Chase shook his head. "You don't get it. With these guys it's all about mental control. Restraining an unwilling victim isn't as erotic as making a person completely surrender her will and self-esteem. They choose the bitches carefully, searching for weaknesses to exploit."

Bryan thought of the pale marks of Butterfly's cutting and wondered what kind of life she'd left behind that was so horrible she believed Gary's control was preferable. "Excuse me. I see someone I need to talk to." He broke off the conversation and escaped the company of the shock groupie, then threaded between the men in suits to look for Butterfly in the hallway beyond.

No luck. A throng of men blocked the entrance to the study. Bryan saw Gary and turned away, but it was too late.

"And here he is. Make room, gentlemen."

The group separated. He held his breath and forced his way through a cloying mix of expensive colognes to reach Gary.

"You're the man of the hour, Bryan Lapahie. Care to say a few words about your creations?" Gary's charm was transparent to Bryan alone, it seemed.

The guests smiled in earnest as he stepped closer to Butterfly's pillar. He'd caught her personality in that hunk of wood. When he'd first put the light washes of color over her form, he worried he'd made her too sure of herself, too strong. But now, gazing into her green eyes and following the line of her expressive mouth, he knew he'd captured her just right. She *was* strong. He only hoped she'd be strong enough to choose the right man tonight... And if she didn't believe this of herself, he'd be there every step of the way to show her how to start believing. To start living.

He reached for the golden ring piercing the nipple closest to him. Tensing, he remembered the day he'd carefully drilled the holes for each of the women's nipples, and how he'd placed a loop in their shy clitorises, too. A tight linking chain hung down from the nipple rings to join the hoop below. He drew it away from the sculpture and met Gary's eyes in challenge.

The threatening half-grin on Gary's face told him to behave in front of his guests. He'd have to choose his words with care.

"I'm sure each of you remembers your first slave. How you selected her carefully and molded her into what you wanted her to be. It's the same with wood. Inside, there's something you want, and you'll try to get it from that chunk of oak or mahogany by any means possible."

His gaze locked with Gary's. "Sometimes the wood obeys. Other times, she's tough. Resilient." He turned to the crowd. "I've had to discard many a good piece of timber when the grain was wrong."

"Or flawed," Gary interrupted.

"I wouldn't say flawed. Not right for the task at hand, perhaps. Or maybe I wasn't the right craftsman to conjure a sculpture from her form."

People must've known the two men weren't talking about carpentry, and an uneasy tension settled in the room. A man coughed. Another loosened his bow tie. Bryan felt heat building under the collar of his shirt, too.

"Well, I think they're stunning," said a guest who raised a martini in Bryan's honor.

"Thanks—"

"Almost as stunning as the real thing." Gary had managed to steal the show again with his interjection. "Thank you, Bryan. Now let's get this party started. To the dungeon!"

A roar of yelps and whistles filled the room as the men lifted their glasses in celebration. The guests left the study and Gary followed. Bryan took one final look around to say good-bye to his creations. His eyes lingered on Butterfly's form. He ran his fingers over the inner curve of an arm that was made to seem like it held a shelf of heavy books.

Don't make them look too happy...

He looked into the wooden woman's eyes. "I can make you happy," he whispered. "If you'll let me."

Where was he? Butterfly's heart thumped against the clear acrylic sheeting that held her still like most of the other women around her. She ached to see him, although she'd feel humiliated when she did. Her breasts ached, too, flattened against the panel screwed into the wall behind her, but this she could ignore. The grease paint obscuring her features had smeared against the acrylic when she'd been placed on display, and this clouded her view as well.

Sapphire stepped into her limited line of vision to offer a guest a drink. The man took a martini from the tray fastened to Sapphire's waist and held upright by chains attached to her tender-looking nipples. Butterfly couldn't tell exactly what happened next—her face was pressed to the side and an annoying pink wig covered most of her vision when her eyes shifted to see—but Sapphire had yelped behind her ball-gag. No doubt the man had fingered her roughly or pinched the sore, red nipples that held her platform of drinks. At least her own breasts were safe behind the see-through barrier.

The guests made the rounds, commenting on the "art" Gary and several other Masters had assembled that afternoon. Plexiglas covered Butterfly and more than a dozen other slaves from waist to head, their breasts flattened, frozen in place at the whim of a so-called body artist who went by the name of Master Deviant. He'd plumped their nipples to the point of pain with suction devices then pressed the clear sheet in place. Rough jute rope coiled over the women's stomachs beneath the acrylic and more held their wrists above their heads from a hook mounted in the wall. Her arms had gone numb long ago, but she supposed things could always be worse... Poor Jasmine dangled from the ceiling with giant dildos filling all three holes.

A tall man shoved the suspended slave, and she bucked as she spun, more toy or plaything than person. Like Butterfly, she must want to get free, but if released might fight back, given her recent behavior. If Butterfly was free, she'd leap into Bryan's strong arms when he walked through the dungeon doors.

Again she wondered where he could be. Days had passed since their interlude on the spanking horse. Had Master forbidden him to return or had Bryan's interest in her simply waned?

Perhaps Gary had rescinded Bryan's party invitation because he'd caught them nearly kissing—for which he hadn't punished her yet. In fact, he hadn't spoken a word about the incident, probably because he knew anticipation was half the torture. There must be something horrible on the agenda for her this evening. Then again, if Bryan didn't come tonight, if he was gone from her life forever, this would be the worst possible punishment. She didn't know if she could bear never seeing him again. Panic churned inside her chest, and her breathing quickened. *Slow down,* she told herself and tried holding her breath. The foggy acrylic cleared slightly, but still no Bryan in sight.

Fingernails scraped into her thighs then trailed up to her pussy. She jumped as best she could while trapped under the plexi and looked at the man who'd come into her single-eyed range of vision. It was the new guy Chase. Although he knew little about the lifestyle her Master and the others led, he always showed up at the parties to hawk his wares. She cringed when he gave her mound a hard pat, then a slap. He didn't ignore her as he did those things like the others usually did. He leaned close to the barrier between them and sought her eyes. When she didn't look away, he threaded his fingers between her outer lips, took hold of her clit and pinched it. And not in a pleasurable way. She refused to shudder or make a sound. His forehead touched the plastic, but her stubborn glare made him break eye contact.

Amateur wannabe. Even Bryan and his gentle ways had more power than a pretender like this guy. She wanted to kick his probing hand away. Already she felt like she belonged to another. To one man. And it wasn't her Master of five years. Thankfully, Chase's fingers retreated, and he backed away into the crowd to find easier prey.

When the one she'd been thinking about finally entered the room, she could see him searching for her among the women on display. Would he recognize her with the wig, the heavy kabuki-style makeup concealing her features and the coils of rope that covered the pale scars of old on her stomach? That and the fresh scratch Jasmine had given her would be his only clue to her identity. All the "framed" women had similar heights and body types—Master Deviant had even gone to the trouble of concealing any moles, tattoos, or other distinguishing marks not hidden by the ropes with makeup.

Her heart racing and yearning toward him, she watched Bryan, studied his tall, well-made body surrounded by chatting guests. He seemed reluctant to set his half-empty glass on Sapphire's tray, so he held it awkwardly as he nodded curtly to the smiling Masters. Butterfly nearly smiled. One-on-one, he was a different person. This was definitely not his crowd. She loved that he wore jeans and a T-shirt, the logo on the chest long since worn to ghostly gray. He stood out in this overdressed crowd, announcing his individuality by his rebellious attire. Bryan was unique among all of Master's friends—for that matter, he was different from all the men she'd ever met in her life. But was she as special to him?

Party guests came and went, tapping on her glass or ignoring her completely. As long as they didn't block her view, she didn't mind. She admired Bryan until Gary clapped his hands to signal the beginning of whatever horrors he had in store for the evening's entertainment. Bile scorched her throat. After that day with Bryan, there'd be hell to pay.

All conversation stopped. His voice sounded muffled through the acrylic, but she could hear every word.

"Gentlemen, this week I was propositioned by my talented carpenter with the most interesting of wagers. This man, whom I invited into my home, planned to pay well and offered the services of my slaves, had the balls to challenge me for one of them."

Butterfly stopped breathing. He wanted her. He hadn't taken his pleasure from her then put her out of his mind. Her heartbeat kicked against her breastbone with both joy and terror. The possibility of leaving with Bryan, leaving everything she knew, horrid as it could be at times, sent her mind reeling. She listened, numb to the core, as Gary continued.

"Needless to say, I was stunned. But, gracious Master that I am, I know well the failings of human nature. I see it every day in my slaves."

A murmur of laughter rolled through the dungeon. "My reputation in this little group of ours is unblemished. Never has a slave asked for her release, and never have I even considered this an option. But a man of Mr. Lapahie's talent deserves to be rewarded, and tonight, should Butterfly choose, she is free to leave with him."

Free to leave. Sweat raced down her temples in rivulets fueled by terror. The gasps of the men—and the slaves who had not been gagged—sounded strange to her ears...and yet familiar. It reminded her of her first experience in a subway, the whoosh of air in the tunnels as trains came and went. In a flash, she was fifteen again, experiencing her first full-blown panic attack, a precursor to those that would later incapacitate her to the point of being unable to function in the world. Her mother's perfect, pointed nails dug deep into her arm, pulling her toward the waiting train, and the screech of harsh words telling her to grow up rang out louder than the noises crashing around her in the dim station.

She took a deep breath. *Leave. Free to leave.* Butterfly gulped and tried to force her racing heart to slow. That freedom would have a price. Bryan might laugh at her—or worse, bring her back once he figured out what a mess of a woman he'd won in this little bet. How would Gary treat her if Bryan did such a thing? But Bryan wouldn't bring her back, not after asking for her... Would he?

Gary's voice came crashing through her thoughts. "So let's see, shall we?"

Bryan nodded stiffly. The tension in his frame was palpable, and that same taut feeling charged the air with an unseen, uninvited guest: dread. Dread for what would happen to her if she stayed behind, the punishments, the regret. Dread for what lay ahead should she rejoin the real world. The living.

With a dramatic pause, Gary added, "Wait. We have to find her first to ask her." He tapped a finger to his chin and surveyed the room. "Now where did I put her? Oh, well, you want her so badly, you must know which slave is your beloved Butterfly." He waved his hands toward the framed women with a flourish. "Choose wisely, Bryan. The one you pick is the one you get to ask."

Bryan didn't open his mouth to protest. Was he so confident that he knew which slave she was? Or perhaps he realized there was no point in arguing with Gary's apparent changing of the rules. But Butterfly's throat let loose a small sound. She tried to wriggle, to let him know where she was. And Gary, ever in control, issued a single command to his peers—"Begin"—and his closest friends came to each woman's side. The men pulled floggers from inside their tuxedo jackets and thrashed away at the "artwork". Her struggles and muffled cries to let Bryan know where she was were lost among the moans, and she writhed as the others did when he walked past to choose.

She tried to stay still. Maybe this would be the clue he needed to pick her out from the others. Then again, as the rhythmic lashing of tails blazed across her skin and the scene around her folded in on itself, all black and white tuxedoes and groaning pink-haired women, she became what she knew best. A slave. Part of something bigger and more important than herself. And maybe she didn't want to be picked to leave at all.

She sank deeper inside herself as the beat of hide against human flesh continued without mercy. He was closer now, so close she could faintly smell his distinctive scent drifting to her even past the barrier of acrylic. But he didn't stare at her for long. The thought that he might not choose her crashed over her exhausted body like a wave. At first, relief, then longing. She couldn't turn her head to beg him to come back. And if he didn't know her, what did that say about him? She pressed into the plexi and took her body's weight from the balls of her feet. She didn't care if the acrylic shattered or if she fell... She only wanted Bryan.

Come back, dammit. She finally saw him again on the far side of the room. He reached in to touch a woman's pussy then withdrew his fingers. *I'm here,* she wanted to scream, but when she did scream, the sound was lost to the others bouncing off the dungeon walls.

"Have you found her?" asked Gary above the din.

Bryan brought his fingers to his face. Gary seemed on the verge of gloating, his chest puffing up, filling his ebony jacket with the anticipation of winning tonight's game.

Game. The word echoed in her mind. Made her feel worthless. Did Gary care so little about her, about her future, that he'd sever whatever twisted relationship they had based on a game, a bet?

Bryan wiped the woman's juices on his jeans and shook his head, much to Gary's obvious dismay. He began a second pass around the room. His gait grew slower, his expression more intense. Like a desperate man on the hunt for a needed thing and not merely a want, he focused on pale thighs and the profiles of their chins.

Come closer. Here... And when he did, the man in front of her stopped his flogger and stepped aside. Bryan cupped her sore mound with his right hand. His callused fingers felt so right on her throbbing skin. He pressed his forehead to the thick acrylic and his mouth made sounds, although his lips barely moved.

"Do you want this?" he asked. "Because if you don't, if you want to stay, I don't want to get you into any more trouble than I probably already have."

The light strokes on her outer lips became a balm for the pain. The eye facing him locked with his gaze and never wavered. She saw the kindness there, the desire. She licked her parched lips.

"Yes," she whispered.

In a quick, graceful movement, he rolled away from the plexi and faced Gary and the roomful of guests. "She goes with me. Now!" Bryan's large body vibrated with energy, with barely-leashed anger. "Give me a goddamn tool so I can get her out."

Master Deviant came forward and began to loosen the bolts holding the clear frame in place. Bryan snatched the wrench away from him and accomplished the job with swift, hard movements, releasing the excruciating tension from her body.

Across the room, Gary looked as if he'd been punched in the stomach. His face, now ashen under the dungeon's faint spotlights, displayed not anger but complete shock.

"How the hell did you know?"

Bryan paused in his efforts to free her, long enough to glance at Gary. "Her eyes. You could've put a hundred women up on these walls and I still would have found her. A little makeup and a wig couldn't conceal her." His gaze met Butterfly's briefly before he turned his attention back to freeing her.

When he released the final bolt, he unwrapped her stomach and wrists to set her free. Butterfly pulled off her wig and cast it aside. She lowered her stiff arms and rubbed them. The rush of blood into her numb hands was like being set on fire. Her legs could barely support her weight after so long on her feet in one position, and her lashed pussy was a burning ache between her legs. She wanted to rub the sore flesh, but wouldn't give any of these men the satisfaction of knowing how much pain she was in. She'd been held up to their ridicule and acted as the source of their amusement for the last time. He took her hand as she found her voice. "Let's go."

Color returned to Gary's face. The red of anger. Of embarrassment. "Not so fast. I believe you owe me something, Mr. Lapahie."

"I didn't forget." Bryan released her hand to tug his wallet out of a tight back pocket. "You can count it, but it's all there."

Gary came to where they stood and held out his palm. "I make many times more than this in one sale of my work, but a bet's a bet." He made a show of counting the bills while Bryan put away his wallet. The look on Bryan's face told her this was a lot of money for him, maybe more than he could afford.

"Wait..." The strength of her voice surprised even her. Men who'd ignored her as a person while they used her as a plaything suddenly looked at her and listened. "If this is a hardship for you—"

"It's not." Bryan caught her hand again. "I'll find other work."

"Not in this city you won't." Gary tucked the money into his pocket and produced a thick piece of paper. "And if I have my way, you won't work anywhere in the state of California. In fact, you might as well take this worthless bitch back to the hole you crawled out of—"

Bryan's fist flew out and slammed into Gary's nose with casual grace. The tuxedoed man stumbled backward into the throng of friends standing behind him. There were a few shouts of surprise and a steady murmur of voices throughout the room. The piece of paper in Gary's hand slid from his fingers. Butterfly stared—not at her pissed off Master—but at the folded sheet. Her contract. Bryan didn't slow down to pick it up as he led her to the door with an arm tight around her waist.

Butterfly half expected the assembled guests to gang up on Bryan, to take him down with floggers and crops in hand. But perhaps they didn't want to get their formalwear messed up. She couldn't help but laugh. Giddiness coursed through her, both from the excitement of the evening and the uncertainty of what lay ahead. She felt on the edge of hysterics, as though she might laugh until she cried then sob until she couldn't breathe and pass out. This was really happening. She was leaving her home of five years and starting a whole new life.

Bryan's firm grip tightened on her still-tingling fingers as they made their way to the front door. His strength soothed her, told her he'd be strong enough to support her through this act of rebellion and help her face her future, whatever it might hold.

"Here. Take my shirt."

He whipped it over his head and covered her naked body with it as they stood on the wide veranda gracing the front of Gary's house. The tee covered her well, to mid-thigh. It hid the fresh marks on her pussy and the scars on her abdomen, but not the raw, red wrists that had remained bound for so long. Bryan took one of her hands between his and rubbed the flesh briskly.

Thus far she hadn't shown any signs of a panic attack, but her sudden quiet worried him. "What are you thinking? Having second thoughts?"

She shook her head, her eyes ever wary of the night around her. "It's dark."

He switched to the other wrist, massaging the blood back into her numb hands then holding them both between his. "Yep. Time to get you home, let you get some sleep. You must be wrecked after going through all that. Christ, the things that guy dreams up to do to women are beyond belief."

Butterfly didn't seem to be hearing him now. She simply stared out into nothing. He didn't want to rush her, but he didn't exactly want to stay on the front stoop of a man he'd just socked in the face either. Silently he berated himself for not doing more research on the web in preparation for tonight. What kinds of reactions should he expect from a released captive—an agoraphobic one at that—and more importantly, how should he deal with them?

"Is it raining?" she asked.

He reached his arm out past the roofline. "Only a little."

She stepped to the edge of the porch and extended her arm as if she were in slow motion. He could see the beads of water gather on her arm then run free over its curves before plunging to the earth below. Even with the depersonalizing effect of the white makeup covering her face, the too-red lips, the black-lined eyes and penciled-in eyebrows, he could see the wonder in her expressive hazel eyes. "You'll get wet," he warned with a smile.

"I haven't felt rain in...years."

He tried not to let this revelation faze him. "Are you ready to see your new home?" Well, temporary home. Without work coming in and no payment for what he'd done for Gary, they may have to move sooner than later. Hell, even a move back to Navajoland was looking like a real possibility. "I really think you'll like Wolf."

Finally she turned to him. Her arms found his neck, and he lifted her, a leg catching on each of his hip bones. Her chest began to heave against his as he darted out into the wide-open space alive with night noises—crickets looking for love and owls calling out from the woods behind the mansion. He pressed her tightly to him, muscles straining with the promise of protection against a new foe, one he couldn't knock in the face or win against in a bet. She did better than he expected, though, and he opened the truck door for her then helped her scoot to the passenger side. When he managed to pry her rigid arms from his neck, he climbed in.

"You did well," he told her. And that deserved a kiss. He slid back into her embrace and coaxed her quivering lips more fully apart. He could almost taste the fear on her tongue, so he kissed her harder. Soon she became liquid against him, all heat and need woven in with her sweet scent.

"Fuck me," she whispered.

He pulled away and made the mistake of looking into her eyes. His hands shot to his zipper, but common sense forced him to hold back. "No, baby. I'm fucking you in my bed tonight, not Gary's driveway."

She tucked her head beneath his chin and nodded, the subtle bob of her head reminding him something fierce of the blowjob she'd bestowed upon him the other day.

"Yeah, let's get you home."

He'd never driven so fast. His cock jumped at each bump in the road and his balls ached like a bitch. He screeched into his parking space and gathered her into his arms. "Hold on, hon."

She never had the chance to start hyperventilating as he carried her up the stairs to his apartment, keyed the lock and kicked open the door. Toenails clattering on the wood floor, Wolf came roaring to the door, barking wildly. It was the way he always welcomed his master home, but it must sound to Butterfly as if they were being attacked.

"Don't be afraid. He's just saying hello," Bryan quickly assured her.

Her arms remained around his neck, but she didn't clutch him any tighter. In fact, she turned her face away from his shoulder to look down at the huge gray and tan beast with the sharp white teeth. "Dog," she murmured to herself as if identifying the animal.

"*Ma'iitsoh*! Stop it!" Bryan barked back at him. "Sit!"

Immediately, Wolf dropped to his haunches and quieted, but his mouth still yawned open and his tail thumped so hard it sounded like a bass drum.

"Really, he just looks like a werewolf, but he's harmless." Bryan maneuvered past the dog, which stayed right where he'd told it to, blocking their way.

"Can I pet him?" She pushed away from him and unclasped her legs from around his hips as she attempted to slide to the ground.

It was nothing short of a miracle. Bryan set her down and watched her go to Wolf and hold out her hand, slowly yet confidently, fingers curled in so he could sniff her hand without being threatened. "I love dogs. My mother would never let me have one. Too messy. But my best friend growing up had a beautiful Malamute. I adored her."

Wolf drenched her hand with licks from his massive tongue. When she scratched between his ears, his eyes closed in rapture and the speed of his wagging tail increased.

"Beautiful boy. How are you?" she crooned.

Bryan simply stood watching her. *Beautiful girl. You're amazing.* She was an incongruous sight in his little apartment with her smudged makeup and naked legs, arms and shoulders displayed fetchingly by his big T-shirt. But he frowned at the glinting silver band around her throat. She still wore her slave collar, the item that proclaimed her Gary's possession. It had to go.

Her hair was flattened from hours beneath a wig, and still looked great and made him want to bury his face in it. Everything about her was adorable and perfect. He wanted to take her to bed and claim her as his own—as if he were as primitive a male animal as Wolf. But despite his pronouncement to her in the truck that he planned to fuck her, Bryan realized tonight wasn't the right time for that. She'd just been through a harrowing ordeal, her body and psyche tormented. She needed to clean up then rest.

Besides, wasn't she due a period of courtship? Proof that

he didn't accept her into his life as a possession, but as a real woman worthy of wooing?

Butterfly sank to her knees beside Wolf and allowed the excited dog to bathe her painted face in worship. She glanced up at Bryan and smiled. The curve of her lips and flash of her teeth was like sunrise and set her face aglow. "You didn't tell me how gorgeous he is! I would've run away with you a lot earlier."

Taken by surprise at her unexpected flash of humor, Bryan burst out laughing. He reached to take her hand and pull her to her feet, then leaned to kiss her, considerably less sloppily than Wolf had done. He pulled away and peered into her eyes. "If I forgot to tell you before, I'm so glad you chose to come with me."

"Me, too." Her smile flickered and suddenly died. "But the money and your business. I didn't want to cause you so much trouble and expense. Master…Gary is a powerful enemy. And he never forgets any slight against him."

He gave her one last quick kiss. "Don't worry about that. I don't want you to let thoughts of him ever bother you again. You're done with him. Got it?" He didn't mean to sound angry, but he could hardly refer to the man without fury flaring up inside him.

She blinked and nodded. Silent.

"I'm not mad at you. I just don't want you to worry," he assured her, attempting to alleviate the deer in the headlights look in her eyes. "One more thing. I want his collar off you. You're no longer the property of Gary Sanderson."

He turned her away from him and examined the back of the silver band. It wasn't locked or soldered in place as he'd feared. She could've taken it off herself at any time, but had chosen to imprison herself.

The simple catch was easily opened with a flick of his finger, and Butterfly was released. As he pulled the silver band from her neck and threw it, harder than he needed to, onto the coffee table, she stood frozen. The room was so quiet he actually heard her swallow as she lifted a hand to her neck and rubbed the skin the collar had covered. A smudged gray ring of tarnish marked the white expanse of her neck.

"It feels funny," she murmured. "So naked."

Afraid to let her dwell on that thought or to start to regret her decision, Bryan took her elbow and steered her toward the bathroom. "Why don't you take a shower while I walk this poor dog and find something for you to wear? I'll leave the clothes right outside the bathroom door for you."

Again she nodded.

He showed her where everything was, handed her a clean towel and some ointment to treat her abrasions and closed the bathroom door behind him. Going to his dresser, he searched for the smallest T-shirt he could find that wasn't too holey or covered with wood stain. As he shook one out and eyed it critically, he realized he'd have to shop for her tomorrow. She couldn't go around in his old clothes for very long.

Bryan kept Wolf's walk much shorter than he normally would have, just long enough to let the dog take a piss and smell a couple of bushes before they went back up the stairs to the apartment. Even so it took about fifteen minutes, and the shower was off when he listened at the bathroom door. The T-shirt and old shorts were where he'd left them.

As a matter of fact, it was completely silent in there. Bryan debated whether Butterfly needed alone time or if she was cowering in a corner from fear at being left alone in a strange place. He knocked softly. "Are you all right?"

He had to strain to hear her soft, "Yes." He tried the knob and it was unlocked.

Entering the room, he found Butterfly, wrapped in a towel, her shower-wet hair dripping down her back and her face flushed and pink as a flower. She sat on the closed lid of the toilet seat, shivering a little despite the steamy heat of the bathroom, and gazed up at him.

"You're not all right," he said. "Are you having a panic attack?"

Her teeth chattered a little. "No. Not really. I just...couldn't open the door. I'm sorry." She sounded near tears.

He crossed the room and wrapped an arm around her, helping her to her feet. "Yeah, it sticks sometimes. I should've warned you. Listen, you don't need to apologize to me. You didn't do anything wrong." He guided her into his room. Her body trembled in the crook of his arm, and he felt useless and inept, unable to protect her from the fears that rose within her.

"Can I take this off you?" he asked before he removed the towel from her body, understanding instinctively that he must let her know right away her body belonged to her. He had no right to gaze at it or touch it unless she allowed it.

Butterfly nodded and lifted her arms, letting him unwind the towel from her body, pat her hair dry with it then help her dress in the T-shirt and shorts, both of which hung ludicrously on her small frame.

"Better?" he asked as he pulled back the covers and helped her into his bed. It was actually made up for a change. He'd put on fresh sheets and aired out the old woven Navajo blanket, just in case Butterfly came home with him that night. It was almost impossible to believe she was really here, settling back against the pillows in his bed.

"I'll get you some tea." Bryan sat on the edge of the bed beside her and held her soft, warm hand. Her silence felt like a barrier he was beating against. She was too overwhelmed to talk, yet he needed to hear her say something. If only she would smile again. His brain clicked on. Wolf had made her not only smile but laugh.

"Look, I'm going to leave you for a minute so I can go to the kitchen and make tea. But Wolf will be right here beside you. Does that help?"

He whistled and the dog rose from his spot on the floor and padded to the bed. "See, he'll sit right here beside the bed until I get back. Okay?" Maybe it was overkill. Maybe she wasn't as freaked out as he thought and maybe he sounded like an idiot telling her his dog would keep watch over her. But the gamble worked. A smile graced her lips the moment Wolf rested his muzzle on the bed. She laid a hand on the dog's head.

"Thank you."

The two words, spoken with such relief and gratitude, made him feel like a gallant knight who'd performed some impossible feat. "No problem." He grinned and left to go to the kitchen.

He brewed the tea then returned to the bedroom with two steaming mugs. Butterfly was already sound asleep, her fingers clasping Wolf's thick ruff. Her lips were slack in sleep, and her eyelashes rested in two pretty crescents against her cheeks.

Wolf whined softly and turned his eyes toward Bryan without moving his head. His tail thumped weakly on the floor as he mutely explained to Bryan he wanted to go lie down in his spot, but was too polite to abandon the woman on the bed.

Bryan set the cups of tea on the nightstand and relieved Wolf. "It's okay, boy. You can go. I'll take over here."

He stripped off his clothes, but put on a pair of boxers to keep his burgeoning erection contained. Although every cell of his being ached for her, he knew she needed time and space before they could even begin to embark on a relationship. It didn't mean he wasn't going to sleep beside her tonight, though. He wanted to be close by if she woke frightened in the night. And, goddamn it, he'd earned the right to at least hold her all night long, hadn't he?

Slipping into the bed beside her, he pulled her body close and whispered, in case she was even slightly awake, "You're home now. You're safe."

His hand roamed up and down her back, cupped her hip, explored the space between each rib through the thin fabric of the shirt. He didn't think he'd ever fall asleep. His nervous system jangled and his blood pumped full of adrenaline.

But he could watch her sleep all night, mark each indrawn and exhaled breath, every beat of her heart pulsing in her delicate wrist. He could guard her like Wolf, a stalwart sentinel against danger and hurt.

He didn't find sleep until the early hours of morning.

Chapter Ten

Where am I? Butterfly's first thought as she surfaced into consciousness was that she wasn't lying on the hard surface of her cot. Her second was that something heavy was pinning her down. Not a bad thing, but she was drenched in sweat from the heat it generated. Trapped, she held very still. She'd learned long ago that struggling against restraints only made them tighter. It wasn't until she woke completely that she realized she wasn't confined or tied, but wedged up against Bryan's body and buried under the weight of his arm and leg. His breath blew moist and hot between her shoulder blades and his erection nestled in the cleft of her buttocks.

She smiled. This was a new and good way to wake up. She wiggled her bottom against the hard bulge pressing into it. Bryan moaned and shifted in his sleep.

Would he like to be awakened with sex? She could keep rubbing against him or dive underneath the covers and take his cock into her mouth. But what if he wanted to sleep in and was annoyed with her for rousing him? It wasn't her place to initiate sex. He would tell her what he wanted, when and how. He was her Master now.

So she held very still while the pressure in her bladder grew increasingly uncomfortable. She needed to pee, and the welts on her pussy simultaneously itched and burned. As much as she enjoyed Bryan's cuddling, his weight was too crushing and hot. She longed to wiggle free, relieve herself and rub more of the ointment Bryan had given her the previous night on her sore vagina. Her stomach was rumbling as well. She hadn't eaten since lunch yesterday. But Butterfly waited patiently for Bryan to wake and tell her what he wanted her to do.

Finally he stirred. The quality of his breathing changed, and she knew he was waking. Her pulse sped up. What would he ask her to do first? As kind and gentle as he'd been with her, she didn't know exactly what to expect now that he was her Master. Would he show another side of himself, become more demanding, rougher, crueler? No. She didn't believe he had that dark and sadistic streak in his character, but what *would* he be like? Master had been the center of her world for so long that the prospect of shaping herself to a new man's desires felt odd and unsettling. What if she failed? What if she wasn't what he'd thought he was getting and he wished he'd never wasted his money on her?

Lips brushed her shoulder. His chest resonated against her back as he murmured, "Morning," in his deep voice. "You awake?"

"Yes. Good morning." She rubbed tentative fingers over the smooth, tan forearm that held her so tightly.

He kissed her shoulder again, and the side of her head. Then he nuzzled into her neck, making her squirm. "I love waking up like this."

She smiled and pressed back against him. "I can feel that," she teased. Her fears from a moment before seemed irrational. This wasn't Gary. This was Bryan, and of course he wouldn't mind if she woke him with sex. She didn't have to wait for his permission for every move she made. And she was no longer Butterfly, she was...not the girl she'd been before she became Butterfly, either, but someone completely new and different. Maybe Bryan would bestow a new name on her.

His arm moved, releasing her from its heavy weight, and his hand settled on her hipbone. He nipped her shoulder lightly.

"I'd like to show you just how much I enjoy having you in my bed, but not right now. For one thing, I have to piss like a racehorse, but I also want to discuss our relationship before we get any deeper into it." He laughed. "Can't believe I'm turning down sex in order to talk. I can feel my testosterone evaporating as I say it." Then he patted her hip. "Go ahead and use the bathroom first if you like. I'll wait."

She turned to look at him over her shoulder. Was this a test? With Gary she'd always had to decipher the meaning of his words, discover if there was hidden subtext or nuances she should be reading. But Bryan just smiled at her, his gaze lingering on her lips a moment before meeting her eyes. His face was as open and warm as sunshine. No hidden secrets or meanings there.

"Thank you." She slipped out of the bed, and Wolf leaped to his feet and came to her side. He pushed his head beneath her hand, demanding a petting.

"Your new best friend," Bryan teased. "Give him an inch and he'll take a mile. Don't even let him get you started on tug-of-war. He'll never let you quit and he might dislocate your arm."

She laughed as the dog escorted her to the bathroom. He would've followed her inside, but Butterfly told him to sit. He dropped to his haunches and gazed at her, tongue lolling. She felt a small swell of power at the animal's instant obedience to her command and smiled. It felt good to give an order instead of receive it for a change.

When she was finished using the toilet and washing her hands and face, she studied her reflection in the mirror for a moment. She straightened the T-shirt that kept slipping to the side to expose one or the other of her shoulders. She looked so pale and plain. What in the world did Bryan see in such a woman, someone who couldn't even make her own decision about getting out of bed to pee in the morning, someone who was proud of herself for something as minor as making a dog sit?

Maybe Bryan liked that weakness in her. Maybe he found vulnerability sexy. He might be kinder and much nicer than her previous Master, but evidently it was her submissive qualities that had attracted him to her. She should probably keep right on acting like a slave as she had in Gary's house.

With that in mind, Butterfly returned to the small bedroom with her head lowered. She glanced up from beneath her brows to see Bryan sitting on the edge of the bed, putting on his tennis shoes. She knelt on the matted brown carpet, studied the foot of the bedpost and waited for him to speak. Wolf lay down by her side, emitting a soft whoosh of air as he dropped to his belly.

"What are you doing?" Bryan crossed the room in two steps and knelt in front of her. He put his finger underneath her chin and raised her face. "This isn't Gary's house. I don't expect you to kneel when you enter a room or keep off the furniture. You're not a slave or a pet. You're a woman." He sounded angry.

She licked her lips and swallowed. Ten minutes into the day and she'd already done something to displease him, however unintentional. She nodded.

"Hey." He smiled. "I'm not yelling at you. I'm just angry at Gary for convincing you this is all you're worth." He rose and pulled her to her feet and close against him. He had on a T-shirt and shorts, but she could still feel his hard muscles through the fabric. "If it makes you feel better, I'll give you a command. No kneeling and no keeping your eyes lowered. When you talk to me, always look me in the eyes. When you come into a room, sit on the furniture. Okay?"

"Okay. I can do that." She lifted her eyes to his. "Just tell me what you expect of me and I'll do it. I want to make you happy."

He paused and she felt this wasn't quite the answer he wanted from her. "You don't have to try, that's the point. Whatever you do is fine as long as it's what *you* choose to do." He shrugged. "Anyway, we can talk more about all this, but right now I've still gotta pee and so does Wolf. I'm afraid I'll have to take him for his morning run, but you'll be all right here by yourself. We won't be more than fifteen minutes."

Butterfly nodded emphatically. "No problem. I'll make breakfast while you're gone."

Bryan smiled and his eyes sparkled like sunlight dancing across shadowy pools. "Sounds great."

After he'd made a bathroom stop, showed her where everything was in the kitchen and leashed Wolf, who was whining with ear-shattering intensity, he left the apartment. The door closed behind them, leaving her alone.

Standing very still, she breathed in the scent of Bryan's apartment. The smells of cooking lingered in the air—spices, frying grease, an overripe banana. She found the offensive fruit on the counter, the brown spots scattered in a Rorschach pattern across it and a few gnats floating above it. Butterfly picked up the squashy banana and located the trash bin underneath the tiny sink—such a small kitchen for such a large man.

The kitchenette opened directly into the living area. A tiny sofa and a TV, and a small bookcase completely filled the floor space. The scarred wooden kitchen table held an outdated computer. On one wall were the doors leading to the bedroom and bathroom. That was the entire apartment.

It was cozy.

She listened to the strained wheeze of the refrigerator, the cars going by on the street outside the open window where a little breeze blew in and gave life to the stuffy air. Walking over to the window, she looked out at a neighborhood. Little girls squatted on the sidewalk, drawing pictures with chalk. One of their mothers came outside and started yelling, pointing at the apartment building behind her. Either the girl wasn't allowed out alone or there was some chore she was supposed to have taken care of before playing. She tossed down a purple chalk, slowly got up and trudged toward her mother. The woman grabbed her arm and dragged her inside.

The scene woke memories of a childhood in which every moment of the day was planned, chock full of activities with no time to breathe. She hoped the girl lived a happier life in that rundown apartment building than she had in her parents' mansion. Butterfly's melancholy at the scene turned to fascination as she caught sight of others walking past. It had been so long since she'd seen regular people going about their daily lives. She felt safe and unseen, watching from her hidden perch on the second floor, half-concealed by the curtain in the window. But standing here staring at a cat sniffing around the edge of a garbage can wasn't getting breakfast cooked.

She returned to the kitchen and surveyed the contents of the nearly empty refrigerator. At least there were eggs and a loaf of bread. After locating a skillet and setting it on the stove to heat, she popped bread in the toaster. No orange juice, but there were coffee packets so she started that brewing.

A moment of indecisiveness swept over her as she tried to fathom whether Bryan would prefer his eggs fried or scrambled, and how hard cooked he might like them. Perhaps he'd like an omelet. Unfortunately, there wasn't any cheese or other ingredients to put in it. Just then the door burst open, and she jumped.

Wolf bounded into the kitchen and over to her. He planted his feet on the floor and stared at her, letting out a deep-throated "woof." Bryan was right behind him. He tossed the leash on the sofa and strode into the kitchen to pull Butterfly against him with one arm. His clothes were damp with sweat, and the pheromones his body emitted made her insides go liquid.

He pulled away, brushing long strands of black hair away from his face—the rest was fastened at the nape of his neck. "Sorry. I know I'm gross. I've got to feed Wolf before he deafens us both, then I'll take a shower." He glanced toward the stove. "Do I have time? It smells wonderful."

"I didn't know what kind of eggs you like."

"Whatever you make." He walked to one of the lower cupboards and pulled out a humongous bag of dog food. Scooping up a portion, he deposited it in Wolf's dish then picked up his water dish to fill it.

Butterfly decided quickly before she could start wavering again. "Fried," she announced.

"I'll make it quick," he said as he headed toward the bathroom. He stripped his shirt over his head as he walked through the living room, and she stared at the rippling muscles of his back, the powerful shoulders and biceps she longed to dig her fingers into.

The door closed. Butterfly waited, listening for the shower to turn on, imagining his body soaking wet under the spray, fantasizing joining him there—but he hadn't invited her. When the water turned off, she waited a few more minutes before breaking a pair of eggs into the sizzling grease. Her timing must be perfect so the eggs would be fresh off the griddle when he sat at the table.

Cooking was one area of her life she felt confident about. She'd organized the meals every day for almost the entire time she'd lived with Gary. Who would take care of that chore now? And if things weren't done exactly as he liked them, who would have to pay the price? Butterfly felt a wave of sadness for the women left behind, and guilt for the rage her leaving would likely bring down on their heads. She felt like a soldier abandoning her buddies on the battlefield to the mercies of a tyrannical general.

Bryan emerged from the bathroom damp but dressed in his standard T-shirt and jeans. The vulnerability of his bare feet beneath the hems of his jeans made her want to caress them. His hair was darker than ever and hung loose around his shoulders. How she longed to touch the silky length, wrap it around her fists and tug a little as she guided his mouth to her breasts.

She squeezed her thighs together against the pulsing of her sex and turned to serve the eggs and toast. When she set his plate before him on the table, Bryan beamed at her as if she'd produced a culinary miracle. "This looks great. Thanks."

Smiling shyly in return, she bobbed her head and stepped away from the table.

"But where's yours?"

"You want me to eat with you?" It had been so long since she'd shared a meal with anyone besides the other slaves that it hadn't even occurred to her that Bryan would naturally want her to sit down at the table with him. "Oh. I..." Her gaze darted to the stove and the skillet. If she cooked her breakfast now, Bryan's would be cold by the time hers was ready. Her heart rate sped up. She'd been stupid, done the wrong thing. "You don't have to wait for me."

"I want to wait for you." He rose from his seat, walked around the tiny kitchen table and put a hand at her waist, cupped her face in his other hand. "Hey, it's no big deal. Your eyes are like saucers." He bent low to meet her eyes and smiled. "I don't care if my food gets cold. As a matter of fact…"

He steered her to his empty seat and pushed on her shoulder until she sat down. "I want you to eat that. I insist on it. You're my guest and here I've had you cooking!"

"But…"

"No." His voice and eyes were suddenly stern, his mouth a straight line. "Eat."

She obediently lifted the fork and cut into the perfect egg.

"Now, I'm going to cook my own breakfast like I always do, while you eat that one. And you're not going to feel guilty or weird. Got it? All you have to do is enjoy the food."

She watched him move around his kitchen, efficiently preparing his own eggs and toast. Once he'd cracked the eggs into the pan, he leaned against the counter and sipped his cup of coffee as he watched her eat. "Listen. I want to talk to you about something, and this is as good a time as any, I guess."

Butterfly swallowed past a sudden lump in her throat. This didn't sound good. While he'd taken his morning run, he'd probably come to his senses, wanted to return her to Gary and try to get his money back. She steeled herself for what he was about to say.

"As I told you before, I won't have you acting like a slave here. What I want is for you to become a confident person again, and I think to accomplish that I'm going to need to set some ground rules. One of them is probably going to be way harder for me than for you." He paused to flip his eggs then walked over to the table and set his coffee down. "I, uh, think we need to abstain from sex for a while. As much as I'd love to…have you in every way, I think it's best for you if we take a break. That means no offering me a blowjob, because I'd have a helluva time not accepting that offer. No touching below the waist at all."

"But why?" It sounded like a child's petulant wail coming from her lips. "I'm happy to do that for you. I *want* to do that for you. Isn't that why I'm here—to please you?"

Bryan gave a growl that made Wolf prick up his ears and growl in answer. "No, that's not why you're here."

"What did you want me for then?"

"Because... Because I like you and I think you deserve a better life than the one you had there. I want to help you be strong enough to make your life your own." He inhaled. "And yes, of course, I'd like to screw you raw, but I don't want any relationship we might possibly have here to be based on that alone."

Butterfly looked up into his earnest eyes and yearned for him to take her right then and there on the kitchen table, to possess her, fill her, use her, hurt her, mold her and make her his very own possession. And she recognized the danger in that. Bryan was right. She must figure out who she was, and if she was even a person any longer, before she could be a fulfilling partner for him.

"I understand," she replied quietly. Picking up her piece of toast, she nibbled one corner.

"Damn! The eggs." Bryan turned back to the stove and rescued his breakfast. A few seconds later, he was seated across from her and devouring his food. "So beyond the 'no sex' rule, we'll make things up as we go along. The important thing is I don't want you to feel like a slave any longer. I don't want you to be afraid to ask me for anything you want or need."

"What if what I want and need is sex?" She delivered the line dead-pan, but her lips trembled with humor.

Bryan grinned. "Don't do me like that, baby. Don't make it any harder than it already is not to throw you down right here, right now, on this table."

Knowing he'd shared her fantasy made her smile grow. "All right. I'll be good."

"As soon as we're finished with breakfast, we're going to go out and get you some clothes. You look too damn sexy wearing my old T-shirt."

Her smile evaporated at the thought of leaving the apartment. "The mall?"

"Sorry. It'll be someplace cheap. I'm pretty well tapped. That's okay, isn't it?"

Guilt stabbed through her at the thought of the money he'd lost because of her. "No. That's fine. It's the going out part I'm not too sure about."

He nodded. "How about today I go out and do the shopping? I need groceries, as you can tell, and I need to stop by my friend Darryl's place and see if he can give me a line on a new job. Tell me your sizes and I'll bring you something back."

She nodded, wondering what her sizes actually were. Had she changed sizes since entering Gary's household?

"Then, a couple of days after you get used to everything, I'm going to want you to shop with me. That is, unless you want a wardrobe full of ugly Hawaiian muumuus. I can't be trusted."

She didn't laugh. The idea of shopping filled her with both excitement and dread. Imagine being able to choose something to wear. Did she even like the types of clothes she used to wear back in college? What kind of bargains could she find that looked good but were easy on Bryan's wallet? And how would she deal with the crowds? She mustn't allow herself to embarrass Bryan in public by having a meltdown. No, she'd fight tooth and nail to keep her anxiety under control.

"It's a date," she finally said.

"Good, because shopping for women's clothes scares the hell out of me. I need you by my side." He smiled and swiped the last dab of egg from his plate with a fragment of toast.

Butterfly smiled, too, enjoying his gentle teasing, his easy-going manner. She could relax around him and be herself...whoever that was.

After they'd cleaned up the kitchen together—she still wasn't quite comfortable with him working by her side—Bryan told her to occupy herself as she wished while he was gone. "I probably don't have any books you'd enjoy, but you're welcome to read what I've got. CDs and stereo are in this cabinet. The remote for the TV is... Where the hell is it?" He dug around in the sofa and found it wedged between the couch cushions.

"Here. I should be back a little after noon, but don't wait for me. Eat whatever you can find for lunch. Take a bath, a nap. Zone out in front of the tube. Do whatever the hell you want, okay? I just want you to be comfortable."

"I am. You've made me feel very safe." Impulsively she threw her arms around him and hugged him tight, breathing in the clean scent of his T-shirt and his own special smell beneath it. "Thank you again for getting me away from...him." She wouldn't call him Master, but couldn't quite bring herself to say his name, either.

"I'll be back soon and then we'll spend the rest of the afternoon together." Bryan kissed the top of her head, and when she tilted her face up to look at him, kissed her mouth, a long, lingering kiss that made her tremble and burn. "Okay." He drew away and sucked in a breath. "I've got to get out of here or I'm not going anywhere."

He turned and left. When the door closed behind him, Butterfly looked at Wolf, who was gazing at the door. "Just you and me for now," she told him. "Let's see what we can do to keep ourselves occupied."

Over the next few hours, she cleaned every room of the house, polishing and wiping down surfaces that probably hadn't been touched since before Bryan moved in. She swept, mopped, dusted, cleaned the toilet, made up the bed, even considered washing the windows, but decided she could save a few tasks for another day. Once more she stood by the window, looking at the world outside.

An old woman with a walker inched down the sidewalk toward some loitering teenagers who blocked her way. She yelled at them. They laughed, but parted to let her pass, calling obscenities after her as she shuffled away. A car pulled up beside the group of teens, engine throbbing, music pounding. Several of them piled in and the car pulled away.

The phone rang, pulling Butterfly out of her rapt surveillance of the neighborhood. Her heart leaped at the sudden intrusion into the silence of the apartment. Should she answer it? She walked to the kitchen and stared at the phone hanging on the wall near the fridge, reached out for it then hesitated. What if it was a friend of Bryan's and he didn't want them to know about her? No, it wasn't her place to answer his phone.

The answering machine clicked on. "This is Bryan Lapahie. Please leave a message. If you have a carpentry need, you may also reach me on my cell, 532-674-5309. Thank you."

"Hi. Are you there?" It was Bryan's voice, already so familiar. "Go ahead and pick up if you can hear me."

She snatched up the phone. "Hello."

"Hi," he repeated. "How's everything going?"

"Great. No problem."

"Look, I hate to do this to you on your first day with me, but Darryl had a tip about some work on a construction site. I really need this job, but I'll knock off by five o'clock no matter what. Will you be okay?"

"Absolutely. I'll have dinner ready for you when you get back. What do you want to eat?"

"Steak, but you're not likely to find that in my fridge, and, unfortunately, I have the damn groceries at Darryl's house in the refrigerator. Why don't you forget trying to put a meal together? We'll order Chinese."

"Don't be silly. I'm a culinary genius. I'll find something in the cupboards. It's the least I can do."

"You'd have to be a genius to find a meal in my kitchen. I'll be back just as soon as I can," he promised. "Call me if you have any problems at all, or even if you just start feeling afraid, okay? I'll have my phone on me."

After she hung up, Butterfly looked around the apartment. It was clean and tidy. She could probably take a break now. God, she wished she had her piano. She needed the tranquility it inspired in her, because she was beginning to feel a little jumpy and displaced in this apartment, safe haven though it might be.

She wandered into the living room, read the back cover blurbs on some of Bryan's books. There were a few on woodworking and some suspense novels by authors like Clive Cussler and Tony Hillerman. A volume on Native American religious practices drew her attention, and it fell open naturally to a section about Navajo shamanism. She took a moment to tune in a classical station on the stereo then curled up on the couch beneath what looked like a hand-woven blanket with bold geometric patterns. Butterfly read the chapter as she idly stroked the slightly rough surface of the blanket.

When she was finished, she thought about Bryan's heritage. There was so little she knew of his culture. What had it been like for him growing up on a reservation? A world away from her privileged upbringing, she was sure. How strange life was that it had brought two people from such opposite backgrounds together. Could they find common ground and maybe even share a life together?

She smiled at that thought as she closed the book. She'd be lucky if he wanted her here for the next month or two, let alone the rest of her life. There had to be a way she could pay him back for what he'd lost. It was time for her to think about crawling out of her shell and getting some kind of a job.

Sections of a newspaper were piled haphazardly on the coffee table by the couch. The want ads were filled with circles of blue ink, and a few were crossed through. She turned the page to find something she may be able to handle, but every job required dealing with the public in some way. Butterfly gave a scornful snort, imagining herself a waitress falling apart the first time she got an order wrong.

Her incomplete college education hadn't prepared her for any career besides an academic one. If she'd carried on in her study of music, she probably would've had a Master's by now and been a professor at some small college. But as it was, she had no marketable skills besides the ability to cook. She perused that area of the classifieds. Line cook. Prep cook. Grill chef.

She folded the paper and tossed it back on the table in frustration. After figuring out how to work the TV remote, she lost herself in a sappy romance as she snuggled beneath the heavy wool blanket. Her eyes drifted closed.

When she jerked awake, Butterfly felt a moment of pure panic before she remembered where she was and that she was supposed to be here. Wolf let out a sharp bark, and the phone shrilled. That was the noise that had woken her. She untangled herself from the blanket and trotted to the kitchen to answer the phone.

"Sorry. I'm running late, but I'll be home in another fifteen minutes or so."

"That's fine." She rubbed the sleep from her eyes and looked at the digital clock on the stove. It was nearly five-thirty. "I'll have something ready for you to eat."

"Don't bother if you haven't already. We can cook together after I bring home groceries. You can show me how it's done." He hung up on that promise.

Fully awake now, Butterfly thought about Bryan coming home to her. She wanted to do something to welcome him, something special. She would've liked to strip and tie herself spread-eagle to the bed as a surprise, but given his edict against sex, that wasn't an option. Besides, tying that last wrist was almost an impossibility.

What would please him the most would be visible proof that she wanted to change and was willing to put forth effort. She'd be sitting and waiting for him at the top of the stairs—outside, a small gesture to indicate that she was ready to re-enter the world.

Taking a deep breath, she walked to the apartment door and unfastened the locks then rested her hand on the knob. The little landing was really an extension of this apartment. She'd be perfectly safe, and if her palms started to sweat and her heartbeat accelerated, she could always retreat back inside. She opened the door and stepped out onto the platform at the top of the stairs.

Warm air brushed her skin. The smell of exhaust fumes made her nostrils quiver. Traffic noise and distant voices seemed loud to someone used to the quiet of indoor life. She gripped the railing and gazed down at the driveway along one side of the apartment. The roof of a blue car, decorated by bird droppings, was directly beneath her.

The sudden push of a furry body against the back of her legs knocked her into the railing. Wolf bounded down the steps as she regained her balance and whirled around.

"No! Come back! Come on, boy. Please?"

She held out her hand, but Wolf was too busy checking out fresh scents while frisking around the patchy grass in front of the apartment. He turned to bark at her, tongue lolling happily, as if to say, "Come on. Let's go!"

"Damn it! Come here!" Butterfly cried. But the dog continued to bark at her, run a few steps, then turn and look at her again.

Bryan would hate her if she lost his dog. She had no choice but to go after him. With shaky hands, she closed the apartment door, making sure it wouldn't lock behind her, then started down the stairs.

Bryan kicked the door of the truck shut while balancing a bag of groceries in each arm. The smaller plastic bag holding Butterfly's dress and sandals hung from his wrist. He hoped she'd like the outfit at least enough to not be embarrassed wearing it to the store tomorrow. That was if she could summon enough courage to face a shopping trip. He wanted to gently nudge her forward, not throw her into water over her head.

He climbed the stairs, set one of the bags on the landing and pulled his key from his pocket one-handed. But before he even got it in the lock, he saw the door wasn't pulled completely closed. Fear twisted his stomach and his throat tightened as he pushed the door open. "Butterfly?"

There was no answer and no Wolf running to welcome him home. The sick feeling in the pit of his stomach grew and his heart pounded. He tossed the bags on the kitchen counter and quickly strode through the small apartment, calling her name. There was no place to hide, not so much as a closet. He even pushed open the shower curtain, half expecting to find her crouched, shivering, in the tub. Butterfly was nowhere in his apartment. And neither was Wolf.

Where the hell are they? He pictured Gary dragging her away. Or maybe she'd called him and begged him to take her back. But neither scenario really explained Wolf's absence. If Gary had taken Butterfly by force, Wolf would have attacked him and there'd be some sign of a struggle, yet the apartment looked more orderly and clean than he'd ever seen it. Maybe she'd left willingly, and the dog had slipped outside and run away. How could he blame her if she had decided to return to the familiarity of the devil she knew? After taking her in and promising to care for her, he'd left her alone all day in a strange place.

He cursed steadily as he threw open the door of the apartment and pounded down the steps. He ran around the truck to the driver's side and had opened the door when Wolf's bark cut through the air. Bryan turned toward the sound in time to see a dark blur. The dog plowed into him, leaping up on hind legs to welcome him home with a blow to the chest. Damn animal had never learned not to jump, mostly because Bryan had enjoyed and allowed his enthusiastic welcoming.

"Down!" he commanded and Wolf instantly dropped to all four paws. But he didn't stay there for long. The dog ran back down the sidewalk, which led to the park where Bryan jogged with him almost every day. A block away, the slender form of a woman in an oversized men's T-shirt sprinted toward him.

"Wolf, come here!" she yelled then froze as she noticed Bryan.

He ran toward her, his legs eating up the yards between them.

"I'm sorry," she said before he even reached her. "He slipped out and wouldn't come back. I've been chasing him. I'm so sorry."

Her face, bright red and sweating, was half-hidden by

damp curls, and her eyes were huge and bright. She took a few more steps toward him, favoring her left leg.

"Are you all right?" He grabbed her shoulders wanting to know she was really there. Although he'd suffered only a few minutes of worry about her, it felt like hours had passed as a dozen different scenarios played out in his head, all of them involving Gary.

"Your foot." He dropped to his knees and lifted it.

"It's fine. I just stepped on a damn pebble."

His gaze shot up to her face. It was the first time he'd heard her curse or, for that matter, express frustration. And she was outside and apparently not experiencing a panic attack. "You're all right." It was a statement of revelation.

"Are you angry? I didn't mean to—"

"No. I'm not mad. I was scared." *Terrified.* "I thought something awful had happened to you."

"It wasn't awful, but it certainly wasn't pleasant, either," she said dryly. "Your dog doesn't mind very well. I stepped out on the landing—to test the waters, see what I could handle— and Wolf made a run for it. And I made a run for him."

"He probably thought you were playing. But you're right—I haven't trained him as well as I should. A big dog like that needs to be kept under control." He stood and took her pink face into his hands. "You ran with him all the way to the park and back? I can't believe it!"

"Well, I didn't know he'd come back on his own or I might not have tried so hard." A slight smile touched her lips.

Bryan couldn't resist kissing it off her mouth. Just a small peck.

"And you went running wearing this." One of her slender shoulders peeked from the low neckline of the tee and her legs were bare. "That took real guts."

Butterfly blinked and looked around at the passing cars and a few staring people. "I guess I was too busy running to have time to fall apart. Or to care about what I had on. I only cared about catching Wolf."

He gave the dog a scratch between the ears then abruptly scooped Butterfly off her feet and into his arms, barbarian style.

Her arms automatically went around his neck. "I can walk," she said.

"I'm not going to make you hobble on your hurt foot." He took his time getting her up the stairs to the apartment, enjoying the weight and warmth of her body pressed against his, the soft curves molding to him and the scent of her sweat and her femininity.

"I have to say, running on a treadmill does *not* give you the same level of exertion as racing after a dog outdoors," she said, her head cocked to the side as she gave him another cheeky smile. "And it's not nearly as exhilarating. If I hadn't been so focused on catching Wolf, I think I might've enjoyed it."

"That's good." He didn't put her down. Not yet. In fact, he held her tighter.

"What's wrong? You're upset, aren't you?"

"No. I was only... I got scared. Scared that Gary had come and taken you against your will. Or maybe you would've gone with him willingly..."

His eyes searched hers. He could see her chewing on this. Wondering how to respond.

"No," she stated quietly.

No, Gary wouldn't have come or no, she wouldn't have left?

She seemed to know what he was asking. "No," she repeated. "I wouldn't go back there. And he wouldn't want me now. I don't need him the same way I used to." A hesitant smile emerged on her beautiful mouth. "After meeting you, I...I grew a backbone. And a woman with a spine is definitely not his type."

They both laughed, but Bryan couldn't help but think of the women left behind with that monster. *Hopefully they'll grow backbones, too,* he prayed. He gave her another quick kiss before setting her down by the sofa. "I'm sorry I kept you waiting all day." He left her to grab the groceries he'd abandoned and began putting items away. "The place looks great, by the way. Thanks."

Butterfly joined him in restocking the fridge and cupboards. "Please don't apologize. You have nothing to be sorry about. I'm the one who should feel guilty. I've ruined your business prospects and drained your finances. You probably wish you'd never met me."

He grabbed her shoulder and turned her around. "Stop. I don't want you to ever feel guilty about anything. I chose you. I'm lucky to have you." He shook his head. "Believe me, I want you and I'm not sorry you're here."

Her eyes searched his, checking them for the truth. Finally she nodded.

"Let's make a deal. No more apologizing." He rested a finger on her mouth. "I don't want to hear 'I'm sorry' pass these lips again, okay?"

"I promise." She smiled. "Not even if I spill hot coffee on you. No apologies."

Bryan laughed. She had an ironic sense of humor now that she wasn't afraid to express herself. He looked forward to watching her unfold. Spread her wings like her namesake.

The cool air from the refrigerator at Butterfly's back washed over them, but he could feel her heat, too. His body strained toward her. He wanted to take her in his arms and kiss her from head to toe, every inch of bared flesh, but knew he'd never be able to stop at kissing. There were so many things he wanted to do to her. Hell, he couldn't exactly remember why he wasn't doing them just at the moment. Not while she was leaning toward him, too, with lust burning in her eyes.

Oh, right, because she was emotionally damaged and needed space and time to set parameters and gain mastery over her own body. When she learned she was worth more than sex to a man, then he could fuck her like a crazed coyote.

Bryan broke off the silent, heated exchange between them. "All right, then. Let's make something to eat. I'm starving." As if on cue, his stomach rumbled. "And I got you a sundress if you want to change."

Butterfly smiled as she took the white dress dotted with yellow flowers from the bag. "It's adorable," she announced, and hurried toward the bedroom to change.

He was folding the paper bags when his phone rang.

"Bryan?" The catch in his grandmother's voice confirmed his worst fears.

"Is he still alive?"

"For now. He slips in and out of consciousness. You should come soon."

"I'll leave right now."

He didn't have to ask if his *acheii* was at the hospital or at home. He knew his grandparents had decided that when the time came it would be in the place he'd loved best. And he'd be buried on the land that was his heart's blood.

He stared at the phone in his hand, but saw Grandpa Butch's weathered face, his, mouth smiling as he told the story about the clever coyote and the foolish rabbit for the hundredth time. *I'm on my way, Grandpa. Just hold on a little longer.*

Butterfly walked into the room, her cheery smile and dress forcing a weak smile from his lips. She noticed his tension right away.

"Who called?" Her eyes were wary.

"Not Gary." He guessed at the cause of her fear. "My family. How do you feel about riding in a car? For about nine hours."

"What's happened?" Concern superseded fear.

"My grandfather... He's dying."

"I'm so sorry, Bryan." She wrapped her arms around him and clutched him tight, then kissed his neck once, long and gentle. He didn't want her warm lips to leave his skin. "I'll help you pack."

"If we leave right now, we should be able to make it by morning. My grandmother says he doesn't have long."

Her arms hugged him even tighter as she murmured her condolences again. "I'm really sorry. Whatever I can do to help..."

Her embrace felt so good, so comforting and wonderful. He reluctantly let her go, corralling his emotions and directing his energy toward what he could accomplish—packing and driving.

After tossing his possessions into a duffle bag, he wondered what to do about the apartment. With a big goose egg in the bank and no work on the horizon, he might as well ditch the place. He didn't have a lease, and the furniture was from a thrift store.

He rang his landlord and explained his family situation. He agreed to hold the place through the next month. If he didn't show up, they'd lease it to the next poor fucker who strolled into town.

When he got off the phone, there was Butterfly and her big, guilty eyes.

"Stop it," he scolded playfully.

A hint of a grin tugged at her lips. "I wasn't doing anything."

"Yes, you were. You were apologizing. Don't worry about the money."

"I didn't say a word."

"Your eyes said it for you."

"Okay, you caught me."

"Yes, I did." And his hands caught her waist. She lifted her head for a kiss. This time he didn't hold back. Because he needed it. Because she was offering it freely. *You were worth every penny,* he wanted to say. *Worth more than I'll ever have.*

When she gave a slight push on his chest, he let her go.

"How's your foot?"

"Much better. Let me put on my new sandals."

He watched as she bent to retrieve them then sat on the bed. Big mistake. The thin sundress crept up her legs, exposing inch after inch of creamy skin he wanted to sink his fingers into. He leaned against the wall to admire the view and nearly groaned when one foot settled on a thigh so she could buckle the strap. He'd forgotten all about buying her some underwear, and the peek of pussy she offered made his cock fill with blood. That made him feel guiltier than ever. How could he still be horny when his grandfather was dying?

"My turn to apologize."

She looked up, blissfully unaware that she'd hiked her dress higher in the process. "What for?"

"I forgot to get you some panties. And a bra." He tore his gaze away from her mound.

Her expression turned saucy. She obviously had figured out what he'd been admiring.

"And here I thought you didn't want me to wear any."

Oh, fuck. His dick throbbed in agony. "I want you to be comfortable." *Even if I'm in absolute fucking misery, I want you to be comfortable.*

"I'm comfortable. Except for…you know. Certain times…"

"Your period?" he offered, thankful for the change of subject. She nodded. "When's it due?" he asked.

"What's the date?"

"The nineteenth."

She contemplated this as she nibbled her bottom lip, probably counting out the days. "Of what month?" she asked quietly. "I know it's summer but…"

She hadn't been counting. Well, maybe at first. Jesus, Gary had really done a number on her. On all of them. How shut off from the world was she?

He sat down beside her and felt the mattress give way under his weight. Her lighter frame shifted snug up against him. "It's August," he said gently.

Chapter Eleven

She flopped back onto the mattress, and was glad when he did the same. There were many reasons why she didn't want to leave his apartment right now... Or his bed. Damn, he was warm. Their shoulders barely touched, but his body gave off a heat she wanted to nestle into deeper. And then there was the smooth velvet of his voice that made her body hum. Made her thoughts stray... Would he talk to her when they finally made love? What kinds of things would he say? When Gary talked dirty to her, his words came without passion. Cold and clinical, his tone betrayed no emotion at all, and his choice of epithets for her body, and for her, were only meant to demean.

She looked into Bryan's eyes. Midnight pupils, wide with care and perhaps lust, filled her vision. Did he want to kiss her as badly as she wanted to kiss him? She licked her lips, not to provoke him, but to feel some contact there. His gaze shot to her mouth, and he licked his own lips. He tipped his head toward her as they lay side by side, his breath teasing her mouth.

"You okay?" he asked.

"Yes." She could almost hear his muscles tense as he played the gentleman for her, holding back his desire to touch her until a later time. She could smell the subtle fragrance of his soap, which blended with the outside August air. *August...* To give a name to time, a number to a day—it seemed so foreign to her now.

He propped himself up on an elbow, casting a shadow over

her face. His large form made him seem so powerful that she felt small and fragile in comparison. Just the thought of his broad hand holding tight to her wrists while his other did whatever it wanted to her body made her wish she were naked. Her toes curled against the straps of her sandals. Other parts of her uncurled, the need deep inside her ready to find release.

But this was not the time for her needs.

"Are you going to be all right to make this trip?"

"I'll be fine, but don't count on me to make much small talk."

When he grinned at her answer, she parted her lips in invitation. He was considering it, she could tell, and as his forehead lowered to hers, her heart trembled beneath her ribs. Nose against nose now, she waited patiently for his lips to take hers, to brush up against them. Claim them gently or fiercely— she didn't care which as long as he touched her there. She closed her eyes and waited some more.

He chuckled. "Good thing one of us has some willpower."

Oh, God. Her racing heart slid to her stomach when she realized he wasn't going to kiss her. Fingers twitching to take matters into her own hands—literally—she debated whether to surprise him with such a bold move, her fist in his gleaming black hair and her mouth lifting to take his.

"What happened to that willpower a few minutes ago?" she teased.

"Oh, that." He laughed. "I was just testing you."

"Did I pass?"

"Not sure. Guess I'll have to retest you later."

"When?"

"Anxious for it, are you? Maybe it'll be your reward for making it to Arizona." Suddenly, the playfulness in his expression faded into sadness.

How selfish of me. "We should go," she said. "Your grandfather..."

"Yeah."

He rolled away from her and stood then offered his hand.

"Are you going to be okay?"

"There's only one way to tell. If I make it there without a panic attack, will I get more than a kiss?"

He didn't answer her, but he already had several ideas about what he wanted to do to her under the wide-open skies of Navajoland. He'd take her to the quiet places and lay her down in the rich, red earth. He hoped he could slowly take away her fears so she could enjoy the beauty of nature once more.

She grabbed the bag of toiletries by the bathroom and followed him to the kitchen. They separated the groceries into piles—one of stuff to take with them and one to throw out so the fridge wouldn't stink when, or if, they returned. After that, he grabbed the blanket his grandmother had made for him and a few of his favorite books and CDs. Wolf knew something was up. He kept by his master's heels, watching, sniffing the air.

"Wanna go for a ride, boy?"

Wolf barked twice and went to wait by the door. Bryan didn't let him out—not quite yet. He loaded his stuff into the truck and hurried back to the apartment in the hopes that she'd still be by the door. And brave. She was standing right where he'd left her.

"Wolf loves riding. Come here, *Ma'iitsoh*." He attached the leash to Wolf's collar, then glanced up at Butterfly. "*Ma'iitsoh* means 'wolf' in Diné."

"Din-a?"

"The Navajo language. Diné is also how we refer to ourselves as a people. I can teach you some on the ride. If you'd like." He waited for her reaction. Simone hadn't been the least bit interested.

She smiled. "I'd like that." But she seemed hesitant.

"You don't have to if you don't want to."

"No—I mean, yes. I do want to. It's just..." She looked at the books he was leaving behind. "There's a book of photographs. Can we take that one, too?"

"Of course." He picked it up and flipped through the pages,

each spread filled with the glorious landscapes of his homeland. It was heavy, so he didn't hand it to her.

"Maybe it will help me get used to all those wide open spaces."

"Yeah." He reached for her hand and slowly led her to the door. It was time. "But a picture isn't like the real thing. And it's time for the real thing. It'll be beautiful, I promise."

She took a deep breath. Wolf threaded between their bodies, waiting.

"Ready?"

She nodded. He held tight to her shaky hand and opened the door. Her eyes closed against the sunlight, and, once he'd locked up, she clenched his palm to the point of pain.

"Steady now. You're doing great."

By the time they got to the truck, sweat slicked every bit of visible skin. He let her in and pulled the seatbelt taut against her panting chest, then climbed in and latched his own. Wolf climbed over him then claimed his space in the middle, tongue wagging, tail slapping the seat behind him. Bryan turned the key in the ignition and pulled out onto the main drag, his eyes peeking over at Butterfly every few hundred yards.

She didn't speak. He didn't pry. But she seemed miserable, her white-knuckled grip on the door handle making his heart pound probably as hard as hers would be. If it wasn't for the seatbelt, she'd probably be curled up in a ball where her feet were.

They rode in silence until he neared Darryl's house. "We need to make a stop," he told her. "My friend Darryl's."

She seemed okay with stopping. Maybe even relieved. He parked and they got out. Darryl, bare-chested and sweaty, showed up at the door to welcome them in.

"Did I catch you at a bad time?" Bryan asked. "You look like you were, um, busy."

Darryl laughed. Butterfly jumped at the loud sound.

"I was, but not anymore. Melanie's a little tied up right now..." Darryl winked, and Butterfly's jawed unhinged ever so slightly. "I'll go get her so she can meet your friend."

Butterfly took in the living room while they waited. The décor was nothing to write home about, a mix of knick-knacks showcased in whatever projects Darryl hadn't found buyers for yet. The craftsmanship was top-notch but the effect all together? Not something you'd see in *Architectural Digest*. He wondered what she was thinking. And what her home growing up had looked like. Then he wondered what she'd think of his grandparent's home. He had a feeling the standards of living back on the Rez would come as quite a shock, especially after Gary's sprawling mansion.

When Darryl returned with a glowing, black-robed Melanie, Bryan hated to tell them this wasn't an extended visit.

"We're leaving. Grampa's near the end."

"Oh, no!" Melanie ran to him and they embraced. He held her tightly until the black silk between their bodies made her slide away from him. When they completely separated, he caught the look on Butterfly's face. He knew that expression. He'd seen it a million times on Simone's face when she had no right to wear it.

Butterfly was jealous.

He bit back a grin and focused on the issue at hand. "I wanted to talk to Darryl before I left town, and... God, this is forward of me, but Butterfly is about your size and I didn't know if you had any clothes she could borrow. I didn't have time to shop for her properly."

Melanie smiled and reached out to Butterfly. And she went forward with the conversation cautiously. Delicately. Too bad the two women couldn't get to know each other. Mel would be good for her. He just knew it.

"I like your name," Mel said softly. "Would you like to come look at my closet, Butterfly?"

"Sylvia," she replied. The word was barely a breath, but it took Bryan's away.

Butterfly—no, Sylvia—glanced over to him. Was she asking for permission, or asserting herself as a person? Either way, it was a good thing. An important milestone.

The grin he fought back earlier came beaming through. A hint of a smile twitched on her lips, and her head lifted an inch. Bryan's heart felt like it was floating.

But after the two women walked away, Bryan's heart stopped its soaring and settled back down into his chest, heavy as iron.

"I hate to ask, Dar, but I need a big favor."

Chapter Twelve

"Ready, Sylvia?"

God, the name seemed so foreign to her now. She hesitated at first, wondering what he'd thought of her revelation. Had he been pleased? He seemed so, especially now as he held her gaze.

She nodded at him and whispered her thanks to Melanie while clutching one of the brown paper bags the woman had so generously filled for her. The bag contained another sundress, shorts, tops and Melanie's gardening sneakers. And socks. She'd missed socks on chilly nights in her cell. Her toes wriggled in her sandals just thinking about soft cotton enveloping her feet at night.

She braced herself for the vast openness of the outside and the rustle of leaves in the wind. She narrowed her eyes to keep the expanse of sky from filling her with panic. Today it worked, mainly because she was hoping to impress Bryan's friends as they walked with them to the truck.

I won't flake out. I won't flake out... Her mantra seemed to be working, and she even managed a genuine smile as Melanie reached through the open truck window to give Wolf a pat. Then she gave Sylvia's shoulder a soft squeeze. "I hope the trip goes okay for you."

So Bryan had told them what a ninny she was and God knows what else. She glanced down at the floorboards, wishing she could hide beneath the mat where it was dark. For all the times Gary had displayed her for his friends, she'd never felt so exposed.

Fingers touched her chin. Lifted her head back up. "Hold your head high, Sylvia." Melanie studied her eyes. "I was an Army brat growing up. My sister hated all the moving, but me, I loved being able to reinvent myself in each new town. Use this trip to help you emerge from your cocoon. Figure out who you really are."

Sylvia nodded numbly. Fear of both the physical journey and the inner one she was about to embark upon sent shivers coursing through her. She'd tried to hold them back on the long walk to the truck and now they came in waves tainted with panic.

Do something. Do anything. She dug through the paper bag for the small golden purse Melanie had given her. It was too dressy to match the casual clothes in her bags, but it had caught her eye. Melanie had pulled it from a shelf, dusted it off, and filled it with whatever she could find that might be useful: lip balm, travel-sized deodorant, a pair of sunglasses... Sylvia slipped those on. The frames were huge, with rhinestones at the temples. They dimmed the early evening sunlight, gave her something to focus on, and she fiddled with them to find the most comfortable position on her nose.

Melanie grinned. "You look very glamorous!"

She peeked in the truck's side mirror. *I look like a star in withdrawal. On my way to rehab, actually, with all the shaking.*

"Thank you. And not just for the clothes and stuff."

"My pleasure."

The men were still talking near the side of the truck. Sylvia saw Darryl thrust a wad of bills toward Bryan. "Just take it. I know you'll pay me back."

"Jesus, Dar. That's more than I—" Red tinged Bryan's cheeks.

"Take it, dammit." Darryl stuffed the bills into his shirt pocket.

Melanie and Darryl backed away from the truck as Bryan got behind the wheel. His sad wave as the truck rolled away made her want to crawl into his lap and hug him. Sylvia raised a hand to the couple and pushed the big sunglasses higher before closing her eyes. Yes, keeping them shut was the best way to go about this. When she'd chased Wolf down the street, she'd been so focused on capturing him she hadn't had time for her anxiety to build. She must use that same focus now to keep her heart rate slow and her breathing normal.

The truck slowed then stopped. Wolf barked, and she squeezed her eyelids tighter. Bryan's warmth came closer, lips against her hair and on her ear.

"You're gonna miss a lot with your eyes closed…Sylvia." He removed her glasses. She didn't stop him, but she didn't open her eyelids.

"You can tell me all about it," she quipped.

"But I can't tell you this," he teased.

"What?"

His tongue clicked against his teeth. "Can't tell ya. A picture is worth a thousand words. You gotta open your eyes."

She did as he asked and rolled them in mock annoyance until she saw what he'd wanted her to look at. A butterfly had flown into the truck's open window and was sitting on the dashboard. Wolf barked, but Bryan shushed him and held him back.

The butterfly, with its big blue wings flickering, seemed at ease on the dash. Hints of dazzling copper dusted the wings as well.

"In Navajo mythology, the butterfly gave horses' hooves their speed." His head cocked to the side as he considered their visitor. "Also, because they're so beautiful, they're considered vain."

"I guess it's a good thing you have another name to introduce me with, then."

Bryan didn't reply. Wolf barked once again, and this time, the butterfly bumped along the windshield looking for an escape until it found the edge of the window. Bryan gently blew on it, and the creature flew away.

He turned back to her, lifted his hand from the excited dog, and offered it to her. "Hi. I'm Bryan Whitehorse Lapahie."

She took his hand while he told her the names of his people's clans and explained which were his maternal grandmother's, his maternal grandfather's and so forth.

"When we meet another Navajo for the first time, we say which clans we're from. You're not Navajo, but I wanted you to know."

The information he shared was important to him; she could tell by the seriousness in his expression. She smiled. "Nice to meet you, Bryan Whitehorse Lapahie."

"And you are Sylvia...?"

She cringed at the pause but told him what he wanted to know. "Sylvia Anne Gibson. From, uh, Hartford."

Not quite as interesting as "Red Running into the Water Clan" and the other things he'd said.

He grinned.

"What?" Was he laughing at her? Did he not believe her?

"I'm just thinking... My ex, her name was Simone." He hesitated, as if trying to decide whether to say his next words. "A good friend once warned me about dating women with similar names. He said it's easy to blurt out the wrong name during the heat of the moment."

She laughed and raised an eyebrow. "Guess we'll need to test your friend's theory one of these days."

He stopped grinning. "Yeah." The sooner the better. *Patience,* he told himself, but this self-imposed waiting game was overrated. No, make that pure hell.

He was too close to her to resist and cradled the back of her head to bring her lips to his. She opened for him, her tongue quickly darting in to tangle with his. Damn, she tasted sweet. It was all he could do to not shove Wolf from the cab and lift that pretty little dress and...

The truck lurched forward. "Shit!" His foot fumbled to find the clutch before they slammed into the parked car in front of them. "Forgot to put the brake on."

"Yes, you did." An impish smile lit her face. "You're under a lot of stress right now. Are you sure there's nothing I can do to help?" She looked past Wolf's large form to the crotch of Bryan's jeans. If Wolf wasn't there, if they weren't parked so close to houses…

"We better go." He shook his head to purge the lustful thoughts racing through his head and fastened his seatbelt. "You know, when your mind's in the gutter, you stay pretty calm."

"Yeah, I was just noticing this myself." She crossed her legs. Squeezed 'em tight. He wanted to pry them apart, make her hike up her hem and let him touch her bare pussy all the way to Highway 89. His mouth parted while he debated telling her this.

She giggled and eased his jaw shut. "Looks like we're both in for a rough ride."

Her touch singed his skin. When she pulled her fingers away, he carefully caught them with his teeth and sucked on the tips. She closed her eyes until he opened up to set her free. After slipping her sunglasses back on, playing it cool, she trailed the wet fingertips over her collarbone and lower, stopping only when she reached the upper curve of one breast.

He let out a groan and released the brake. Soon they were heading east with only the engine's hum and occasional rattle—and Wolf's panting—to break the silence. Sylvia kept her head down for the first hour and stayed focused on petting the dog whose head rested on her thigh.

The lack of conversation reminded him of something he needed to tell her. "I'll probably be a little different around my family."

"Oh. Well, I understand. Your grandfather's…"

He waited to see how she'd say the word. She never did.

"Already you think like a Navajo, afraid to say the word." He smiled and took her hand. "As quiet as you often are, you're probably more like my people than I am. Where we're going, silence is considered a good thing. I'm a chatterbox compared to my kin."

"I like that you talk. I like it a lot."

So he kept talking. The miles flew by. The hours, too, the landscape ever changing as the last rays of sun slowly faded from the sky and a bright full moon rose to take its place. Sylvia didn't take her hand away as he pointed out the ghostly shapes of familiar landmarks in the growing darkness and talked about his childhood. Well, some of it, anyway. The mother part, the fatherless part... These things he didn't mention.

She noticed. She asked questions.

He tried not to sound bitter while answering. After telling her the story of how he almost got kicked out of the Army—for trying to steal a vehicle, while drunk, so he could rescue his mom yet again from some bad situation—her hand clutched his tighter. She didn't let go unless they stopped for a rest break or to walk Wolf.

"How about you?" Her gentle questions had gotten him to share more than he'd intended, and finally he turned the spotlight on her. "Tell me a little about your family and your life before..." he could barely say the name, "Gary."

"Oh." Her eyes widened, gleaming in the dashboard lights. The sunglasses had long since been put away as the black velvet desert night enveloped them.

"Please. I'd really like to know everything about you." He knew she couldn't resist his request and waited patiently for her to respond.

After a while her voice floated through the darkness, quiet but clear above the truck's loud engine. "I'm an only child. My parents...I think they loved me in their own way, but success and being the best at something meant everything to them. Average just wasn't acceptable."

Bryan nodded. He'd figured a psychological profile of Butterfly...Sylvia would include trying to please parents with impossible expectations.

Her laughter was cool and brittle. "I'd like to share some

interesting life stories like you did, but honestly mine was nothing but lessons and practice. Every minute of the day was planned. You'd think with all that focus I'd be an expert at something, that the tennis or piano lessons would've paid off and given my mother the star she wanted, but I was never special or brilliant at anything."

"I heard you play the piano. You sounded amazing."

"I'm no prodigy." There was a long pause as she stared out the window. After a few moments, he rested his hand on her forearm and rubbed it lightly, encouraging her to go on.

"When I was twelve, my mother took me to see Pasterovsky, a famous pianist. I'd never heard music so beautiful and passionate in my life. It was almost surreal in its perfection. But at the same time that I was enchanted by the music, I remember feeling actually nauseous, because I knew I could never attain that level of excellence. As we walked from the concert hall, my mother said to me, 'Why can't you play like that? Sylvia, if you'd just try a little harder and apply yourself, you could be a real pianist.'"

She laughed again. "I play adequately. I could probably have a career on stage if I wasn't terrified of crowds. But I could never be a Pasterovsky. Never. That was the moment I realized that no matter what I did, it would never be enough to please her. Yet I kept trying year after year to be the daughter she wanted."

"When you left home things didn't get better?"

Sylvia shook her head. "I thought I'd have a fresh start, but Mother's voice was still in my head driving me. Cutting was the only way to gain control over my own life, you see?"

He didn't, but kept silent and continued to stroke the soft skin of her arm.

"College is a time of change and pressure for any kid, and I didn't handle it well. By the time I met Gary I felt completely exhausted, tired of making decisions, tired of making an effort, tired of myself and my issues. He offered freedom. All I had to do was give myself over to him completely and I could stop worrying, wondering...even thinking. All I had to do was obey."

She turned to Bryan. "It was such a relief. Can you understand that?"

"Maybe. A little."

"I simply gave everything over to him...and I lost five years of my life." This time her laughter sounded more like a sob. "God, I'm sorry. I didn't mean to spill all this on you."

"I wanted to know and I'm glad you trust me enough to tell me."

There was a pause. Sylvia changed the radio station which had become static-filled white noise to the lone broadcast here in no man's land. Country music filled the cab with its cheerful simplicity. The music made Bryan think of Sylvia's playing.

"You're going to miss your piano. I'm sorry. I know that music meant everything to you."

"Not everything." She smiled and squeezed his hand. "I can always find someplace to play if I want to badly enough."

Pianos weren't plentiful, especially where they were headed. Bryan wondered if he could convince her to contact her parents, let them know she was alive and maybe ask for help getting back on her feet. He didn't know how much use he was going to be to her while he was living on money borrowed from Darryl. As a kid, he'd always dreamed of going away from the Rez and coming back filthy rich, but here he was, once again driving home in a rattletrap truck with nothing to show for his years away.

Sylvia needed a fresh start. She deserved more than he could give her, which, at this point, was nothing but his protection and care.

All the talking had taken them right up to the edge of morning. The sky was growing light in the east, the moon fading away for another day. Cast in ghostly shades of gray, the landscape of rocky dunes, boulders and vast stretches of open land spread out before them.

"See that?" He pointed out the open window. "That's the Little Painted Desert. When it's light out you'll see the buttes are banded in a paint box full of colors."

She bravely looked, her hand now clammy and cold from earlier bouts of sweating in his.

"You're doing much better than I'd expected." He said the words softly, afraid he'd jinx her with the saying of them. But he wanted to know how she felt. How she really felt.

"I noticed that, too. With you I feel safe. I can't explain it."

He pulled over. The view wasn't as good as it could've been if he'd taken a detour into the park, but he needed to stop. He hadn't forgotten the reward he'd promised when they reached Arizona.

"What's wrong?" she asked.

"Nothing." He climbed from the truck and went around to her side. Opened the door. She let him pull her outside. Wolf wanted some fresh air, too.

"Stay."

The dog obeyed. Bryan shut the door and drew Sylvia into his arms. "Kiss me." *Kiss me in my country.*

And he welcomed her to it with the most tender of kisses, as if testing her, testing them. What would she be like with his family, and they with her? Her mouth opened wider. She'd be fine, he realized, then claimed her with a fiercer kiss. Her head tilted back to give him what he wanted. His erection snaked across his abdomen, the length of it plumping, growing hot against his flesh. He released her mouth to lick her neck.

"So if I kiss you all night, you'll go camping with me, right?"

She laughed. "Baby steps."

Yeah, tread carefully, he warned himself. He pushed away from her and held her at arm's length. "I wonder how it'll be for you here. I took Simone home once."

"And?"

"She wasn't impressed."

Sylvia looked past his shoulder at the panoramic view. "I'm impressed."

He kissed her temple. "And I'm impressed that you're doing okay out here."

"You should hear my heartbeat. I think it's going to explode."

They laughed, and he pulled her close again. "You're going to be an outsider. I mean, people will be nice enough, it's just that..."

"You don't have to explain."

He couldn't help it. Simone's reaction had told him without a doubt that if he ever brought another woman here, he'd damn sure better prepare her for what lay ahead.

"There's a lot of poverty. So much that you'll wonder if you're still in America. It's that bad."

Her fingers brushed his lips and pressed against them. "It's okay. God knows what they'll think of me." She gave a tiny gulp. "Did you tell them? About what I was before I met you?"

He wasn't sure whether to grin or what, but in the end he decided she'd take it well, with humor.

"They don't even know you exist."

Chapter Thirteen

Sylvia wasn't sure what to say to that. "Oh."

She thought of how she could present herself to his family. *I teach piano at a local community college. I'm a graphic designer working at a major firm in California...* No. Lying was too difficult. The less said the better. He'd mentioned the Diné were a quiet people... Maybe his family wouldn't ask too many questions.

"Ready?" he asked.

"How far are we?"

"We're close. Real close." He helped her back into the truck and took his place behind the wheel again. "We should've picked up some fast food at the last exit, because we won't be able to get anything but a gas station burrito for the next forty miles."

"I'm not hungry," Sylvia lied. "Besides, snack foods are part of a road trip, aren't they? The important thing is that we get there fast. I'd offer to drive for a while, but it's been years since I was behind the wheel." She gazed at the highway rolling endlessly toward the horizon. Although mesas and buttes rose around them, the road was flat, straight and empty enough that she probably could manage to drive it. Slipping behind the wheel and taking control sounded exciting.

"We get off the highway soon and it's pretty rough going after that. The roads on the Rez aren't what you'd call maintained."

Several miles later they stopped at a station that was little more than a weathered shack with one ancient gas pump. From inside the car, she watched Bryan chat with the woman who ran the place. She was short, plump and wore jeans and a Western style shirt. Her long, black hair hung in a single braid down her back. She eyed Sylvia while speaking to Bryan.

When he returned to the car, he said, "Mrs. Nizhoni. She paid her respects to my grandfather a couple of days ago. She says Grandma's holding up and my mom's staying with her...for now." His mouth was a grim line.

Sylvia reached across Wolf's furry body to hold Bryan's hand, offering what comfort she could. From his stories, she knew seeing his mother again would be nearly as upsetting for him as facing his grandfather's death. Having her own family issues, she understood and wondered if she'd ever be brave enough to face her mother again.

They turned onto a dirt road, which became a rutted trail through the wilderness. The truck bounced over pits in the road and Sylvia's teeth clicked together.

The eastern sky lit up with one fiery color after another, salmon, mauve, gold and brilliant orange. By the time they'd jolted over forty minutes worth of road, the sun had emerged above the folds of rocky mesas to illuminate the vista of the barren yet beautiful land. The buttes glowed in shades of violet, blue, red and gold that rivaled the sunrise. All that empty terrain should've started her pulse racing, but instead she was struck by the primal beauty of the scene, which had probably remained unchanged for thousands of years.

"The colors are caused by minerals and decayed matter compressed into strata. All the red dirt is clay we use in pottery. Coal, petroleum and uranium mining have all taken place here at one time or another." Bryan recited the facts absently as if guiding a tour. "My grandfather's cancer is probably courtesy of the time he spent in a uranium mine. Gramps only worked there part-time when times were tough. He's already outlived most of his friends, who mined their entire lives."

"I'm sorry," she offered, rubbing his forearm.

They rounded an abutment of rock, and several miles

ahead was a cluster of buildings marring the untouched splendor of the land.

"My grandparents' house," he announced as they drew closer.

There was a trailer with extra rooms added onto one side, a couple of sheds, a fenced area and several vehicles parked in front. The trailer was a faded turquoise and white set on cement blocks. The wood add-on was weathered gray boards with a tin roof. A few hens pecked in the fenced yard near their coop. A skinny dog crawled out from beneath the trailer and ambled toward the truck as Bryan pulled to a stop. Wolf lunged across Sylvia, scraping her arm with his toenails, and barked at the other dog through the window.

"Hey! Calm down." She rested a hand on his bristling ruff.

"*Ma'iitsoh*! Quiet!" Bryan commanded.

Wolf whined, but retreated off Sylvia's lap to sit alert and shivering with excitement in his place between them.

"I didn't think about Naalnish. It'll take the dogs a few minutes to get used to one another." Bryan turned off the engine and the silence was broken only by Wolf's panting and whining.

Bryan's face was set and still. His eyes flicked over the house and yard then met hers. "The place is more rundown than it used to be. I should've come here a long time ago. I should've helped."

"You're here now," she said. "You can help now. Don't think about the past."

"My grandfather taught me carpentry while building the add-on." He nodded toward the back half of the trailer. "I was only about seven or eight, but he taught me to measure and cut boards and nail them, and where to place the supports to keep the structure sturdy. He taught me that it's worth it to take your time and do things right—measure twice, cut once. I know the place doesn't look like much, but it's sound, watertight and wind-proof." He paused. "It's a good house."

"Yes, it is. It's just fine."

He shook himself from his memories. "I'll introduce Wolf to Naalnish and then we'll go inside."

Bryan got out of the truck. Wolf bounded after him and raced toward the other dog, circling and barking at it ferociously. The older dog's hackles rose, but she didn't snarl, just watched the much larger Wolf rant at her. Then, abruptly, she sprang on him and nipped his neck. The big dog yelped in surprise and scrambled away.

Sylvia laughed. The old bitch was a force to be reckoned with. Unbuckling her belt, she opened the door then stepped down from the cab.

The dry desert heat enveloped her, and sweat beaded on her skin. It seemed every last drop of moisture instantly evaporated from her body and her throat became parched. Her body vibrated with the need to retreat back into the confines of the truck. Despite the heat, her hands were clammy and a shiver passed through her.

Bryan called a cowering Wolf to heel and ruffled Naalnish between the ears then glanced at Sylvia. "You're out of the truck! Are you okay?"

She gazed at the yard, the house, the vast empty land and then at Bryan. Swallowing down the flutter of nerves, she smiled at him and walked over to take his hand. "I'm fine. Don't worry about me. Let's go inside and see how your family is doing."

Chapter Fourteen

Everything here seemed smaller than he'd remembered—everything except the land itself with its towering rock formations rising from the flat plain. Bryan knew this was a common feeling for someone returning home after a long absence, but it didn't make him feel any less strange. Having Sylvia with him added another element of surrealism. He saw the place through her eyes, and it looked like crap.

Plus he worried about how she was doing, his emotions torn between focusing on her and on his family. All that combined with too many cups of coffee had his stomach churning.

Sylvia squeezed his hand. "It's going to be all right."

They mounted the two narrow steps to the front door. The boards were weak, sagging beneath their weight. Dangerous. He must replace them before Grandma fell and broke her hip or something. Why hadn't he checked on his grandparents sooner? There was so much he could have done to make life easier for them.

When he opened the front door and inhaled the scent of fry bread, a wave of nostalgia swept over him. He may have walked away from this world, but it was still home. As Grandma used to say, "A coyote may howl at the moon and dream of flying through the heavens like an owl, but at the end of the night he returns to his den." He used to think she was just trying to keep him on the Rez. Now he understood she'd been saying a man couldn't cut his connection to family no matter how far he traveled.

The living room was only steps from the front door. Grandma Naomi and Mom sat on either side of the bed on which Grandpa Butch lay. Bryan took a few steps toward them then stopped. His pulse raced faster and his chest ached. *I don't want to see this.*

He only realized he was gripping Sylvia's hand like a vise when she made a small sound and her hand shifted in his. He glanced at her and let go. "Sorry."

"It's okay." She took his hand again and together they walked into the living room.

Grandma Naomi looked up. She was old, he realized with a shock, her skin as gnarled and weathered as the trunk of a juniper. She was only sixty-five. When had she started to look so old? His mom was an image of Grandma a dozen years earlier. The two hard-boned, round faces, both with their hair pulled back and braided, were so alike no one could mistake them as anything besides mother and daughter. And the sorrow in their dark eyes as they looked at him only added to the similarity.

"*Shiyáázh.*" His grandmother's voice calling him her son was as low and soothing as a wood flute. "You made it."

"*Shimá sání.*" Bryan released Sylvia's hand and crossed the final few steps to pull his grandmother to her feet and into his embrace.

She hugged him hard. Her body seemed almost fragile despite its sturdy fullness.

"I'm sorry," he whispered.

His gaze settled on his grandfather. If Grandma seemed old, Grandpa Butch was ancient and so gray-tinged he appeared already dead. Only the harsh breaths wheezing in and out of his open mouth confirmed that he still lived. He'd been a big man, towering over his grandson until Bryan finally reached his full growth—and even then they'd stood eye to eye. Now, he was diminished. His mahogany flesh was like crepe paper draped over his bones.

Bryan watched his mother lean forward and dampen his lips with a moist towel. She looked clear-eyed and clean, but then she'd had good spells before, sometimes for as long as a year. They never lasted.

Bryan released his grandmother and took her chair beside the bed. He glanced at Sylvia, standing near the foot of the bed, acting so much braver than he'd hoped she could be. Throughout the long drive and now faced with people she'd never met, she remained composed. Being catapulted from captivity to this family drama couldn't be easy, but she was handling it well.

"This is Sylvia. My girlfriend." His eyes locked with hers to gauge her reaction. Color filled her cheeks, and she didn't look away. A good sign.

His family murmured greetings while he turned back to his grandfather and took his hand. Bryan tried to imagine Grandpa Butch could actually hear him. "I'm sorry I kept you waiting, *shicheii*. I'm here now."

He paused, wondering how he could encompass everything he needed to say in mere words. "I want you to know how much I love you, how much I learned from you. If I can become anything like the man you are, I'll be proud."

There was no change on the slack face. Another harsh breath rattled from his chest. Bryan glanced at his mother across the still body between them.

She smiled at him. "You must be hungry after driving all night. I'll get you something to eat." Rising from her chair, she walked toward the kitchen, inviting Sylvia to go with her.

Bryan felt a rush of gratitude to Sylvia for making this so easy. He wouldn't have imagined bringing her home to meet his family, but she appeared at ease, nothing like high-maintenance Simone. God, what a disaster that visit had been! What had possessed him to think he could show Simone where he came from and expect her *not* to be appalled by it?

A light hand dropped on his shoulder and Bryan glanced up at Grandma Naomi by his side. He covered her hand with his. "How are you doing?"

"Not good. I knew it would be hard, but helping him cross over is worse than I imagined."

"Couldn't the doctor—"

"Your Grandpa and I agreed when the time came there'd be no hospital, no doctors or drugs. It's how he wanted it."

"But, *shimá sání,* the passing could be so much easier with a morphine drip."

She stroked his hair with her other hand. "Sometimes a transition requires struggle. Remember the butterfly?"

How could he forget? As a child, he'd found a butterfly emerging from a cocoon. He'd tried to help it by prying open the husk to set the insect free. It had lain in the sun, beating its wings as they dried, but had never flown and soon died. His grandmother explained the butterfly needed to go through the difficulty of freeing itself in order to have the strength to fly.

Bryan couldn't help but hope his grandfather's end would be soon, because the struggle for each breath was agonizing to watch. "Shall I carry him outside?" he asked.

"Yes. I don't think there's much time left."

It wasn't Diné custom to die indoors where the spirit might continue to haunt the living. Releasing the soul to the open sky was important. Bryan lifted the old man's body, frail but still heavy and awkward to gather into his arms.

Outdoors, Bryan's spirit lifted. The sky was an aching blue from one horizon to the other. The painted hills rose all around them and a breeze ruffled his grandfather's hair. This was exactly where Butch would want to die, in the midst of the land that was a part of him.

Bryan laid him on a woven blanket his grandmother had spread in the shade of the only tree for miles. He recognized the pattern of the blanket, which had covered him many times in his childhood. The familiarity was a simple comfort.

He sat on his heels and listened to Grandpa's labored breathing and the echoing cry of a hawk somewhere in the distance. Grandma Naomi lowered herself to the ground on the other side of her husband.

"Sing with me. Help me send him on his way." She began the song of passing, her flutelike voice nasal as she chanted. The words were repetitive, so, although Bryan had never sung the death song before, he could soon join in. Together they wished the spirit traveler well and prayed his guide would lead him safely to the other world.

The song wound round like the endless seasons, the steady drone putting Bryan in a near trance. Peace came upon his spirit and with it, the release of tension.

Grandpa exhaled another rattling breath then fell silent. Bryan stopped singing and waited, one second, two, three, four, but his grandfather didn't inhale again. It was over. A mingled sense of relief and sadness washed over him. No matter where he'd traveled or what he'd done, he'd always known his grandfather would be here if he needed him. Now the comforting blanket of his presence was gone.

Grandma Naomi's eyes glistened with tears, but her face was calm. "It is good. He suffered too long."

They sat for several minutes gazing at the shell of the man they had loved and listening to the lonely cry of the hawk overhead. Neither touched him. Old beliefs were too ingrained for that, but they shared the moment, offering comfort to one another in complete silence.

"Leave me now." Her tone was abrupt. He knew her too well to offer to hold her right now. She wanted to be alone in her grief. Later there would be time for hugs and tears.

Bryan rose, squeezed her shoulder and walked back toward the house. Wolf appeared from wherever he'd been exploring and pushed his head under his master's hand. The dog panted heavily from running. He needed water.

"Stay," Bryan ordered when he reached the steps. Wolf settled on his haunches as his master abandoned him to go inside.

In the kitchen, Sylvia was rolling out pieces of dough, and his mom fried them.

"It's over," he announced, suddenly feeling nothing but exhaustion.

His mother turned from the stove to embrace him. He stood stiffly, nothing forgotten or forgiven. He would've liked to have been a bigger man than that, but there was too much history between them for him to want to return her hug.

After a moment, she released him. "I'll go check on Mom." She left the kitchen.

Sylvia wiped her hands on a dishtowel and walked toward him. Hers was an embrace he was glad to accept. He wrapped his arms around her slender body and held on tight, nuzzling his face into the side of her hair, wishing they could curl up together and rest right now. He hadn't an ounce of energy left as the tension of the last few days caught up with him. The drama in Gary's dungeon seemed light years and a lifetime away. The long drive to Arizona was like a river that separated this world from the other he'd been living in. Here, he had to be a different man than the carpenter from San Diego.

He wasn't ready to face the emotional ride of the funeral, to see all the relatives and friends he'd left behind, and hear their words of sympathy. God, he needed sleep.

"I'm so sorry, Bryan. Whatever I can do to help, let me know." Sylvia's voice was music to him, soft and soothing.

"Just be here," he whispered.

"I'm here."

For a long while, he simply relaxed into her comforting embrace. He may have fallen asleep standing up, because his eyes suddenly opened and his consciousness returned. He pulled away from Sylvia.

"The funeral will probably be tomorrow. Our people believe in getting the spirit on its journey as soon as possible so it doesn't linger or get trapped here."

She nodded. "What will happen next?"

He drew a deep breath. "We call the radio station to make an announcement since not everyone has phone service, and we make a lot of calls to relatives. Some will arrive as early as today. Others have to travel from a long way. The burial process is kind of complicated since traditional and modern ways are often at odds. If the family is Christian, they'll have it at the church, if not, a funeral parlor or at home. My grandma hasn't told me what she wants done yet."

Sylvia removed the frying pan from the stove, flipping the burnt flatbread into the trash and setting the pan aside. "What's the traditional way?"

"My people fear being haunted by the dead. If things aren't done right, the spirit might return from the underworld. In the past, a couple of men would prepare and bury the body while the family mourned at a safe distance. The gravediggers would be naked except for a coating of ash to ward off evil spirits, and there had to be a cleansing ritual performed on them afterward. Now we usually use a funeral home run by Anglos."

He accepted the glass of water Sylvia handed him and a piece of fry bread. His stomach rumbled loudly. Life went on amidst death. Stomachs still had to be filled. He wolfed down the bread.

"Anyway, now many Diné are Christian, but they still do everything in their power to make sure the dead stay buried."

"I can help with the cooking or anything else you need done. I want to be here for you."

"Thank you." He kissed the anxious frown from her forehead and stroked her soft, fine hair then he pulled away abruptly. "Crap! I forgot about Wolf. He needs water."

"I'll go out and see to him. You go to your family."

"Outside by yourself again?" He raised an eyebrow. "You've come a long way in just a few days."

She smiled. "Didn't say I'd like it out there, but I'll be fine. Please, let me do this for you. I want to be useful."

He leaned to give her another kiss, on the mouth this time, slipping his tongue between her lips to taste her sweetness, lingering to delay the moment when he'd have to go back outside and deal with death.

Chapter Fifteen

How good it was to be in the shelter of his arms again. She wished she could cling to him for a long time, maybe find a soft bed to lie in and curl up together and just sleep. She was so very tired. Her life as Butterfly seemed a world away from this place, and occasionally she experienced a flash of homesickness for it. How horrible that the familiarity of her cell, her routine and seeing the same few people every day had been a comfort as much as a curse.

She pulled away from Bryan's kiss and his embrace. "All right now. Let's do what we have to do. Your family needs you, and Wolf's thirsty."

His dark eyes shone as he gazed at her. "You're a miracle, do you know that? So much stronger than you think, and so concerned about others' needs."

His praise set a warm glow burning in her and made her smile. It had been very rare in her life for anyone to acknowledge her good points. She'd mostly believed she didn't have any. But standing here being admired wasn't getting Wolf watered or fed.

"Go on. Keep moving," she ordered. Even though she was only teasing, she would never have imagined a month ago she could dare talk to a man like that. Gary's indoctrination making her believe she was a mere object for his sexual entertainment seemed ridiculous now. How could she have fallen under his spell? The slave mentality of the past five years of her life was rapidly falling away like an outgrown cocoon as she emerged stronger, braver and better than ever before. She owed everything to Bryan, including her very life. Everything changing in her was due to him.

She watched his broad back as he left the house then looked through the cupboards for a bowl to use for the dog's water. After filling an old metal mixing bowl from the tap, she walked to the door and hesitated with her hand on the knob. She could do this. She'd chased Wolf down the street and walked to and from Bryan's truck numerous times. She'd gone to his friends' house, to public restrooms in gas stations along the way and entered his family's house without more than a rapid racing of her heart and sweaty palms. She'd managed to travel hundreds of miles without a debilitating panic attack. She could certainly go outside and give Wolf his water.

The metal knob turned beneath her palm, and once more she faced the eye-searing sun of the Arizona desert and the wide-open land that both awed and frightened her. Across the yard, Bryan and his family were clustered together in an open shed where a potting wheel stood. Wolf was with him, but when the dog saw her, he raced toward the house. His tongue lolled as he frisked around her.

"Poor baby, you must be so thirsty with that heavy coat." Sylvia crouched beside him, and he nearly knocked the bowl from her hands as she placed it on the ground. He lapped the water, pushing his muzzle in too deeply and snorting.

She pushed her hand into his thick ruff, feeling muscle under the soft fur. She'd left her sandals in the house and her bare toes dug into the red dirt—such a bright brick color it seemed like she was on Mars. The dirt was hot. The sun on her head was hot. The very air she inhaled was like a dry sauna. Sweat beaded on her forehead and trickled down her back.

Sylvia glanced up from the dog to the Lapahie family. Bryan's mom, Janice, seemed like a very nice woman. She'd introduced herself to Sylvia, dark eyes quickly assessing but not judging her, before she invited her to help in the kitchen.

"I know this is a very uncomfortable way for you to meet our family." She'd smiled grimly. "It would be awkward under the best of circumstances since Bryan and I haven't really talked in years. I don't blame him."

Bryan had only mentioned briefly that his mother's addictions left his grandparents to raise him. Now it appeared Janice was ready to make peace with her son. She'd confided to Sylvia that she'd been clean for almost two years, living with her parents for the last twelve months and making and selling beaded jewelry. She wanted to build a new relationship with her son. But Sylvia had seen how Bryan rebuffed his mother's embrace. Would he be able to forgive her?

Wolf looked up from the water and bounded away in pursuit of a scent. His nose stayed low to the ground and Sylvia imagined he was tracking a prairie dog—if they had prairie dogs here. The land looked too inhospitable so support any life. A few twisted shrubs grew between the stones, and a lone tree pierced the horizon where the grandfather's shrouded body lay, but mostly it was just rock and red soil.

A sharp cry came from above and she looked up. A hawk sailed high overhead. It was the first time Sylvia had really taken in the vast blue canvas of sky. She was transfixed and horrified by it. She felt vulnerable and exposed, as if that hawk might drop down a thousand feet and attack her. Her heart beat faster.

Time to go in before the anxious feeling turned into a full blown panic attack. She retreated into the safety of the small house and fought her racing pulse under control.

By mid-day, the Red Running into the Water Clan began arriving. Bryan had explained to Sylvia the structure of the family was matriarchal and cousins were called sisters and brothers. There was a vast pool of people one was related to, and marriages could only be made with members of other clans. His huge extended family as well as friends and neighbors pulled into the yard in pickups, rusty sedans and outdated minivans. Men set up tables and women laid out food and drink.

The Lapahies had contacted a gravedigger, a white man

who was used to doing this kind of work for the tribe at a moment's notice. He'd known about Butch's impending death and arrived early with his partner to dig the grave and wrap the body in a woven blanket Naomi had provided. The plot was about a hundred yards from the house.

Sylvia stayed indoors, watching the progress of the event from the window. She studied the faces of the people as they arrived, all similar in their heritage, but each unique.

Occasionally one of the women would come to use the kitchen to put a dish in the fridge or heat something on the stove. The first time Sylvia saw someone heading for the house, she hid in the bathroom like a child until she heard them leave again. Ashamed of her cowardice, she forced herself to meet and greet the next relative to come inside. It was the lady from the gas station, Mrs. Nizhoni.

"Hi." The woman's deep set eyes examined her intently.

Sylvia cringed inside, but she forced a smile. "Hello. My name's Sylvia. Is there anything I can do to help you?"

"I brought some chicken for grilling." The woman offered a Styrofoam cooler.

Together they unpacked the meat and found room for it in the overcrowded refrigerator. The chicken looked fresh-killed, scalded and plucked rather than neatly bound in plastic wrap. Sylvia imagined these birds had run around a yard not too long ago.

Mrs. Nizhoni chatted with Sylvia a few moments before returning outside with a large container of instant lemonade for the kids to drink.

As people continued to come in and drop off casseroles or cakes, Sylvia greeted each one politely, learned their relationship to Bryan and offered her thumbnail profile. "I'm a friend of Bryan's from San Diego. So sorry for your loss."

Periodically, throughout the afternoon, Bryan came in and touched base with her. "Still okay?" He wrapped an arm around her waist and pulled her to him.

"I told you not to worry about me. I'm content here in the

kitchen. I've met some of your family, and I'm doing just fine. You don't need to keep checking on me."

He lowered his lips to graze the skin below her jaw. "Maybe I *want* to keep checking on you. Maybe these breaks are the only thing that's helping me make it through the day."

"I like you sneaking away to see me, but your family needs—"

He captured her lips in a long, slow kiss, his fingers kneading the flesh beneath her dress. She didn't need to be flush against him to know his cock was stone-hard. He brought her closer, until the heat of his crotch burned through to her stomach. The smell of the outdoors was on him and she inhaled deeply as she melted into his body.

The sound of the trailer door opening broke them apart. Sylvia gasped at the sudden absence of his mouth on hers.

Footsteps approached and a man's tall figure filled the kitchen doorway. He carried a paper sack in each arm, and his eyes brightened when he saw Bryan. "Brother! It's been a helluva long time!"

"Mike!" Bryan crossed the kitchen to take the bags from him then introduced him to Sylvia as one of his cousins.

Mike's eyes flicked back and forth between them before he offered a greeting.

Sylvia smiled then returned to her casserole preparation while the two men talked about their lives. Mike had married Jackie from the Near the Mountain Clan right out of high school and already had four kids. He was a trucker and lived in Tuba City.

"Grandfather was a great old guy. Remember when he used to take us fishing in that stream up by Wolf Rock?"

The pair reminisced about their boyhood for a while then Mike asked Bryan to come out and meet his family. "You, too," he invited Sylvia.

Her chest tightened as she searched for a way to decline that wouldn't give him the impression she was avoiding or snubbing the Lapahie clan.

"Sylvia doesn't do well in the heat and the sun," Bryan said as he slipped an arm around her waist. "I'm sure she'll get to know everyone eventually."

She exhaled in relief and relaxed into his supporting embrace. "Please tell your wife I'd love to meet her if she wouldn't mind coming in here."

Before Bryan followed his friend outdoors, he gave her a last squeeze and dropped a kiss on her cheek. "I'll be back in a while for a taste of that casserole." His grin told her it was more than casserole he intended to taste.

He walked through the doorway and barely cleared it with his height. When she peered out the window again, he was standing with his kin, sometimes chatting, sometimes not. Although they clustered in small groups, talking, his people gave the impression of quiet stillness, just like he'd said. She liked their relaxed demeanors. Sure, kids played off to the side, their antics wearing down after a long day of travel and sunshine—plus chasing the two dogs—but the whole scene seemed subdued. At least from where she stood watching.

Bryan returned about an hour later as promised and scooped a chunk of the casserole onto a small plate he'd snatched from a cupboard. "Here."

"Oh, no. You messed it up for me." She grabbed the spoon. "Put it back."

He lifted the plate over her head and pressed her against the counter. His free hand rifled through a drawer until he found a fork. "You probably haven't eaten all day."

She hadn't. "It's no big deal—"

He speared a small morsel. "The cook has to eat, too. Open up."

So she relaxed against the counter and did as he asked. Bite by bite, he fed her. "More?"

She loved the caring his act signified, but she was full and shook her head. He reached over and helped himself to a plateful. The brown gooey mixture wasn't fancy—there hadn't been much to work with in the house—but it was filling.

"Is it okay, me being in here instead of out meeting your family?"

"Everyone's speaking Diné. Well, except for the kids. You'd probably feel a little strange, but no one thinks you're being rude or anything."

"But I want to be there for you."

"You'll comfort me tonight." He gave her a suggestive smile and slowly sucked the last of the casserole from his fork. Then he moved away from her, taking his body heat with him.

"You forgot the casserole." She held it out to him.

He came back for it, and for one more kiss.

Chapter Sixteen

Bryan didn't come indoors until late, after the chaos of getting an entire encampment of people settled for the night. He smelled of wood smoke from the blazing bonfire. Sylvia drew him into her arms and breathed him in, nestling her head against his chest.

He sighed, his breath stirring her hair. "There will be more family coming in tomorrow. We'll have the funeral in the afternoon."

She pulled away to look up into his face. There were dark circles beneath his eyes. Without a word, she took his hand and led him to the pallet on the kitchen floor that Grandma Naomi had helped her make up. Other bodies filled the living room, older people who didn't sleep as well outdoors on the hard ground as they used to. The kitchen was the only space left and, to tell the truth, she was glad to have that bit of privacy.

There was no "comforting" as she had hoped, or maybe she had imagined the innuendo. She had only his warmth and deep snores as he slept beside her. Occasionally, he'd mutter something in his sleep. Navajo words. She felt helpless to soothe him, and could only wrap the blankets around him tighter.

"I like waking up beside you." The words were in English this time and they dragged her into consciousness.

"Morning already?" She groaned and snuggled deeper into his arms. Keeping watch over his restless sleep had taken more out of her than she'd expected. She inspected his features. The dark half-moons under his eyes were still there.

"You didn't rest well."

"I'm fine." He got up and offered her a hand, then pulled her close. Quiet voices down the hall made her back away from his morning kiss.

"They can't see us."

"I know, but someone could come in here any second."

His warm chuckle made her insides go weak. "I kind of like the thought of that. Besides, you're irresistible in that big T-shirt of mine."

She gave in to a quick kiss then grabbed the bag of Melanie's donations he'd brought in last night before disappearing into the little bathroom to wash up. When she emerged, Bryan had already left the house to greet his relatives. Another vehicle drove up outside. He had another long day ahead.

Janice watched her from the kitchen as she folded Bryan's tee. "You can come outside if you'd like. We all speak English. It's no trouble to switch back and forth."

"Thank you." Sylvia looked down and tucked the shirt into the rumpled paper bag. An egg sizzled in the background, and the smell reminded her of how little she'd eaten yesterday.

"Come. Sit with me." Janice turned off the burner. "I want to learn about the woman my son loves."

Loves? "I'm not so sure about that."

"Why wouldn't I want to get to know you? I've missed out on so much of his life." Sadness darkened the woman's face.

"I'm not that interesting." *And what do I say?* Her heartbeat accelerated. "I meant I'm not sure about him loving me."

Janice set the plates on the table and motioned for her to sit. She obeyed.

"I see how he looks at you." She smiled. "Him always coming back to the house yesterday, or looking at the window to see if you're still standing there cooking. I enjoyed your casserole, by the way. So, how did you two meet?"

Sylvia chewed the fried egg and wondered how to respond. When she couldn't think of a good answer, she stabbed another bit of egg.

Janice laughed. "It's okay. I've met many men under less than perfect circumstances. Bars, parties, you name it." Her jovial tone faded. "But I'm sure Bryan has told you about those days."

Swallowing the egg was tough. It seemed to keep growing inside her dry mouth. Finally, she forced it down. "He told me some things."

Janice looked away for a second, shame briefly clouding her features before she made eye contact again. "I'm really better this time."

"It's okay. I wasn't passing judgment. Honestly."

"I forgot the coffee." Bryan's mom left the table and returned with two steaming mugs. "You take sugar? I think we're out of milk."

"Black is fine." Sylvia took a sip and felt it warm her bones. "I just hope... I mean, I know Bryan isn't ready..."

"Oh, I know. I don't blame him. It will take a lot of time. But enough about me. Tell me about yourself."

She took another drink to stall then decided to keep it simple. "I'm a pianist."

"Do you play professionally or teach?"

She shook her head. "Neither, but I'd like to teach kids to play one day." It wasn't a lie.

"That's wonderful. You know, if you and Bryan settle down here, you could probably teach children at the church. They have a piano there."

"I, uh, I'm not sure what Bryan's plans are. We haven't really discussed anything."

Janice stretched her hand across the table to pat Sylvia's. "It's okay. I just want you to feel welcome." She glanced at her watch. "I should get going."

"I'll clean up." Sylvia stood and reached for Janice's plate.

"Oh, no. You come outside today. Everyone wants to meet

you."

Egg turned to rock in her gut. All day outside? All those people?

Janice took her hand. "Come. Please?"

Her feet refused to move. Going outside with Bryan by her side was tolerable, but without him...

Janice studied her eyes then ran her thumb through the sweat gathering on Sylvia's palm. She released her hand and nodded.

"You stay inside. I'll bring some people in to meet you."

Relief washed through Sylvia like a flood, and she closed her eyes in embarrassment. When she opened them, Janice still watched her, a sympathetic smile curving her lips.

"Yes. You stay inside."

Once the dishes and pans were clean, Sylvia set about making another casserole. Bryan didn't take as many breaks as yesterday, but she often looked out at him talking with his friends and family. Was the pretty woman in the flowing purple dress an old girlfriend? He spoke to her a lot. It took a moment for Sylvia to recognize the strange, uneasy feeling welling up inside her. With Gary, she wasn't allowed to feel jealousy, and now the idea of Bryan being attracted to another woman made her feel...possessive. As if she should dash outside and stand beside him. Let the woman know he belonged to her.

Many people made their way in and out of the kitchen, introducing themselves to Sylvia and making small talk, usually centered around food.

By mid-afternoon, a throng of people milled in the front yard, and she guessed it was almost time for the funeral. Sylvia steeled herself for the prospect of standing by Bryan's side during the ceremony. She would gladly do it for him, face the open sky and a group of strangers. But she received an unexpected reprieve when Bryan came into the kitchen followed by the woman in the purple dress with a sleeping toddler in her arms.

"Sylvia, this is my cousin Mandy. Her little boy is wiped out and we wondered if you'd be okay with looking after him and a couple of the other little ones if they napped in the living room."

She nodded. "Sure, but don't you want me with you at the funeral?"

His smile was warm and sweet, and his eyes lingered on her face. "I really appreciate that, but if you could help with the kids, that would be great."

She was glad to obey his wishes and happy to be of use to his family.

"Thanks." Mandy's pretty smile made Sylvia very glad she was a cousin. She carried her child into the other room.

Sylvia put her arms around Bryan's waist, hugging him tight. Without a word, she tried to give him her support for the difficult ceremony ahead.

His hands roamed up her back and sifted through her hair. Cupping the back of her head, he pulled away from her embrace so he could kiss her. Light as the whisper of a breeze, his lips settled on hers and teased them open. A quick flick of his tongue, a promise for later, and then he stepped away. "Okay. I'll be back soon."

She walked him to the door and saw him out, then went into the living room where several young children were sound asleep on couch cushions or sleeping bags.

Mandy settled her little boy in a nest of blankets on the floor. The child's pudgy face was slack in sleep, his mouth open. Tendrils of hair clung to his sweaty forehead.

"He should stay sacked out for a lot longer than the service will take. Rick's a whirlwind, but when he crashes, he doesn't move for hours."

"He's adorable. How old?"

"Four." The woman continued to stand there.

Sylvia flicked a nervous glance at her.

Mandy's eyes were assessing. "Look. The rest of the family is too traditional, meaning too polite to talk plainly, so I'll make up for them. Bryan may have chosen to leave here, but a person can't reject family so easily. We'll always be a part of him and vice versa. That's what it means to be a tribe. I don't know if he told you about that girl Simone. She did a real number on his head. Made him feel bad about himself."

Sylvia's pulse thudded under Mandy's direct stare and frank words.

"Don't expect him to change. He is who he is, and this is where he comes from. Okay?"

"Yes," she replied meekly.

She understood Mandy intended to be blunt, not mean, but the unexpected confrontation made her stomach churn.

The black-haired woman nodded and turned to go.

"Just so you know. I wouldn't want or expect Bryan to change. I like him exactly the way he is."

Pausing with her hand on the doorknob, Mandy looked back and smiled faintly. "Well, all right then. Just so we're clear."

After she left, Sylvia checked on the sleeping children then returned to the kitchen to wash another sink full of dirty dishes. As she rinsed and stacked, she listened to the faint sound of singing from outside, "Amazing Grace" rather than the Native American chant Bryan and his grandmother sang the day before.

If she pressed close to the window, she could see the group gathered near the grave. A soft cough made her whirl around from the window.

A round-faced child stood sucking its thumb and staring at her with bright eyes. It could've been a girl or boy as the jeans and T-shirt would suffice for either.

"Hi! Can I get you something? Need a drink?" She poured a glass of tap water and offered it to the little one, who continued to gaze at her. "Thirsty?"

Sylvia wasn't used to children. She hadn't been around them for the past five years, but even before that, she'd never had a babysitting job or any reason to be near kids. The idea of having one of her own had crossed her mind occasionally, but she knew she was too screwed up to ever be a mother.

Pulling the thumb from its mouth with a pop, the child announced, "I gotta go potty."

"Okay. It's right over here." Sylvia took the chubby hand in hers and led the child to the bathroom. The sweaty and sticky palm clung to hers, the little fingers curled around her hand. Her heart twisted at the vulnerability of children and how the adults in their lives could hurt them.

If she and Bryan had a child, would it look something like this little one? Her melancholy grew stronger, as she dismissed the impossible thought and opened the bathroom door. "Do you need help or can you do it by yourself?"

The kid looked up at her with disdain. "I wipe my own pee-pee now. I'm a big girl, not a baby."

Girl then. "Of course, you are. Pardon me." Sylvia nodded gravely.

The little girl went into the bathroom and closed the door behind her.

After the service, Bryan stopped by the kitchen to see her again, but then there was more socializing and eating to be done until late that evening.

As daylight shifted into night, some vehicles drove off, but others stayed. The crowd drew nearer to the house to gather around a pit fire.

She watched Bryan until she ached with emptiness at being apart from him. She rested her forehead against the door and listened. The fire crackled. Barking from Wolf or the other dog interrupted a chorus of crickets looking for love in the Arizona twilight. She wrapped her moist hand around the doorknob and practiced giving it a good, hard twist. When Bryan's deep baritone rose above the conversation, she found the strength to twist and pull.

She spotted him near the corner of the trailer. He'd been standing for most of the day, and she could see the rhythm of his body as weariness and fortitude battled in his muscles.

196

Eventually he leaned against the trailer for support, a casual pose, but the way he sagged into the siding told her he needed rest.

She crept around the opposite side of the dwelling until she could see his broad, strong back. "*Pssst.*"

Bryan didn't hear her, but Wolf did. He and the other dog bounded around the corner. She wiped her damp palms off on her dress and gave them some attention. When they were ready to explore the next night sound off in the distance, she looked at Bryan. He stared right at her from between the bend of his bicep and forearm.

She crooked her finger.

He called out some parting words to his family and came to her.

"What are you doing out here?"

He didn't give her a chance to answer, leading her to the rear of the house and covering her mouth with his. She kissed back, tamping down on the fear still rocking her belly. He broke the kiss to tilt her head away and lick her collarbone.

"Come with me," she said.

"I don't want to go to the kitchen and sleep. Not yet."

"Then we'll go somewhere else."

He worked his way up her neck to the corner of her mouth. "Hmmm. Where are you taking me?"

"You once spoke to me about how you loved to camp out—"

His head popped up. "You can't be serious."

"Yeah." She grinned up at him. "I think I am."

He swept her into his arms and carried her to his truck parked near the pottery shed.

Once they were several hundred yards away from his family, he hit the gas. They had the road to themselves, except for a few nocturnal animals, their eyes flashing bright as they scampered across the road.

Bryan slowed to avoid hitting an armadillo and took her hand in his. "You really okay with this?"

"I'd do anything to get you a good night's rest. Even brave leaving your grandparent's house to sleep under the stars."

He smiled. "So I take it you got blankets and stuff and threw 'em in the back?"

Oh, crap. She gave her forehead a light smack. "Um…no. Sorry. Should we turn around?"

He lifted her hand to his lips, kissed the back of it, then rolled her palm over and open. The softness of his lips made her body hum with anticipation. Made her think of other places she wanted him to kiss…

"Just teasing. I always keep a sleeping bag and blankets in back, so no worries there."

She gave him a mock pout, and he immediately leaned in to kiss her. "Hey! Watch the road, silly."

"What road?" he asked against her cheek.

She glanced out the window. He'd pulled off the road, and a small scrub of a bush lay directly in their path. "Look out for that tree."

Bryan hit the brakes. "Hey!"

Her tongue darted out. "Payback."

He put the truck in park and unbuckled her belt. The roar of the engine matched the thrum of her pussy as he pulled her across the seat. "Payback, eh? Careful. I just might up the stakes."

I don't want to be careful. Not with your arms around me and the smell of you and the heat melting me from the inside out…

Keys jingled as he fumbled to turn off the ignition. She brought her leg up over his and wiggled her way into his lap.

"Jesus, woman," he murmured into her mouth.

She ate up those words, every syllable, and pressed into his erection to force more from his lips. Tonight she felt powerful. God, he made her feel so much.

When he inched his head away, he was panting. "We should wait."

"No!" She took back the vehemence of her protest by adding, "I mean, out of respect for your grandfather, maybe. But not for anything else."

He shook his head and took hold of her hips to untangle their bodies. "Five years of damage is a helluva lot. I can't just snap my fingers and undo what he did to you. You need time."

I need you. "Show me. Show me the right way to know pleasure. You've already done it once. Do it again."

She'd beg if that's what he wanted, on her knees or by lying prostrate before him. "Tell me what I need to do to make you want me."

He laughed and planted a sweet kiss on her forehead. "You know I want you. Soon, Sylvia. I promise."

He hopped out of the truck. After catching her breath and willing her watery bones to move, she joined him. Together they layered a few blankets in the truck bed then crawled into a sleeping bag.

"Ready to zip up?"

She snuggled closer to him and folded her hands against his hard chest. "Yes."

"Sorry it's so tight."

"I don't mind." She wished she could see his eyes in the absolute darkness of the night. She'd give anything to see the desire there. "We'll be warm."

"Yeah. Warm," he muttered.

She chuckled and shifted against him. He was definitely warm—in all the right places. Her hands went lower, across tight abs and thick denim...

"Hey, look up."

"Trying to distract me?"

"Yes and no. Just look."

She stifled a frustrated sigh and rolled to her back. "Wow."

The black velvet expanse above them was sprinkled with diamonds that pulsed and glowed more brightly than any stars she'd ever seen.

"Amazing, isn't it? You don't get this kind of night sky in the city."

And you don't get it in the confines of a place like Gary's... She blocked the rest of the thought. It was time to let go of the past, or at least start trying. She waited for the usual feelings of helplessness to overtake her, to drag her down into panic and despair. Secure in Bryan's arms, she felt none of these things.

"See that star there?"

She did, and he told her the story of it, a tale passed down from generation to generation here on this brick red earth. Her fingers found his lips, felt them move from one piece of sky to another while he shared the lore of his people. She held on to wakefulness for as long as she could then let her fingers drift. The stories still flowed from his mouth, now in Diné, and she dreamed of drifting through the skies on the back of mischievous Coyote spreading stardust along the Milky Way.

Chapter Seventeen

"Bryan. Bryan!"

She was rocking the boat. Wait, no boat. A bed?

"Huh?"

"I think we're surrounded." Sylvia was shaking him now. And he'd been having such a good dream...

"What's wrong?"

"I hear things. Alive things."

He popped one eye open. "We're outside. Relax." He pulled her closer. "There's tons of critters out there."

"*Tons?*"

Uh-oh, he was freaking her out. "Don't be afraid. Heck, they're more afraid of us than—"

"I'm not so sure. Listen."

He focused on the night noises around them. The skittering of something not so little rounded the back of the truck. It was curious, but not daring to jump in.

"Probably a fox. Remember, we're sleeping out in their territory. We're the uninvited guests." He heard her suck in a sob-like breath. Obviously his explanation hadn't done much to ease her mind. "Want me to tell you another story?"

"Do you have any that don't involve 'critters' of any size or shape?"

He laughed. Damn, she was hard to resist, clinging to him for dear life. "What happened to my brave one?"

"She left when the 'critters' came out," came her muffled

reply.

He chuckled. She'd tunneled deep into the sleeping bag. A very hot sleeping bag. Between the thermal rating and their combined body heat, he was swimming in sweat.

"Well, this can't be too attractive. Sorry." He unzipped the bag and peeled off the soaked T-shirt. She dropped her head right back onto his chest. "Want me to air out first?"

Apparently not. She practically pushed him back down into the bag then lay quiet and shivering against him. Maybe he should keep her talking, keep her mind off wild things. But his thoughts stayed centered on coarser subject matter, like what he wanted to do to her once she was ready. They could talk about it, just not do anything...right?

"So what are your limits?" he asked quietly.

"You mean besides the outdoors?" The words came out between chattering teeth. "I guess no high places, not until I get used to the lay of the land. It's bad enough to have sky above, but to have it below, too..."

"Sexual limits."

She didn't speak for a while, and he wondered where her mind had wandered to. Probably back to Gary's dungeon, reliving some bad moment.

"I don't have any," she whispered.

Anger boiled up inside him so fiercely that the field of stars blurred with his rage. How many times had he punched that bastard? Obviously not enough.

"Well, you should. Gary never ever allowed you to say no?"

"Never."

He cradled her chin in his hand and brought her face to his. "I have limits. And I'm almost afraid to tell you what they are. After all the hardcore stuff Gary did to you—and I'm assuming you liked at least some of it—the way I want to do things might pale in comparison. I'm not sure what you'll think of me. I'm nothing like him."

"And I'm so, so glad."

She cuddled closer to him, and he gave her a small hug.

Then he rolled her away from him and hopped out of the truck bed. To think. To move around. Staying that near her body would only tempt him further.

She sat up. "What's wrong, Bryan?"

He stopped pacing and gripped the edge of the bed to keep from jumping right back in and fucking her senseless.

"I want you to tell me what you want."

"I want whatever you want," she replied.

Christ, the automatic reply made his blood heat with fury again. "That's not the answer I need here. I guess... I want your honest reaction when I say I won't be using whips on you—maybe a soft flogger—but nothing that will cut you, not after what you've been through. And I'm not going to tie you up for hours and walk away. What we end up doing, we do *together*. Is that enough for you?"

Her answer was immediate. "Yes, it is."

"Then get out of the truck."

"What?!"

"Whatever was out here is gone. I want you to trust me, and I want you to get out of the truck. Now."

"Yes...Sir."

"No 'sir' shit with me. I don't want you to call me that."

She tried again. "Okay." There was the soft shuffle of the sleeping bag and the shifting of her weight in the truck.

"And I want you naked. Come to the edge."

"The edge?" Her teeth were chattering.

"The edge of the truck bed. Are you cold?"

She stepped closer until he could catch hold of her calves. She didn't feel cold.

"No, I'm fine. Just..."

"Say what's on your mind. I want to hear it all." He walked her closer to the end of the bed and wasn't satisfied until her toes curled and uncurled nervously over it.

A nervous laugh escaped her. "I'm getting naked out here in the middle of nowhere. On the edge of a truck."

He tightened his grip on her legs then stroked up to the backs of her knees. "I've got you." He couldn't have seen much of her unfastening her dress in the moonless night, but he closed his eyes anyway. Were her fingers trembling at each button? Did she miss one in her eagerness to strip for him?

The dress slid down her body and covered his arms. "Find my shoulders."

When ten tiny fingers dug into him, he lifted her down to the dirt and walked backward, small steps at first, taking her farther away from the false security of the truck. He cupped a breast as he went, feeling for the stiff nipple or the hoop dangling from it. She groaned against his arm when he found it. The wind danced around and between them, setting his hair in motion. She caught a fistful of it.

"Did it grow back fast after the Army?"

"Fast enough. It's had about eight years to grow." He laughed. "Is that all that's on your mind? My hair?"

"If I think about what you might do to me, I'll spontaneously combust."

A growl echoed in his chest. "I'd like to see that."

He let go of her nipple, of her body, and stepped back. His pupils were fully accustomed to the darkness now, and he admired her rigid form in the black night. He took another step backward, and another. She reminded him of the statue he'd carved of her.

"Bryan?"

He knew she could see him. She just needed to hear his voice. "I'm right here."

Again at her side, he now knew how to handle tonight. No more anxiety over how he'd perform this first act of dominance or how he'd please her—he'd love her like he loved the wood he carved, compel it to open up to him and share its secrets as he worked it.

He traced the curve of her hip to prove it and trailed that finger completely around her, taking in every detail. The small swell of her belly and the dark butterfly wings at her lower back… The long hair curling at the ends right above the tats and the dimples in her ass cheeks. He made his way to the front of her body and picked her up. Her legs wrapped around his hips in a perfect fit. When they reached the truck, he set her there and pushed her down.

"Spread for me."

He leaned down between her wide open legs to kiss her belly. She tried to coax him away from that spot, but he wouldn't budge. There he found her old scars with the tip of his tongue. He kissed every one he could feel then he moved down to the top of her thighs and showered them with kisses, too. The scent of her pussy lured him in, and a patch of short, bristly hair pricked his lips. Licking her lightly, he savored each squirm she gave beneath him.

"Wood doesn't move." His voice came out low and rough. Proof he was struggling to maintain control. Had she noticed? She'd stopped her movements and sat up.

"Wood?"

"Yes. When I put my tools to wood, I'm looking for something deep inside. Something intimate and beautiful. Tonight, I'm going to find this inside you. With my hands. You need to feel these things deep down. Are you ready?"

She gave a little shudder. "Yes."

"Then lie back down."

She didn't expect Bryan to climb up into the truck with her. And she didn't expect him to head for the utility box and dig through his things. She wondered what he was looking for. With her back to him, she couldn't make sense of the sounds— maybe the loud clunks were scrap wood and the ping was something metal. The mysterious sounds set her senses on edge. With Gary, the toys were always the same. Expensive. Black. Predictable.

Tonight had been anything but predictable. From her own behavior to his decision to finally play with her, this night was meant for surprises.

The rasp of his zipper made her heart pound faster. She wanted to see the denim uncover his hard cock and firm thighs. She wanted to be the one stripping him off—he wouldn't have to do a thing but stand there while she took care of him.

He walked to where she lay. A mass of bungee cords dangled from his hand. What she could see in the low light made her pulse beat even faster; she prayed her heart wouldn't explode. The moon had risen late tonight and it peeked over the horizon to her right. Its subtle radiance painted him in light. His cock glistened at the tip, and she had to claw into the sleeping bag to keep from reaching for it.

"Did I say you could turn your head?" He was smiling.

She replied with a smile of her own. "No." She turned back to the twinkling stars.

He sat over the wheel hub and dropped the tangle of cords. Disappointment washed through her. She'd never been tied up in anything like them before...

"Come to me."

She rolled to all fours in a flash and crawled to where he sat, her lips mere millimeters from the drop of liquid on the slit of his cockhead. It reminded her of a delicate star. Her lips parted, and he didn't have to say a word or guide her head to where he wanted it. She knew what he wanted. The tiny pearl of pre-come taunted her. She lapped at it, but didn't swallow. Instead she let it mingle with her saliva to ease his shaft's unrushed slide into her mouth. She felt his hand on her hair and the outside curve of her ear. His fingers seemed to be peeling back her layers, teasing out her need to please him with just a fingertip.

The limited contact let her concentrate on the two points of connection, mouth to cock and fingers now at her earlobe. When his finger spiraled inside her ear to press at the small, sensitive hole, her pussy clenched. He forced the finger deeper, not enough to hurt but to let her know he would control the tempo. The finger guided her up and down his length as fast or as slow as he pleased.

"You like that, don't you?"

Her eyes fluttered open. They told him that she did.

He fingered her other ear. Night sounds muffled, all thoughts on him, she relaxed as he gently twisted her head along his cock and nearly broke free of her lips. She licked at him, eager and greedy, then surged forward to take him inside her mouth again. His fingers held her back to show her who was in control.

Then he let her go.

He's teasing me. And she loved it. Loved every long, drawn-out moment in the sensuous dance unfolding between them. He moved behind her. Turned her around. She closed her eyes as he tenderly pressed her face down to the blankets and circled her limbs with the cords. Her heart dropped with each tug until he had her like he wanted—immobile, but nowhere near uncomfortable with her wrists bound to her ankles, her bottom wriggling and arched up toward the sky.

His palm met her ass. "All tied up and still she moves." Fingers feathered over her exposed pussy. She gasped, and he laughed. "Keep wiggling and you won't get any more of that."

Oh, she wanted more. A lot more. But it was so damn hard not to jump when his nails raked one bare foot, or when teeth grazed her hip. He even placed a kiss right next to the entrance to her ass. He followed each tantalizing touch with a long pause. She'd hear him shuffle around, calculating his next move. A hand thrust past her stomach to taunt her nipple with the slightest dusting of fingertips. A hot tongue made a quick landing on her accessible clit. She moaned her pleasure, her frustration. That only made him slow the tempo more.

It wasn't until she was shivering with lust and the need to find release that his finger outlined the inner lips of her drenched pussy. When the finger slid inside, she began quaking, a teeth-rattling earthquake of emotion and longing. He added another finger then a third. She'd never felt so full...so fulfilled. And when those fingers curved into her long-neglected G-spot to rub and rub and rub, she shattered like stardust across the Milky Way, every cell of her being becoming one with night and air and soil.

Tears came. So did his gentle words, "You okay?"

She couldn't talk. But she managed a whimper and a nod against their bedding still thick with his sweet scent.

The cords came off. The rustle of foil permeated her consciousness. Then his hardness pressed into her liquid center and fucked her soft and raw and perfect. His hands covered her limp ones and stretched her flat, his weight a burden she never wanted to be free of. He brushed her hair from her face and kissed her cheek as they lay, him moving inside her, her taking every inch. When he laced his fingers through hers, she knew he was close. She found the strength to tighten her cunt's grip on his cock and push him over the edge, one spasm at a time.

Bryan released with a long, low groan, and she felt his relief as if it were her own. He'd needed a release so badly after the stress of the past days, needed the comfort her body could give him. Sylvia was filled with joy to be fulfilling her purpose, pleasing her lover. It was the one thing in her life she excelled at.

Bryan's weight settled even more heavily on her, cupping her back and buttocks. His breath hitched harshly in and out, puffing warm against her skin. His sweat-slicked chest slid against her back. Brushing her hair aside, he kissed her shoulder, between her shoulder blades and the back of her neck.

"I should move. I'm going to flatten you." His husky murmur held a glitter of humor. Oh, how she loved his teasing playfulness—so different from Gary's dark, demanding nature.

"It's all right. I like your weight. It makes me feel safe." Like being bound tight and kept in an enclosed space where nothing could harm her. She felt like she was a butterfly again in Bryan's safe cocoon of protection.

And so they stayed that way, although Sylvia was stretched out flat, and Bryan shifted partially to the side to take some of his weight off her. They lay melded together on the rumpled sleeping bag. Bryan pulled the extra blanket up over them against the chill of the night wind, but Sylvia didn't even need it. He was her blanket, her comforter, radiating boundless heat and security.

They didn't move until the sun came up. Under him, under his warmth, she didn't want to move ever again. Like the wood he carved, she lay there still and waiting. Waiting for what he would think to do to her next.

Chapter Eighteen

Bryan sat at on the ridge, gazing across the panorama of the arroyo. The striations of color in the rocks were different at every moment of the day: brilliant at sunrise and sunset, washed out in the brightness of noon. He had seen the progress of the sun across the sky and the way it changed the land below for the first half of his life, but he'd been away for a few years—it was like discovering the desert all over again.

As a boy, how many times had he sat on this flat boulder, perched above the deep gorge like an eagle surveying its kingdom? He and Mike, Billy Naja and Jake Orono had camped here on the crest of the hill dozens of times—more if he counted the times he'd come alone. From boyhood through angry teen years when they'd smoked weed and daydreamed their freedom from the Rez, this had been a special place.

Billy Naja was dead now—killed in Iraq. Jake Orono was a car dealer in Phoenix and doing really well for himself, Mike had heard. And Mike was still here, married to Jackie as they'd all expected he would be, with four kids and an income that barely met his family's needs. It was a typical life for those who stayed on the Rez—minus the booze and drugs that made lives more miserable than they had to be.

As beautiful as the desert was, Bryan knew he couldn't stay here. There was no work for him, and he couldn't imagine Sylvia living in poverty. When he was finished fixing things around the homestead and helping his grandmother through the aftermath of Grandpa Butch's death, he'd take Sylvia to

Phoenix. The city was close enough that he could come home quickly if needed, but large and wealthy enough to support his specialized carpentry work.

The idea he'd never return to California didn't bother him at all. He'd always felt like a visitor in San Diego, and now believed it was inevitable he'd end up back in Arizona. The red earth really was in his blood.

He rose from the sun-baked rock to start his trek back down the mountain...to Sylvia, who was never far from his mind now. The other night, under the magical influence of the desert sky, it had been impossible for him to resist the elemental pull of her body. The magnetism between them was powerful, and his spirit was weak from the stressful day. He'd wanted her with a bone-crushing need and had given in to his body's demands despite his vow to give her time to rediscover herself.

The morning after their truck-bed tryst, they'd hurried home to see off the relatives. It wasn't until late afternoon that the last straggler left. Grandma had been sagging with exhaustion and after a light supper, they'd all gone to sleep almost before the sun set.

Waking in the night, Bryan could've sworn his grandfather's voice had pulled him from sleep. In the dark house, old superstitions seized him. He'd burrowed back under the blanket, pulling Sylvia's sleeping body tight to his, her warmth easing him back to sleep.

Today, with his body rested and his mind clear, he made a vague promise to resume his program of chastity, for a while, at least. Sylvia should stand strong on her own instead of depending on him. But Bryan knew he would give into temptation again. She was a drug and he an addict. If she so much as smiled at him, he was aroused.

Her soft, pale skin, her large, luminous eyes, and, God help him, her compliance were irresistible. Even now a sharp stab of lust went through him at the image of her face pressed to the truck bed and her ass thrust into the air as she awaited his touch. So sweet and loving, so tender and vulnerable, she made him feel more powerful, more a man than he'd ever felt before.

His boot heels skidded in gravel as he wove his way between boulders and sagebrush, following the narrow trail downhill. The clean, sharp scent of sage filled his nose. It was the smell of his youth, the smell of home. He should burn some on the campfire tonight, another cleansing ritual to send Grandpa on his way.

When Bryan entered the house, he followed the sound of feminine voices to the kitchen where his mother had Sylvia cooking again. Their backs were to him and he lounged in the doorway, watching. He didn't like how Janice had seduced Sylvia into trusting her. The younger woman was naïve enough to take his mom at face value, but Bryan knew better. Her upswings never lasted and when she started her inevitable downward spiral, he didn't want Sylvia caught up in it. Hopefully, they'd be out of here before that happened.

"What you making?" He interrupted their conversation.

Both turned toward him. They were like relief images of one another—light and dark, petite and tall, fresh youth and hard-lived middle age.

"Bryan!" Sylvia said his name like a caress, her face full of pleasure at the sight of him. "Come and look at this. It's adorable."

"Adorable food?" He crossed the kitchen to see what they were looking at. A shoebox sat on the counter and in a nest of cloth huddled a baby rabbit, shivering and twitching. Its fur was damp and matted.

"Where'd you find it?"

"Wolf carried it in and dropped it at my feet," Sylvia explained. "No tooth marks that we could find. Other than being terrified, I think it's all right."

Janice laughed, stroking the brown fur with the tip of her finger. "Remember that rabbit you found when you were little, *Shiyáázh*? You were so excited and determined to take care of it."

Bryan grunted. Didn't she remember how it had ended up?

The fucking rabbit had died. He cried, and she screamed at him to shut the hell up because she had a hangover. Then her current boyfriend had tossed the rabbit's tiny body to his dogs and they'd ripped it to pieces. Hell, Janice probably *didn't* remember how upset Bryan had been or what exactly had happened to the baby bunny, she'd been so out of it. Shortly after that she'd dumped Bryan with her parents—for the first time.

He looked from the quivering rabbit to Sylvia's enchanted smile. "Don't get too attached, okay? It probably won't make it through the night."

She frowned. "Maybe not, but we have to at least try to take care of it, to help it grow stronger then let it go."

He knew the animal was too small to survive without its mother. Trying to nurse it to adulthood was an impossible task, but he swallowed his instant negative response, not wanting to upset her. She'd be upset soon enough when the little animal died.

Bryan changed the subject. "Want to leave the rabbit to rest and come outside with me? You can see my grandma's pottery."

"Sure." Sylvia didn't hesitate. He wondered if she'd overcome her fear of the outdoors so quickly or if she merely wanted to please him. With a last gentle touch of the rabbit, she smiled at Janice. "Take care of our little one."

Bryan met his mother's eyes. Hers were clear, the circles beneath them gone, and her complexion had a ruddy glow. The frantic edginess that had always sizzled around her had quieted. The tapping fingers and darting eyes were still.

For how long?

Turning away, he slipped an arm around Sylvia's waist and escorted her from the room. He didn't want her under his mother's influence. Besides, he needed her to himself for a few minutes.

Outside, she grasped his hand, their fingers twined together, and that simple touch of skin on skin was so erotic Bryan's cock went hard. He was such an animal where she was concerned, as hungry for her as a starved dog.

"Your mom is nice. She's made me feel so welcome." Sylvia squeezed his hand.

He shrugged. "Today she's nice. Tomorrow, who knows?"

She kicked a pebble with the toe of her sandal. It shot across the dusty yard and into a tangle of weeds. "From what she's told me, she's changed her life completely. She's a different person from who she was. It's possible, you know. Maybe you should talk to her."

A flicker of anger burned in his chest. His jaw tightened. Sylvia had been completely snowed by the woman. "You've known her only a few days. Don't give me advice on my mother."

She winced as though his sharp voice were a physical blow.

He glanced at the top of her head. She was staring at the ground as they walked. "Hey, don't mind me. It's just Janice is kind of a sensitive subject."

She nodded, but her eyes remained focused downward.

Bryan stopped walking, took her shoulders and turned her to face him. He put a finger under her chin and raised it.

"Sylvia. It's all right. You're allowed to have an opinion, but I have the right to disagree and to ask you to stop talking about it. Sometimes couples argue. Please don't start thinking of me as 'sir' again. I thought we were past that. I'm not your Master. The kind of games we play during sex don't have to influence every facet of our lives."

He couldn't read her eyes. Did she really understand that she was allowed to think for herself, or had five years of living like a pet stripped her of that ability? Maybe full-time slavery— that level of control—was the kind of relationship she wanted in her life. Maybe Bryan wasn't the right partner for her at all.

"May I keep the baby bunny and look after it?" The abrupt change of subject took him by surprise.

"Of course. You can do whatever you want. I just told you, I don't own you." He stroked his fingers over her soft cheek, the light skin already flushing in the midmorning heat. "You can do what you like, any time you like." He smiled and teased a little, "I'm not the boss of you—except in bed."

"All right...Sir," the title came out a seductive drawl rather than a formal title, "in that case, what I'd like, after we see your grandma, is to have some alone time. Is there any place we can go for a quickie?"

His smile widened. Her teasing him back was a good sign. "Actually, there is." He pressed a light kiss to her mouth, no more than that or they'd get distracted from their destination.

When he pulled away, she whispered, "Good. 'Cause I've been thinking about the other night all morning. I want you so much I think I'm suffering some kind of withdrawal."

He laughed, and the sweet sound of her joyful laughter combined with his. Just then Wolf came charging up from wherever he'd been foraging. He raced around them in a circle, his coat a dusty red from rolling in the dirt.

"Whoa, buddy, slow down before you drop from heat stroke." Bryan ordered him to sit, and Wolf reluctantly dropped to his haunches. "Take a cue from Naalnish and relax a little." He gestured at the old bitch, lying in the shade at the side of the house. She'd dug herself a deep furrow in the dirt over the years and only her head peeked out. "There will always be more rabbits to chase."

"And poor baby bunnies to kidnap, you bad dog!" Sylvia scolded.

"Hey, he was just following his hunting instinct. Lucky he didn't snap its spine," Bryan pointed out. "Have to give him credit for treating it gently. City dog doesn't know what he's supposed to do with wild game."

"Ooh, stop! I don't even want to imagine that."

He smiled at her tender-heartedness and put his arm around her shoulders. As they continued toward the pottery shed, Wolf padded beside them, until something caught his attention and he tore off across the ground.

Grandma Naomi's shed housed her wheel—a modern nod to her arthritis—a bucket of raw clay and a low shelf where pieces of pottery awaited pit firing. Buckets of water to moisten the clay had to be hauled from the house. Bryan had done it today. He didn't think Grandma could carry full water buckets any longer and wondered if his mom had been doing it since she'd been home.

Grandma Naomi bent over her wheel, humming one of her work songs. The smell of clay and the tune were a strong reminder of his boyhood. It made him miss his grandfather with a sudden, sharp ache.

"'Love Me Tender'?" Sylvia identified the melody.

"Yeah, Grandma's a huge Elvis fan."

"Hello!" His grandmother greeted them, as she straightened and let her wheel slow to a lazy spin.

"Don't stop. Sylvia wants to see you in action."

She kicked the wheel back to life—she'd refused to upgrade to a motorized one when Bryan made the offer—dipped her hands in water and cupped the red lump of clay in the center of the table. It was already rounded. As they watched, she drew it taller while dipping her fingers in the center to make a hollow. Sylvia moved closer to watch.

He wondered how many pots, vases, mugs and bowls Grandma had made over the years. He understood perfectly why she was out here throwing clay only a couple of days after her husband's death. Her work was a comfort. Better than the daunting task of clearing out Grandpa's closet and packing his things away.

She glanced up at Sylvia. "Want to try?"

"Oh, I couldn't. I'd mess it up."

"Nothing wrong with that. Come on." Grandma rose from her seat and ushered Sylvia into it, offering her a smock to cover her clothes.

"You're balancing the speed of the wheel and the pressure of your hands, while making sure you keep the clay wet enough, but not too wet. Sounds simple, but that's a lot of factors. Here, use the heel of your hand. Like this."

Her brown hands cupped Sylvia's long, pale ones. For a

moment or two, the clay grew taller and rounder, then the growing column began to wobble off-center. Finally it collapsed in on itself.

"Oh, no! I knew I'd wreck it." Sylvia sounded distressed beyond what a piece of pottery deserved.

Grandma laughed. "I told you, it's all right. The great thing about clay is it can be kneaded and re-shaped into something new. It's pliable until you fire it. Go ahead. Try again."

"No. Please, I'd rather not." Sylvia rose and rinsed her hands in the water bucket then dried them on the smock. She looked adorable in a clay-smeared apron, and he imagined taking her while she wore nothing but that.

Bryan grabbed her damp hand and kissed it, tasting a trace of clay along with her skin. Together they watched Naomi resume her place at the wheel. She folded the ruined pot in on itself, pummeled it with all her strength back to a solid lump, rinsed the table and planted the lump firmly back in the center. Soon, she had another smoothly even bowl inching to greater and greater heights.

"Amazing," Sylvia sighed. "You make it look so effortless."

"Just like you make playing the piano *sound* effortless," Bryan said. "Grandma, you should hear her."

"I'd love to. Maybe one day we can drive to the tribal hall. The piano there is old and usually out of tune, but you're welcome to play it."

He'd forgotten that piano. Sylvia's smile brightened, and Bryan felt bad about his inability to supply her with a piano of her own. He'd love to be able to give her anything she wanted, to have Gary's wealth to lavish on her. At least at the tribal hall, she'd have access to the thing she loved most, even if it wasn't in good shape.

They stayed a few minutes longer. Sylvia asked questions, and Grandma answered in detail while glazing her work with pinion tree sap.

"Well, I've let enough of the day slip by," Bryan finally said. "I'd better get up on the roof and check it out." *Then there's fencing to repair, the outbuildings need work and the plumbing in the bathroom is sluggish. I could be here a long time.*

He linked hands with Sylvia and they crossed the yard again. "This way." He tugged her off course. "I'll show you a rock shaped like a bear if you want to see it."

"What happened to repairing the roof?" She smiled at him.

"Plenty of time for that later. I believe there's something I promised to do for you first."

He dragged her around the edge of a big boulder, out of sight of the house. The day offered very little shade, but when he pressed Sylvia up against the flat side of the rock and leaned in close to her, they both stood in its shadow.

Even so, the sunlight reflected off every available surface, bathing them in heat and light. He hoped Sylvia's fair skin wouldn't burn from this brief exposure to the harsh UV rays. Strands of her light brown hair shone copper and blond and her cheeks were bright pink. A sheen of perspiration glistened all over her face and arms. It looked good on her. He, on the other hand, probably looked like a big, sweaty beast. His hair clung to his forehead and a bead of sweat rolled down his cheek.

"Should've taken the truck out for a drive. At least there'd be air conditioning." He bent his head to lick the pool of moisture that had gathered over her collarbone. She tasted salty. He wanted more.

Taking her by the wrists, he pinned her hands against the rock on either side of her head. When he let go, she remained as he had placed her. She watched him, lips slightly parted, waiting to see what he would do next.

Her sundress had little buttons down the front, and Bryan smiled at the possibilities. If he had a knife handy and her clothing options weren't limited, he'd love to cut off that row of buttons one by one, exposing her damp, rosy flesh by inches. But going back to the house with her front gaping open wouldn't be too cool, so he satisfied himself with unbuttoning each tiny white disc. Her skin was hot beneath his nuzzling lips as he kissed his way down her chest and stomach.

She wore no bra, and he fanned the bodice open to reveal

her small breasts. Her erect nipples still sported small golden hoops, courtesy of Gary. Bryan frowned when he saw them. As hot as she looked in them, he wanted them off her. Like her silver slave collar and the cluster of butterfly tattoos on her back, they were a connection to her old life. He couldn't change the tats, but he could remove the nipple and pussy jewelry, those reminders of her servitude to another man.

He tapped one of the gold rings. "Do you like these?"

Sylvia glanced down. "I've worn them so long I almost forgot they were there. You don't like them?"

Bryan shrugged. "They're pretty and sexy, but...they're his."

She nodded. "Please, take them off."

He carefully unhooked one ring and eased it through the pierced hole in her firm nipple. As his fingers brushed the sensitive nub, she shifted and made a soft sound in her throat.

"Okay?" he asked.

"Mm-hm. You're turning me on."

He grinned in satisfaction and turned to the other nipple, stripping it bare. When he was finished, he took both red nipples between his forefingers and thumbs and rubbed them.

She thrust her breasts toward him, begging for more.

He obliged by licking and sucking each one briefly then he moved his attention down to her pussy. He pulled the sundress over her hips and let it drop in a puddle around her feet. Kneeling, he unhooked the gold hoop decorating her pussy.

She stiffened at his touch, her thighs tensing and releasing. He placed the tip of his finger on her clit and gave it a little wiggle, eliciting a push of her hips and a soft whimper. He brushed a finger over the light brown stubble growing on her mound.

"I'm sorry. I need to wax. I haven't had a chance."

"Don't. Let the hair grow back," he said. "I like it natural. You don't need to shave or wax for me." He cupped his hand over her crotch. "This is who you are—a real woman, not a little girl or a plastic doll."

"Oh." It was more a catch of her breath than an exclamation. Emotions passed over her face like clouds crossing a blue sky. A small smile and a relaxing of her eyes told him she was pleased. "All right."

Honestly, he didn't mind a smooth pussy. They were pretty sexy. But he thought it was good for Sylvia's growth that she stopped trying to change herself to please a man. Bryan pressed a kiss to her clit while he slipped his fingers between the folds of her labia to test her readiness. She was soaking wet and open for him. Her muscles tightened around his probing fingers as through trying to suck them deeper. He stroked in and out of her—just a hint of what was to come—before he took his hand away. With a last flick of his tongue over her clit, he rose to his feet.

He pushed his body against hers from head to toe, his fingers lacing with hers. The warm rock scraped his knuckles. His cock was hard and straining at the seam of his fly. He rubbed against Sylvia's mound, sucking in a breath at the jolt of pleasure that raced from his erection all the way through him. He kissed her softly, teasing her lips to part for him. His tongue slid over hers, and he angled his head to take firmer control of her mouth, pressing her head against the rock.

Having her nude body trapped between him and the unyielding rock was a big turn on. How did the sun-warmed stone scraping her spine feel, the heat baking into her flattened cheeks?

"You like it out here?" he murmured as he rocked against her. "Even under the sky and in the middle of the wilderness?"

"It's not scary with you." Her voice caught on a gasp as he nudged her legs farther apart with his knee.

"How does it feel to be naked and pinned against a rock?"

"Hot. Uncomfortable, but in a good way. Arousing."

"Do you know how sexy you look like this?" He lowered his head and kissed her shoulder, so soft beneath his mouth, then trailed kisses across her chest and over the swell of each breast. He licked the slope of her breast to the pointed nipple and drew it into his mouth, rolling his tongue across it. Latching on, he suckled greedily while he clutched her other breast, squeezing lightly then toying with the nipple.

Sylvia whined and wiggled. Without his permission, she released her wrists from their imaginary shackles and plunged her hands into his hair. She unfastened the tie that held it back from his face and combed her fingers through its length. "Love your hair," she murmured. "It's so soft. Love the way it tickles my skin."

At her words, he moved his head so his hair brushed her chest and belly, making her twitch. He transferred his attention to her other breast, sucking the rosy nipple until it was bright red and glistening.

Bryan reached for the front of his jeans, unzipping and pulling out his cock as fast as a gunslinger drawing his weapon. Foreplay was good, but the day was blazing hot and he didn't want his girl burning to a crisp. He scooped his hands beneath her bottom and lifted her. Her legs went around his waist and she gripped his shoulders. She was so little and light, he felt like a hulking brute. It seemed impossible his entire length could be sheathed inside her petite body, yet he knew from the other night that it could. He set his cock at her entrance and let gravity pull her onto him.

His eyes nearly closed as he was swallowed into her hot, moist channel. He sucked in a breath as her inner muscles clenched around him, drawing him even deeper. He wished his clothes were off so their sweat-slicked skin could slide together. Her nipples would feel like heaven against his chest.

Her body took in every last bit of him it could until he was seated deep inside her. He gazed into her eyes, so close he could see the striations of dark green mingled with the gray. Her pupils were contracted from the bright outdoor light, and he could even see the ghost of his face reflected in her eyes.

Such a pretty, delicate thing she was, perched on his cock like a butterfly resting on some dark limb. His hands dug into her soft ass, lifting her up as he pulled out.

Only when he drove back into her once more did he realize he wasn't wearing protection and hadn't thought to put any in his pocket. Bryan pulled out, cursing.

"What?" Her eyes widened.

"No condoms."

"It's all right. I've been tested and I'm on birth control." Her voice was urgent. "Gary had us all on Depo-Provera."

"And I haven't been with anyone since Simone," he offered. He'd gone for testing afterward because of her cheating. It may have been only one guy or several, but he hadn't wanted to take any chances.

She thrust her hips, and he sank deeper into her. Giving up any further protest, he pumped vigorously in and out. As much as he liked to take his time and play games, he also enjoyed the rushed exhilaration of a stolen moment like this.

Sylvia spurred him on by murmuring encouragements like "fuck me" and "fuck me harder". He loved the sound of her cultured voice saying crude things. It was like a whip to his flank driving him faster and harder. He grunted and thrust.

Mine now. Mine. Mine. The thought pounded with his heartbeat and with every stroke of his cock.

Sweat poured off his body, soaking his shirt so it clung to him. His dark blue jeans bound his legs like hot shackles. The discomfort of the heat and of his knees hitting the rock as he bucked and plunged added to his primitive passion. A few strokes more and his climax hurtled through him.

"Aw, fuck," he panted as tremors spasmed in his body. His chest heaved like a winded horse. He pressed his lips against Sylvia's sweaty neck and breathed in her scent. From the way she trembled in his arms, he thought she'd come, too.

She untangled her hands from his hair, and he set her down on her feet, holding her steady while her quivering legs found balance. He helped her pull on her dress and fastened the long row of buttons for her then slipped her sandals on her feet. Crouching there, he looked up at her flushed face.

"Feeling good? Not nervous out here anymore?"

"Not with you. I don't even know where I'm at. I lose myself in you."

She smiled, and his heart clenched hard. His feelings for her were too intense for so early in a relationship. He barely knew her, but he knew he felt something deep and powerful—if not love then something close to it.

"Hopefully you won't need a map."

She chuckled at his reply, but he could tell she was looking for a different response. He held her, needing a map himself. This was definitely uncharted territory.

Chapter Nineteen

Sylvia dreamed she was playing the piano. The smooth black and white keys felt good beneath her fingers. The flow of music surrounded her like a protective veil giving her security and peace. She was glad to be playing. Her only regret was that Bryan wasn't with her. She missed and longed for him, but he had disappeared.

You have to do this alone. He can't help you now. This is your journey.

She knew it was time to stand up, to leave the piano behind and do some important task.

"One more piece. Just one more then I'll go." Mendelssohn's *Rondo in E major* rippled beneath her fingers. In her dream she could play better than she ever had in her life—as effortlessly as the prodigy her mother had wanted her to be. She closed her eyes and surrendered to the joy of the music.

While she played, hands touched her naked body, fondling her breasts, sliding down her belly to her pussy. Her sex became wet. The presence behind her was powerful, dangerous and seductive, and she leaned back into it. Glimmers of arousal shot through her, tingling in her breasts and cunt from the relentless pressure of the masterful hands.

The exuberant eroticism of the dream changed, the mood darkening as the hands grew harsh and hurtful. She knew instinctively the demanding, demeaning force was Master. He'd come to take her back. Without words she heard the litany of worthlessness he'd drummed into her. She was less than nothing and had no right to be playing without his permission. She would never be free to love or belong to Bryan. Once more she was Master's butterfly.

Sylvia jerked awake, crying out. She sat bolt upright, blinking in the darkness as she tried to recall where she was. In her cell? No, although the surface she slept on was as hard as her cot. She took stock of her surroundings. *Sleeping bag. Floor. Bryan beside her, warm and solid.* Her thoughts quickly assembled into comprehension. She was safe.

"What?" His sleepy mumble let her know she hadn't really wakened him. He slept heavily, rather like a hibernating bear. She snuggled beside him once more. Her racing pulse slowed and the tightness in her chest eased as she soaked in his warmth. He put his heavy arm around her, the weight pinning her down and making her feel secure.

But she couldn't fall back to sleep. Although the details of the dream were already drifting away, her mind was restless and uneasy. She recalled something about a piano and the feeling that she'd never be free.

Despite the comfort of Bryan's presence, her anxiety grew stronger. What was going to happen next? It should have been enough that she'd found a wonderful, gentle man whom she adored, who had taken her into his care. But her controlled life had gone topsy-turvy over the past week. She felt bombarded by the sudden changes that had brought her here.

Bryan kept telling her not to think of herself as his slave, but she didn't know how else to define herself except in relation to him. She might not be Bryan's butterfly, but she wasn't the Sylvia she used to be, either. Who was she now? And what possible function could she serve except as a man's plaything?

Bryan didn't need her depending on him financially. She must think about what kind of work she could do, and that required going back out into a world she'd turned her back on for five long years. Could she function in a normal workplace—even a job as simple as fast food service? How could she help Bryan get back on his feet after he'd given up everything he had for her? Gary probably wouldn't pursue his intent to ruin him, not as far away as Arizona, but still Bryan was starting over with nothing because of her.

She gazed at the black square of window over the kitchen sink until it shone pearly gray and then dusky rose. She checked on the rabbit then tunneled back under the covers and Bryan's arm. Once settled in, she examined his sleeping face—the strong bones, the soot-black lashes and sensuous mouth. Although she'd known him such a brief time, his features were dear and familiar to her.

She touched her fingers to his lower lip. His mouth moved in response and he muttered something.

Her chest ached with the sudden depth of her emotion, and in that moment, with the early morning sunlight illuminating Bryan's sleeping face, Sylvia knew she was in love. This feeling burning inside her was more than just gratitude to a man who had saved her. It was purer than lust for his body, and stronger than her desire to be possessed and controlled. The deep sense of connection must be real love, because she'd never felt anything like it in her life.

Just then his dark eyes opened, their blackness catching a glimmer of light and shining at her. It took a moment for him to focus then a slow smile curved his mouth. "Morning, *she'at'eed.*"

She grinned at the endearment he'd taught her yesterday. *My girl.*

"Good morning." She lifted her face for a kiss, and he didn't disappoint her. His warm mouth settled lightly on hers, bestowing a series of little, nibbling kisses before he pulled away.

"Mm. Sorry, I need to use the bathroom first. Be right back." He climbed out from under the covers and walked across the kitchen.

She watched his tall, lean body, naked but for a pair of jersey shorts, which clung to his ass. His broad shoulders and narrow hips, the long line of his back, the sinews of his thighs, calves and arms, his flowing black hair—every part of him turned her into an aching puddle of want.

When they'd both crawled back into the warmth of blankets, Sylvia nestled her head in the crook of his shoulder. She turned her face toward his chest to breathe in his scent.

"What are you going to do today?" she asked.

"Roof's finished. Guess I'll replace the front steps. Just a few rotted boards, so maybe three hours tops. After that, the chicken coop needs some work. I should give Grandpa's car an oil change, too."

"There's a lot of work to do here. I wish there was more I could do to help out."

"You're doing fine." He kissed the top of her head. "Cooking and cleaning are important. Besides, you have that rabbit to take care of, right?"

"Which I should check on." She started to sit up, but he pulled her back down.

"Bunny can wait. This won't take long. Damn, I'll be glad when we have some privacy and can really take our time. There are things I want to do to you..." He let the thought trail off suggestively as he kissed her throat.

A delicious shiver of anticipation tingled through her. There were things she'd like him to do to her, given a length of rope, a four-poster bed and plenty of time. But they didn't have the leisure for intensive play right now. A quick joining before Janice or Naomi came into the kitchen was all they could manage.

Bryan rolled her to her side, facing him. The length of their bodies pressed together, legs tangled, arms wrapped around each other. He pushed up her T-shirt and cupped one of her breasts. The pad of his thumb pressed flat against her nipple and made agonizingly slow circles.

She shivered at the tension that ran straight from her breast down to her pussy. Leaning into Bryan's chest, she found his hardened nipple with her mouth and latched on. Her hand roamed restlessly up and down his arm, feeling the biceps beneath her palm then hooking over his massive shoulder. She licked his areola and nipped his nipple until he hissed and shifted. She had to burrow deep to find the other one. Bryan turned his body to allow her access to it. Again she licked, nipped, sucked until he groaned softly.

The sound of bedsprings creaking and a quiet cough came from the far end of the house. They froze, Bryan's hand cupped around her breast, Sylvia's mouth on his nipple, and waited for footsteps. Adrenalin raced through her body, making her heart pound.

The house subsided back into silence, leaving behind a sense of urgency. No time for foreplay. No time to linger. Bryan reached between her legs, testing her wetness. She could feel the slippery wetness, her readiness for him.

"Hurry. I want you inside me." She was shaking with need now. Jesus, she had it bad for him. Did he like her eager? Not that it mattered—she wouldn't be able to hide it anyway. Hopefully he didn't mind.

He sat up and let the covers fall away. "You're just afraid we'll get caught."

"That, too."

He leaned back down to press slow kisses along her neck. "You're turning into a demanding little thing, telling me to hurry like that." The seconds between each steamy kiss grew longer. More sounds of waking relatives filled the air. "I should make you wait. Make you *really* want it."

"I do really want it."

His fingers tested her dampness again. She was awash in her juices, and her scent invaded her lungs. He brought his hand up to taste her. The sight of him sucking those thick fingers clean nearly undid her. Then his mouth covered hers, sharing her flavor, tongue probing deep. She opened her legs for him, and he slid between her thighs to guide his cock into her entrance.

The lips of her pussy stretched around him, the friction of his passing sending a wave of pleasure through her. How good and full she was with him inside, pressing deep and deeper into her, filling her completely with his hot, thick shaft. He pushed hard and fast, racing against a possible interruption. Sylvia loved the urgency of it and embraced the small pang of pain as he drilled her deep.

In and out, swiftly yet quietly. Only his harsh breathing disturbed the silence of the kitchen. Suppressing her moans and whimpers, Sylvia bit down on her lip and arched her hips, accepting his cock again and again.

He rolled them onto their sides. Facing each other this way gave a sense of intimacy, as though they were having a conversation—a silent conversation between their two bodies. She wrapped her leg around his, grabbed his ass in her hand and pulled him ever closer to her.

A few strokes later and he stopped moving, his body shuddering, his breath hitching in his chest. She smiled and burrowed her face into the hollow of his throat, feeling his cock pulsing inside her and happy to be able to give him pleasure. She might be good for little else, but it was one thing she could do for him.

They clung together a while longer before more noises from one of the bedrooms broke them apart. Bryan pulled out of her and tucked his cock back in his shorts. Sylvia tugged the T-shirt down to cover herself and slipped on a pair of sweat pants over her naked lower half. By the time Grandma Naomi arrived in the kitchen, Bryan had rolled up the bedding.

Sylvia bent over the rabbit's box and pulled aside the cloth they'd put in the bottom for a nest. Her fingers touched soft, brown fur and felt a pulse of movement and warmth. The animal shifted beneath her touch. She smiled smugly. *Hah, Bryan! Still alive. This little one is stronger than you think.*

"How's your little friend?" Naomi asked.

"Hungry, I hope." Sylvia went to the fridge and got out some milk. Watering it down as Janice had suggested, she warmed the liquid in the microwave for just a few seconds. They'd devised an awkward but somewhat effective method of feeding the rabbit, dipping a tight twist of cloth in the milk and putting it near its mouth. After a moment, the rabbit latched onto the cloth and nibbled at it. The process took awhile and the bunny's bedding ended up with more milk on it than the animal probably ingested, but it was the best she could do.

As she finished and rose from her crouch beside the box, Bryan came up beside her. He looked down at the rabbit burrowing back beneath the piece of rag. "Don't get your hopes too high," he warned. "Wild things don't do well when you try to care for them."

A mix of sadness and irritation shot through her. Did he think she didn't know that? Just because the rabbit might not survive was no reason to abandon it. What did he want her to do, put it outdoors and let nature finish it off?

He seemed to catch her mood and added, "Just saying."

Well, don't! She swallowed back the retort. She could never say such a thing to him. He was her protector, her lover, her new master—whether he thought of himself that way or not. She owed him her life and her respect.

Sylvia gave him a small smile before heading for the bathroom. She wanted to help Naomi prepare breakfast, to stay busy and not think of the rabbit.

He caught up with her in the narrow hallway and grabbed her gently by the arm. "Now I get a smile, eh?"

She gave him another one, wider this time. And she scrunched up her eyes so it'd look genuine. He studied her.

"Don't fake anything with me. Please?" He bent his head to her ear. "I saw your anger. Or something. Something real. Gary may have programmed you not to show what you feel, but I want to see it. Even if I don't feel the same way."

She was too surprised to reply. Was she that transparent? Or was he that perceptive? He kissed her temple and released his hold on her. When he walked away, her whisper followed him.

"I'm afraid."

He turned back. "I know. Allowing yourself to feel, to think your own thoughts, is scary, isn't it?"

She nodded. "It's like I'm opening myself up to someone else for the first time." She met his eyes. "You may not like what I have to offer."

He took her hand. Squeezed it. "I know we met under pretty

strange circumstances, but you have to believe I wouldn't have taken you out of there if I didn't think we were connected in some way. You know that, right?"

"Yes."

"Then if we want to make this real, a real relationship, we have to open up to each other. And stay open."

She nodded, still a little frightened, but now more sure of herself. *Baby steps...*

The moment lasted only a second more before Janice appeared from the living room. She hesitated as they broke apart to let her pass.

"Sorry," Sylvia mumbled and pressed flat against the wall. Bryan did the same.

There was no mistaking the look on his face as his mother walked by. The blank expression, the forced apathy. He'd opened up to her, but his mom?

No, that relationship had miles to go before it healed.

Throughout the morning as she helped clean the house, Sylvia could hear Bryan working on the new steps out in the front yard. The saw buzzed, the hammer pounded—comforting sounds that let her know he was nearby.

She helped Janice move her father's bed back into the bedroom. The family had set it up in the living room when he got sick for easier access. They had to disassemble the frame to get it through the door then put it back together again. Janice brought in the sheets she'd hung to dry on the clothesline. They were crisp and crackly, unlike bedding dried in a machine with a fabric softener sheet.

She breathed in their fresh scent while she and Janice made the bed, tucking in the sheets and the hand-woven blankets.

Sylvia ran her hand over the blues and blacks woven in geometric shapes. "This pattern is beautiful."

"It's a pretty standard Navajo design. My great-aunt Alice wove this one. See this?" Janice indicated a marred place where the pattern was broken, blue replaced with gray. "It's the custom to leave an imperfection, the idea being that if perfection was attained there'd be nothing left to strive for."

Sylvia smiled and touched the mistake in the blanket. "I like that. I wish someone had shared that theory with my mom."

"A perfectionist?"

Sylvia nodded.

"Well, that's one thing Bryan can't fault me for." Janice laughed. "I never expected him to be perfect, and I sure as hell wasn't. I have a son who's practically a stranger to me and no one to blame for it but myself." She paused then continued. "I notice you talk about your mother in the past tense. Is she still alive?"

"I haven't seen or talked to either of my parents in years. I imagine she is." How awful it sounded that she didn't even know if her own mother was alive or not. "I've lived a very strange life the past five years. I've kind of been out of touch with the world."

Janice stuffed a pillow into its case and shook it down. "You can tell me about it if you want to. Whatever you say, trust me, I won't judge. I've been a complete screw-up as a mother and as a person. Nothing you can say would shock me."

The words, spoken with such sincerity, made her heart lift. Sylvia realized she wanted to tell Janice everything. She needed to bounce all her conflicting thoughts and feelings off someone besides Bryan, an impartial person who wasn't part of the riot of emotions tumbling through her.

"I'll tell you what," Janice said. "Our cupboards are about bare. Let's drive to the store. Would you want to do that? I know you don't really care to go out much."

Shopping was near the bottom of her list of things she wanted to suffer through. But if she was going to function in the world and help instead of hinder Bryan, going to buy groceries was a good beginning.

"Sure. I'd love to go with you."

Bryan had disappeared by the time they went outside. Naomi said he'd taken Butch's truck for a short drive to hear how the engine ran. She and Janice loaded the trunk of Janice's car with bowls, pitchers and beaded jewelry to take to the dealer who sold their work.

Sylvia looked down the road, searching for a puff of dust that would indicate Bryan's return. She had some misgivings about going to town without his permission, but then she remembered this morning's conversation. It was okay to try something new. To let herself open up to things and make her own decisions.

Sylvia got into the passenger seat of the car, and Janice drove toward town, the opposite direction from where Bryan had gone.

The drive to Tuba City took over an hour. Janice told a little more about her life and as much of Bryan's childhood as she'd been a part of. Sylvia wasn't ready to talk about Gary yet, but shared a little about growing up with her mother's constant demands and the feeling that she was never good enough.

The shopping trip turned out to involve much more than buying groceries. In addition to delivering pottery and jewelry to the dealer, Janice sent a package from the post office, picked up supplies at the auto parts store and stopped at the hardware. By the time they'd made all these purchases, she suggested they eat lunch before getting the groceries.

It was while they waited for their food at the restaurant that Sylvia finally spoke about her college years and how she'd given her life to Gary. At first the words came out broken and hesitant, but once she began talking, she found she couldn't stop.

Janice listened quietly to all she had to say about the journey that led her into Gary's world and how Bryan had set her free. Finally Sylvia fell silent, wishing she hadn't said so much. What would Janice make of the sordid tale of her life?

"Honey, there's nothing I dislike worse than people who offer advice where it's not wanted, so before I say anything, do you want my opinion or did you just need to talk?"

Sylvia gazed into the deep black eyes and thought how similar they were to Bryan's. She sensed warmth and caring concern and, as Janice had promised, no judgment. "Yes. I want to hear what you think."

"Bryan probably told you I've been clean and sober before. In the past, I always slid back after a while, mostly, I think, because I was still broken inside." She shook her head. "I don't even have the excuse of a bad childhood. My parents were very loving. All my problems were in my own mind. I won't use a genetic tendency toward chemical dependence as an excuse."

She paused as the waitress arrived with their food. After she'd gone, Janice continued. "The point is, I knew I needed a different kind of healing than I could get at a rehab clinic. This time I went back to my roots. I've been seeing a tribal shaman. I went through a healing ceremony, and I'm feeling better, clearer and more centered than I ever have before."

Sylvia nodded, uncertain what to say.

"It might sound superstitious to you. Maybe you aren't into alternative healing and maybe this isn't something you'd be interested in, but if you want I can introduce you to John Kayani, our shaman. He's great at listening and can suggest some herbs to help you."

Sylvia thought of the nightmare involving the piano she'd had the previous night. "Yes, I'd be open to that. Let me talk to Bryan about it first and see what he thinks."

"Bryan knows John very well. From what Mom's told me, Bryan even trained with him briefly a long time ago. I guess he was fascinated with the healing arts when he was about fourteen." She gave a sad smile, no doubt at the years of her son's life she'd missed. "Even though he left the Rez behind, I imagine he still respects Kayani enough to appreciate what he can do for you."

"Let me think about it." She wondered if turning to medicine—even natural herbs—was too similar to what she'd sought with Gary. Something artificial to take the edge off, to give her control when she felt she had none. Then again, she

234

wanted to be able to function in the world and not be a burden to Bryan.

"I haven't seen a sign of your agoraphobia all day. You've been doing great." Janice smiled. "If you're anxious, I can't tell."

Sylvia glanced around the crowded restaurant. The tightness in her chest and the fluttering pulse weren't plaguing her today, but she knew how quickly an episode could flare up with no particular provocation. It was hard for those who didn't suffer from panic attacks to understand that they could seize a person unexpectedly. However, dwelling on the idea of an attack was likely to get one started, so she pulled her mind away from the topic.

"It seems your shaman has really helped you. What is the healing ceremony like? What do you have to do?"

Janice gave a brief description of the Night Chant, while they ate. "It's the idea of building self-worth that's so important. People can do a lot of foolish things to themselves all for lack of self esteem."

By the time they'd filled a shopping cart full of groceries and made the long drive back through the desert, the sun was turning the striated rock brilliant shades of crimson, orange, purple and gold. The land around them blazed with color. Sylvia ached with the beauty of it.

"I can't imagine wanting to leave here," she said. "It so gorgeous, and there's such a sense of peace."

"Believe me, when you're a teenager, anyplace seems better than the Rez. There are no decent jobs, nothing to do but hang out and get drunk with your friends. It seems like a real dead-end life." Janice smiled. "It took me twenty years of searching to find that all the things I really needed were here: family, true friends, some honest work, plenty of open sky. The quiet life doesn't seem so bad when you're older."

Sylvia returned her smile. "It doesn't seem so bad to me now. I like things quiet."

It was sunset by the time Janice stopped the sedan in front

of the house. Sylvia got out and waited while the other woman unlocked the trunk and handed her a couple of bags of groceries. After barking a greeting, Wolf frisked around them.

The front door flew open and Bryan stormed out, glaring at his mom from where he towered over her on the top step. "Where the hell have you been? It doesn't take this long to pick up a few groceries!"

Sylvia's heart pounded, and she cringed, taken aback by his unexpected anger—an emotion she'd only seen directed at Gary up until now. His dark brows were knit together in a scowl. His mouth was a grim line. Wolf whined and slunk away, joining the older dog in her dugout den beside the house.

"Relax, *shiyáázh.* We had other errands to run and we stopped for lunch." Janice's voice held the kind of reasonable calm that makes an irate man even angrier.

Bryan turned to Sylvia and fixed his forceful gaze on her. "I don't like you spending time with her." He jabbed a finger at Janice. "You can't trust her."

Sylvia swallowed. She wanted to tell him he was wrong. Janice was a good person, despite what she'd done in the past, but her mouth felt like it was glued shut. She bobbed her head and waited with a grocery sack in each arm for him to give her permission to move. Her eyes were fixed on the ground. She was incapable of looking beyond his knees.

"Here, let me take those." His boots strode closer. She surrendered the bags to him and stood awaiting further instruction. "Go inside. I'll get the rest of the groceries," he ordered.

"Bryan, we were just shopping for God's sake. Your grandma told you where we were." Janice's exasperation began to show.

"I don't care. I don't want her around you. Besides, it's almost dark. You had us scared to death you'd been in an accident."

"Really? I don't see Mom out here throwing a fit."

Sylvia risked a glance at the pair of them, squaring off

against each other, identical stubborn expressions twisting their features. Then, obeying Bryan's direction, she hurried into the house.

Closing the door behind her, she pressed a hand to her chest. Her heart pounded against her palm. She'd screwed up, done the wrong thing and made Bryan angry. Hell, she'd even managed to make the situation between him and his mother worse. Why had she chosen to ignore his warning and follow her intuition to trust Janice? Her eyes scanned the room while she tried to control her racing pulse.

Shit! She'd forgotten about the rabbit. Again.

She dashed to the box and sighed with relief to see it breathing. Her fingers stroked the soft fur as she tried to make sense of the day's events.

"I'm sorry I left for so long, little one." She noticed the box was clean and full of fresh grass and new cloth.

"Someone else isn't ready to give up on you, either," she whispered. So Bryan couldn't make up his mind about the rabbit...or about whether she was allowed her own opinions or not.

I took a pretty big step today, she thought as a hollow sadness settled into her chest. *How could he not see that?* And for such a caring, perceptive guy, why couldn't he see what he was doing to his mom? She debated whether to go outside and give him her opinion of all this right then and there, but the loud, angry-sounding words in his native tongue made her stay inside.

She gave the bunny another stroke. "Yeah, I think I'll stay inside with you."

Chapter Twenty

Bryan knew he was wrong, but the words wouldn't stop flowing from his mouth. Or maybe his heart. Grandma had told him before she left for her bingo night that he was being unreasonable and ridiculous and should expect the trip to take a long time. A drive to Tuba City always lasted most of the day. There was never just one errand to run, and the travel time alone was several hours. But, damn it, Sylvia should have asked him first! She knew how he felt about Janice. Hadn't he made it clear?

His mother, standing straight and tall before him, took every rage-fueled word he flung her way until he stopped.

"Well, what do you have to say for yourself?" In English. If Sylvia was eavesdropping, he wanted her to understand when his mom admitted she'd been wrong.

"I'm so sorry, son."

"You should be, taking her off like that." He switched back to Diné. "She's delicate. I know her, know when she needs my help. You can't just trot off to Tuba City with Sylvia whenever you feel like it. In fact, I don't want you spending any time with her."

Janice raised her hand to silence him. "You didn't let me finish."

He looked away from her face. The sun, sinking low into the sky, cast a long shadow behind the woman, and the wind blew her long calico skirt around her legs. "Then say what you will. I'm tired of talking."

"I'm sorry I wasn't there for you. And I'm sorry you don't trust people because of what I did—"

"I do trust people. I just don't trust you."

"You sure about that? You don't trust Sylvia to make her own decisions. What if your grandma had invited her to Tuba City? I think you'd still be upset."

A little, he admitted to himself. "Careful. She can hear you," he said in Diné. "What's your point?"

She climbed up the steps and stopped beside him, her arm grazing his. He wouldn't turn to face her.

"Sylvia is much stronger than you give her credit for."

Shit. He prayed Sylvia wasn't in the kitchen listening to them talk. "Jesus, Mom. Say it in Diné."

"I'm fifty-three years old, and I'll talk in any language I choose. Perhaps she needs to hear those words."

"From *me.* And I've told her. I just... Dammit. I'm the one who saved her from...a really bad situation and—"

"She told me, son. She told me everything."

He felt her looking at him, but he still wouldn't face her. He didn't want to see compassion or understanding there. He didn't want to see into her soul.

"I think part of you wants her to be whole again, but another part is worried about the changes in Sylvia—like maybe she won't need you anymore. I remember that time you were in the Army. How you wanted to come save me when you heard J.D. put me in the hospital after a binge. You like to play the hero."

"Yeah? Well, it didn't work for you."

"No, because I finally figured out I had to save myself." She slipped back into Diné as she continued. "Forget the past, Bryan. Or at least don't let it screw up the present."

He held his tongue. Not out of anger now, but because he'd have to confess she'd hit too close to home. A picture of him carrying Butterfly out of Gary's house through the rain entered his mind. He'd been so scared, but rescuing her felt good, like a rush he'd never experienced before. He hoped he'd done it for all the right reasons.

"By the way, I know we can't afford a Night Chant for her, but there are things we can do. There's a tribal sing in a few days for John's cousin. Maybe she could come by and see the sand painting, listen and share the food." She smiled. "Maybe just by her being there, her *hózhó* can begin to be restored."

Bryan felt his jaw clench with fresh rage.

"You have a problem with that idea?" she asked.

Only the fact that he hadn't thought of it. Frankly, participating in a ceremony to help her find balance and harmony might be a great way to get her ready for Phoenix.

"No."

"Good. It's up to her of course, but I'm glad you'll be supportive if she decides to explore this."

"Yeah. Well, I'd better get the groceries in the house and check on her. I think I scared her by yelling."

"I'll help you and then I'm heading over to a friend's house."

After carrying the purchases to the house, he told his mom he'd put them away if she wanted to get going. He wanted to be alone when he apologized to Sylvia.

For a few silent moments, he and his mother stood together in the yard, all the words they'd spoken hanging between them. He knew she wanted to hug him, but she wouldn't reach out first this time. She'd wait for him to show he was ready. The thought of giving her a real son-to-mother hug made him ache deep in his chest. He shut his eyes and remembered wanting this closeness as a kid...to be tucked in at night or snuggled in a towel after a bath. It hurt. It hurt like hell.

He finally turned to her and met her patient gaze. *If I open up to you, if I allow myself to feel and you fail me again, I don't think I can take it,* he wanted to say. He forced his hands to relax and reach for her.

Her calm demeanor melted, her lips parting with surprise and her breaths increasing. "Oh, Bryan."

He gathered her into his arms and held tight. Like trust, his mom was an elusive thing. If he didn't let go, she couldn't abandon him again. So he kept holding her until the sunlight faded completely.

"I don't want to go, son, but my friend…"

"Who is he?"

"John."

He stepped back and gripped her shoulders. "Jonny from Salt Water Clan? The hell you are! He gave you nothing but trouble—"

"John Kayani."

"Oh."

When he didn't release her shoulders, she caught hold of his wrists and gave a gentle squeeze. "Relax. I'm not stupid."

He let go. "Sorry. I just assumed…"

"As you have a right to. It takes time to build up trust after how I treated you."

His hands fell away. "I'm thick-headed, you know. It's gonna take a while."

She cupped his face. Even though he towered over her, he felt two inches high. "If you weren't stubborn, you would've given up on me all those years ago. I never said thanks for caring about me, even when you should've turned off any feelings for me."

He laughed softly. "Stubborn. Yep, that's me."

"It's a good trait to have. At least in moderation."

She let go of his cheeks. Part of him wanted to hold her hands there, let her palms' heat warm his soul forever. He watched her leave, her long skirt waving as she walked.

"Don't expect me back tonight," she called. When she reached her car, she turned to shoo him inside the house with a grin. "Go check on Sylvia. Grandma's moving the beans around tonight, right?"

Moving the what? Jesus, he'd forgotten so much. "Oh, yeah. She's playing bingo at the church and staying the night at Mary Nizhoni's afterward."

Janice gave him a wink.

Bryan waved goodbye then turned and practically ran into the house. A few hours alone with Sylvia. An actual bed, well, sofa bed… Although he really wanted to set her up on the kitchen counter and fuck her long and slow that way—he'd thought about it every time he watched her cook.

"Sylvia?"

She didn't answer, but a noise came from the bathroom. He knocked on the door. "Honey, you don't need to wash up, in fact I'd rather you didn't—"

She wasn't bathing. But she was sitting in the tub.

"Sweetheart, what's wrong?" He stepped into the rust-ringed tub behind her huddled body and held her as sobs wracked her chest.

"God, I'm sorry I yelled, hon. And I knew Mom shouldn't have taken you out all day. It was too much for you. Too overwhelming."

"No, it wasn't."

He could barely hear her at first, but when she repeated the words, it hit him that she'd heard everything he'd said outside. He pried her gently out of the tight ball she'd curled into and turned her to face him.

"Baby, you *are* strong. I know it. It's just that I can be overprotective sometimes of the people I love—"

She gave him a funny look.

"I know I was an ass out there, but…" Wait, maybe the word *love* had made her give that reaction. "I do think I love you, you know."

"I think I love you, too," she whispered between sniffles.

He fought the urge to kiss her. Hard. The admission, even though tempered with an *I think,* made his heart want to burst. "So I'm sorry if you overheard—"

"I didn't hear anything. Only voices."

"Then going out today—all day—was really the reason for you being upset?" He took a deep breath. *Hide the anger. You're mending fences, remember?* When she didn't answer, he lifted her chin and touched his nose to hers. "Look, when someone says they're running out to the store on the Rez, it's pretty much an all-day thing. It kinda bothered me that you took off. I want to be there for you."

"I need to spread my wings, Bryan. I need to challenge myself to get out and manage my fears."

"I know. And I need to rein myself in when I want to play the hero. I just think I'm a pretty perceptive guy, and when we're out together I can read the signals, see what you need, that kind of thing."

"Perceptive, eh?"

"Yeah." He grinned and gave her a quick peck on the lips then each cheek.

Her head edged out of range. "The jury's still out on that one."

"Huh?"

She offered him a sad smile and brought her hands up between their bodies. Bryan sucked in air. *Shit.* The small ball of brown fur she held was still and quiet.

"I'm so sorry. I didn't see—"

"He seemed fine when I came in. I shouldn't have gone off today. I shouldn't have..."

"Shhh." He stroked the fur peeking out from between her fingers for a few minutes while he pondered what to do. She'd kept a cloth around the bottom of it, probably to keep it warm.

"Can we bury it?"

"Sure, hon." He didn't mention that the dogs would probably dig it up soon afterwards. Maybe if he drove her out to the desert tomorrow, that'd be a better way to handle it. This way she wouldn't see the hole they'd make or, God forbid, small bunny bones strewn across the yard.

"Let's drive out tomorrow. There's a ridge with a great view where we can lay him to rest."

"Okay."

He got up and helped her out of the tub. "The way I smell, I need this."

She gave a quiet, unconvincing laugh.

"Want to join me?"

She nodded and tenderly put the rabbit back in its box. After covering the creature with the cloth used for its bed, she set the box on the floor. She needed to keep the rabbit close. To touch the soft fur one more time. When she returned to Bryan, she grabbed the hem of his T-shirt, stretched it taut and pulled it up. He lifted his arms to let her undress him. Small shaky fingers caught his belt buckle. He caught his breath.

"We don't have to make love if you don't want," he offered.

"I know."

The confidence in her voice would've turned his cock to stone any other time, but in this moment, sex didn't feel right. She needed his support, to simply be there for her.

As he pulled her into his arms, her next words confirmed this.

"In the past when I felt pain, I turned to sex to make it better. I don't want to do that anymore. But I do want to be close to you."

"I'm here for you. Always."

He undressed her slowly, with as much care as she'd displayed with the bunny. But the solemn motions of his doing so uncovered a surprise—her bare waist was encircled by a string of beads. He took the dangling tassel of small turquoise and coral spheres and let them drop back beside her belly button.

"Where'd you get this?"

"Your mom gave me some beads to work with the other day." She fingered the tassel and inspected her handiwork. "I need to work on my knots."

"You did a fine job."

Ignoring his compliment, she dropped to her knees. One quick tug brought his jeans to the floor, but not off. His boots were still on.

"Lift your leg."

He leaned back against the wall while she removed one

boot then the other. The underwear he took care of himself. Holding back became a little hell that he endured alone, for her sake. He turned away and willed his cock to stay limp, and started the shower.

"I want to wash you." *Take care of you.* No, help her learn to take care of herself. His mother's words came back to him. *You like to play the hero.*

As he reached down to test the water's temperature, he studied her features. The gentle curve of her jaw seemed stronger. Maybe it was a trick of the shadows in the room, but once he met her gaze, the determination was there as well.

"You're a lot stronger than you know."

She offered a weak smile and slipped behind the curtain and into the tiny puffs of steam filling the small space. The old shower was loud, so he felt safe in saying the rest of his thoughts before joining her.

"Once you realize how strong you are, will you still need me?"

He stepped into the warm water. She had her back against the tiles, her face in profile, her jaw somehow softer now.

"Maybe not," she whispered.

His heart plummeted to his knees.

She faced him. Opened her arms to him.

"But I'll want you," she added. "I think I'll always want you."

"Jesus, you scared me." And she had. The fear that she'd grow strong and leave him to explore her new self, her new world—without him—scared him shitless.

Some days I think I need you more than you need me. He couldn't bring himself to admit that out loud. He wondered if she could sense it, tell by the way he crushed her body against his and breathed in the smell of her hair.

She wiggled away from him to grab the soap and washed his back. He took care of his other parts, then returned the favor, taking his time with her until she relaxed a bit.

When they'd finished, he held her face in his waterlogged

hands and touched her nose with his.

"I don't want to leave the water," he sighed, "but we'd probably be more comfortable in bed. We've both had long days."

She nodded against his shoulder and let him lift her from the tub. After drying her then himself, he carried her naked to the living room and pulled out the sofa bed. She wasn't looking quite so sad. A good thing. She was taking the creature's death well.

"Hang on a sec."

Sylvia waited, those huge eyes filling her face in the dim room. Once he returned with the sheets and a blanket, she rolled off the bed and helped him with the bedding. Then he lay down and opened his arms to her. She climbed into his embrace.

Bryan stayed awake until he heard her breathing steadily.

"When you find your wings, don't fly away," he whispered.

Chapter Twenty-one

Bryan was still sleeping hard after Sylvia woke the next morning, ate and dressed. He didn't wake even when someone knocked on the door.

"Good morning!"

It was Janice. The two women exchanged a hug, and Sylvia opened the door wide to let her inside. "You don't have to knock. You live here."

"I knew you two would be alone this morning." The older woman winked. "Didn't want to come too early."

Sylvia bit back a giggle. "No worries. He's still asleep."

Janice peeked down the hall to see her sleeping son sprawled on the sofa bed, his legs tangled in the blankets, with one foot sticking out.

"He always did that. I'd come home, late as usual—when I'd come home at all—and cover up that little foot." Her eyes turned red. Moist. She looked away. "I'd give anything to go back. To be the one who tucked him in or to see that foot poking out again in the morning."

Sylvia wasn't sure what to say. She focused on a dent in the linoleum and let the silence draw out into long, painful seconds.

Janice smiled. "You're more like the Navajo than me, I think. Understanding the need for quiet at times... Me, I'm a chatterbox."

Sylvia smiled, wanly at first, then widely and earnestly.

"Just like Bryan sometimes."

"Yes!" Janice was laughing now, and Sylvia joined in. The sleeping man in the room beyond didn't stir.

Janice took her hand as their giggles faded. "Did you mention the sing to him?"

"Yes."

She'd awoken around midnight to find Bryan watching her. That's when she'd asked him about it. What it entailed. If it would help. He'd been hesitant at first, but then said it was a good idea.

"And?"

"He said it'd be great."

"I'm so glad. Listen, John gave me something for you. I hope that's okay." Janice fished a small parcel from her pocket. "Make an infusion with hot water. It's like brewing a cup of tea, but more concentrated. There are instructions inside."

"What will it do?"

"It's no Xanax, but it should help you feel calmer. All the ingredients are natural, dried plant leaves and ground roots. You shouldn't have any side effects. Just drink a cup when you feel anxiety coming on and it takes the edge off before panic can take hold. Although, as well as you've been doing, I don't know if you'll need it." She smiled again, that brilliant smile that reminded Sylvia so much of Bryan. "You're a strong woman and you're doing really good."

Sylvia smiled, flushing at the compliment. She was still unused to receiving them, although Bryan had done a lot to remedy that in the short time she'd known him. She reached for the packet, a small plastic bag of off-white powder. "Thank you. I'll—"

"What's this?" Bryan's loud voice from the kitchen doorway startled her and she whirled around.

His expression was thunderous. A frown knit his dark brows. His hard jaw and fierce scowl set her stomach rolling as it had last night. What had she done this time to anger him?

She couldn't find words to respond as he crossed the

kitchen and snatched the bag from her hand.

"What the hell is this? What are you giving her, Mom?"

Sylvia's gaze immediately went to the floor, and she fought her training which told her to prostrate herself before him like a disobedient dog. Her heart pounded, and her mouth went dry. All Sylvia could see was his bare feet and the bottoms of his jeans, but she could feel his huge, angry presence filling the entire kitchen.

"Jesus Christ! It never changes with you. I don't know why I ever believe you."

"Bryan, calm down. This isn't what you think." Janice's level voice was lost in the storm of his anger.

"But this time you're not just dragging yourself down, you're trying to bring Sylvia with you." He stepped between them. "Just keep the hell away from her. Do you hear me? I don't want you to have anything more to do with her!"

She wanted to say something, to support Janice, who'd been so kind to her, but Sylvia stood frozen, incapable of speaking a word.

"You get this from your dealer or are you the one selling this shit? Right under Grandma's nose, while Grandpa's dying, you're running drugs from their house." His anger, disgust and hurt was so raw and painful it hurt her ears.

"Son, listen to me!" Janice entreated him.

"Bryan." Sylvia lifted her gaze from his feet to his broad back.

He shook the little bag of powder at his mother. "Fucking drugs! It never ends."

"Bryan!" Sylvia said louder. She raised her hand and touched his back.

But he was oblivious to her touch, his fury concentrated on Janice. "Why don't you get the hell out of this house, before you break Grandma's heart again."

"It's not coke—" Janice's voice raised as she struggled to be heard, but Sylvia knew he didn't really want to hear her.

"Bryan, stop it!" Sylvia shouted as loud as she could.

Both of the Lapahies fell silent. Bryan turned toward her, his expression surprised, as if he'd almost forgotten she was there.

"Stop it," she repeated more quietly, sounding amazingly calm when her heart was pounding so hard it deafened her. "It isn't what you think. Those are herbs for anxiety. Not drugs. Not coke."

His dark eyes went from her face to the little bag clutched in his fist. His mouth opened and he paused. Sylvia could almost see his mind working. He wanted Janice to be wrong so he could be right.

"Is that what she told you?" He shook his head and his tone was scoffing. "Herbs? She just wants to get you hooked or—"

"I'm not an idiot," Sylvia snapped, as if a different woman had taken control of her mouth, a confident, brave woman who wasn't afraid to stand up for what was right. "But you're acting like one, accusing without even finding out the facts. It doesn't even make sense. Why in the world would she want to give me coke? This is only a packet from the shaman."

"Trust me, Bryan, I would never give Sylvia drugs. I might fuck up my own life, but I wouldn't deliberately ruin someone else's."

He faced her again. "Well, you sure as hell wrecked mine. Over and over again."

"And I'm sorry for that." Her voice broke. "Like I said yesterday I'm sorry I destroyed your trust in me so completely that you're immediately ready to believe the worst of me."

Sylvia took Bryan's arm and gazed into his face, her eyes and voice steady even if her legs were shaking. "Janice didn't do anything wrong. She's trying to help me. Check with John if you're in doubt. But I would hope you'd have enough faith in me to trust my judgment."

"I don't like you spending so much time with her." His tone was sullen. "Even if this isn't drugs, she's...she's not good for you to be around. I don't trust her, and I'm telling you to keep away from her."

"You're ordering me?"

His jaw clenched. "Yes. I'm ordering you."

Sylvia squeezed his arm tight, willing him to hear her—to really hear her. "You keep telling me I don't belong to you, not like I did to Gary. You tell me you think I'm strong. You encourage me to stand up for myself, and then you take it all back again."

She breathed slowly, searching for words. "You've set me free, and I can't be caged again."

He reached out and touched her hair lightly. The tension in his face relaxed a little, but his eyes were still intense. "I know that. I just want to protect you, to keep you from being hurt."

"And I love that about you, but, Bryan..." She paused again, making sure she got it just right. "Making mistakes, failing and trying again is what life is about. It's what I have to learn to do. I can't have you protecting me from the world, even if you're doing it because you care about me. In the end, it's no better than letting Gary control me. Do you see that?"

His eyes widened and he pulled back as if she'd slapped him. It hurt her to see his reaction, but she'd gotten his attention.

"Please trust my judgment. Your mom is a good woman. She's changed." Sylvia rubbed her hand down his arm. He hadn't yet put his shirt on and his skin was warm. She prayed she hadn't angered him enough to make him turn her away. She couldn't bear it if he did, but she wouldn't back down and become pliant little Butterfly again.

"If you love someone, you can't limit how many chances you give them," she added softly.

He looked at her hand on his arm then back at her face. He frowned and nodded. "I know." After weighing the little bag of herbs on his palm, he offered it to her.

She took it.

Bryan turned to his mom and cleared his throat. "I'm sorry I, uh, jumped to conclusions."

"I understand why."

For a moment, the tension in the room spun out then Janice broke it with a low chuckle. Sylvia held up the little packet. "Can I brew you both some tea? It's supposed to be good for reducing stress."

Her irony earned a smile from both Bryan and Sylvia...and then a laugh.

"I'll make coffee," Bryan offered. "A little family drama isn't enough to jumpstart my day. I need caffeine to make me even edgier."

The lopsided grin that Sylvia loved twisted his mouth. He was so different from Gary, willing to accept when he'd made a mistake and apologize for it instead of clinging to the certainty he must always be right. The fact that he was able to see the humor in the situation and laugh about it made her adore him, and her tension dissipated.

Bryan took Janice's hand and squeezed it before turning to Sylvia. "I'm sorry. I seem to keep yelling at you. Don't let me get away with it, okay?"

"I won't," she promised, rising up on her toes to kiss him.

Her heart expanded, growing more open and full of joy than ever. She'd stood up for Janice and spoken up for herself and she felt powerful, strong and confident, all the things she'd always wanted to be, but hadn't been able to draw out of herself. And apparently Bryan liked her that way. He really wanted her to air her feelings and respected them.

It was a good feeling, to beat her wings and find out they were strong enough to lift her and hold her aloft.

Sylvia held the shoebox with the dead baby rabbit and watched Bryan's shoulders bunch as he worked the shovelhead into the rocky, red earth. It was hard digging, and he stopped to mop off the sweat and exchanged a look with her.

"Guess we should've waited until evening when it's cooler." He glanced at the box. "On the other hand, I don't know how much longer the poor bunny could've held up in this heat."

She grimaced. "Don't."

"Sorry, but that's life, sweetheart. Things are born then they die and decompose. You can't argue with nature."

"I know." The rabbit's death had made her think of the ephemeral nature of life. It was certainly too short to waste. She would've regretted the time she'd spent with Gary, except that it had led her to Bryan. And she did regret all the years she'd been estranged from her parents. Watching Bryan and Janice attempt to heal their rift reminded her it was past time for her to call her own mother and father. For all she knew, one of them might be dead without her ever having had a chance to talk to them again.

"Are you ready?" Bryan tossed the shovel aside and faced her. The small pit at his feet was a couple of feet deep and wide.

Sylvia nodded and stooped to place the box into the hole. When she rose, Bryan began the chant he'd sung at his grandfather's passing. He'd explained to her what the words meant—a wish for the deceased to travel safely in the spirit world and find its destination. If Bryan felt a funeral for a rabbit was silly, he gave no sign, treating with respect her desire to lay the animal to rest.

His rich baritone was as soothing as a caress. She half closed her eyes against the glare of the sun and listened to the rise and fall of his song, as she prayed for all souls searching for their place in both this life and whatever came next.

Afterward, Bryan filled in the hole and tamped down the earth. Together they placed a little pyre of rocks on top of the grave to keep the coyotes out, and then Bryan slipped an arm around her waist. "Are you doing okay out here?"

"Good." She looked inside herself—not a flutter of anxiety even though they were standing on a hillside under the arching sky. With Bryan's arm around her, she felt sheltered. Perhaps her agoraphobia had been brought on by Gary's treatment of her. She hadn't had a problem with it until she'd gone into his home. Plenty of other issues, yeah, but not that one. Maybe her pre-slavery panic attacks had less to do with open space and more with anxiety in general, like the cutting. Gary's repeated reminders that she was safe only with him and his use of those outdoor concerts as punishment had quickly reduced her to a quivering mass of jelly at the very thought of going outside her comfort zone—or outside, period.

Now she could stand with Bryan and gaze at the world around her without panic rising inside.

"It's a beautiful day," she added.

Over the next couple of days, Sylvia found a routine while living with the Lapahies. She devoted herself to the cleaning and cooking, while Naomi created pottery, Janice beaded and Bryan worked through his fix-it list. She thought hard about her future and how she'd like to spend it—other than in Bryan's arms, which was a given. Music had always been important in her life. It must somehow play a part in whatever she did. She couldn't afford to return to college to finish her degree, but there were other music-related jobs she could do, perhaps be a salesperson in a music store, a church organist or piano teacher. When she and Bryan moved to the city, there would be opportunities like that. She could picture herself teaching children piano. Spreading the joy of music could be very rewarding.

"Come with me." Bryan pulled her away from folding laundry one afternoon. "I want to take you someplace."

Sylvia smiled. A midday quickie in any of the secluded spots they'd found was always welcome. But he led her to his truck.

"Oh, you mean really go somewhere—like on a date. Where are we going?"

He grinned, but refused to answer. "I hope you like it."

The truck bounced over the rough road in the direction she and Janice had taken to Tuba City, but Bryan turned the opposite way when they reached the highway. A thrill of anticipation filled her at the mystery.

"So, you and your mom are getting along better." She filled the silence.

He nodded. "A lot better. But I'll always... I'll never

completely trust her, you know. I can't tell you how many times I've seen her get better then backslide over the years. To have your hopes built up then dashed that often takes it out of you."

"I understand. With my parents, there are different issues, but I know how hard it is to let go of the past. Every day I think I'll call them. It's time to lay the past to rest and see if we can forge some type of a relationship, but I've been letting day after day slip by without making the call."

"We're quite a pair." Bryan laughed.

She smiled, glad to be part of a pair with him.

"I'm thinking it's about time to move on. I've gotten the place in pretty good shape and I think Grandma and Mom are going to be okay here by themselves. I'd like to go to Phoenix and start a new business." He glanced at her and she caught his tension as he asked, "How would you feel about that?"

"Phoenix?" She imagined the noise of a big city, and her immediate reaction was negative. But they had to leave this cocoon eventually, and Tuba City wouldn't have enough clients for Bryan's specialty woodworking. "I've never been there. It should be interesting."

"I've been wondering if you might have plans of your own, someplace you want to go. I'd love to have you live with me, but I don't want to hold you back from pursuing whatever it is you want to do."

She laughed. "My 'plans' are pretty open-ended right now. The only certainty I've been able to come to is that I'd like my work to have something to do with music."

Bryan nodded. "I thought you might be missing your piano. That's why we're here." He pulled the truck into the dirt parking lot in front of a long, low building. It was basically a large pole barn attached to a smaller building, in front of which a tall cross was planted.

"The tribal hall," Bryan explained. "It's a center for meetings and social gatherings. It's also where Grandma plays bingo and, since she acts as a caller and events coordinator, we have a key. The piano here's a pile of crap after what you're used to, but I thought you'd like a chance to play anyway."

She squeezed his hand. "I can't believe you went to all this trouble. Driving clear over here just for me."

"For me, too. I wanted to hear you play—not from a distance this time, but a private concert. Will you play for me?" His husky tone imbued the words with extra meaning.

Excitement and pleasure bubbled up inside her. "I would love to play for you."

Inside the hall, Bryan switched on fluorescent lights that cast a harsh white glow over rows of scarred folding tables. The stale smell of cigarette smoke hung in the stuffy air. The walls were decorated with tribal symbols. At the far end of the room was a raised dais on which sat the bingo machine and the caller's chair. Behind the platform a serving counter separated the kitchen from the rest of the room.

In a corner sat an upright piano. Sylvia moved toward it as if magnetically drawn. She was barely aware of Bryan making apologies for the quality of the instrument and the venue. If she'd been presented with a grand piano, she couldn't have been happier.

Seating herself on the wobbly stool, she lifted the lid. The keyboard was old and damaged like the piano's wood finish. The white keys were yellowed and some of the veneers chipped off, but when she played a few scales, the instrument wasn't too horribly out of tune.

Sylvia tapped the high C, listening to the buzzing vibration that accompanied it.

"I told you it's a shitty piano. I'm sorry I couldn't find anything better."

She glanced at Bryan's embarrassed face. "This is fine. Thank you." Then she turned her attention to the piano and began to play.

Chopin flowed like water from her fingers. Without sheet music to prompt her memory, she hadn't been sure she'd be able to play an entire piece. But the melancholy *Nocturne in E minor* seemed to be embedded in her hands, which performed without conscious direction from her mind. When the last note floated away, she paused then began a more upbeat piece by

Haydn.

Sylvia became lost in the music, the ebb and flow of rippling notes, the subtle and more obvious mood changes within each composition. She played one song after another, forgetting where she was and who she was with until a small shift of Bryan's body brought her attention back to him.

"I'm sorry. You must be bored to tears."

His eyes were riveted on her face and he shook his head. "No. I'm in fucking awe is what I am. I knew you were good, but the fact you make sounds like that on this beat-up old piano is amazing."

Her cheeks burned and she couldn't stop smiling. In all her years of playing, she'd never received such heartfelt enjoyment from a listener. Her teachers and parents had been too busy pointing out the flaws in technique she needed to correct if she wished to reach concert performance level. Gary had occasionally complimented her, but with the air of a man praising a clever pet. She knew he didn't really care about music. He just liked to show her off to his friends.

"I should've asked Grandma and Mom along to hear you play. They'd love it. But I wanted to have you all to myself today." Bryan rose from the folding chair he was straddling. "I want to do things to you that aren't appropriate for an audience." He leaned against the piano. "Although, come to think of it, having an audience could be really sexy—just not one that includes my family."

"What kinds of things did you have in mind?" Sylvia teased.

Bryan's eyes were hooded as he reached for one of her hands and brought it to his lips. He pressed a kiss to the back and then the palm.

"Feel free to tell me 'no' if the idea reminds you too much of Gary's concerts. I don't want you to do anything that will bring back unhappy memories, but..." He hesitated and she thought his cheeks were flushed, too, although it was hard to tell with his tan skin. "I'd like to make love to you while you play."

She smiled. His desire was tame compared to many of the acts she'd performed for Gary or his guests, but she appreciated that Bryan asked her first, especially given what she'd told him about those punishments involving her piano.

"I don't know how long I'm going to be able to concentrate on playing while you're touching me. But yes, I'll hold out as long as I can."

She began a slow and simple piece, but was aware of Bryan's movements. He moved to stand behind her without touching her, simply listening to the soft notes for several moments. Sylvia felt his heat against her back and waited for him to touch her. When, at last, his hands settled lightly on her shoulders, she exhaled a breath she hadn't known she was holding.

The weight of his warm hands on her shoulders broke her concentration, but she knew the melody well enough to keep going without pause. However, when his hands slid down her chest to cup her breasts through thin cotton, she stumbled over a couple of notes.

He pressed a kiss to the top of her head, his breath stirring her hair, and he kneaded her breasts and pulled on her erect nipples with his fingertips.

She moaned quietly, but didn't miss a beat.

Bryan unfastened the front of her dress and slipped his hands inside against her bare skin. It was a great deal harder to concentrate when his fingers pulled and twisted her nipples without the barrier of fabric. Her pussy clenched and creamed.

A particularly difficult passage was coming up. Sylvia tightened her thighs against her growing arousal and focused on the notes. The rough, veneerless G key felt odd beneath the pad of her finger. Bryan's mouth was hot as he kissed her neck. His pulling, pinching fingers sent pangs from her nipples to her sex. But she filtered all these physical distractions from her creative mind and played on.

Her chest was completely exposed now. He'd pulled the bodice as far down her shoulders as he could without forcing her to take her hands from the keyboard. The air in the room wasn't cool, yet Sylvia's skin prickled and a shiver went through her as her flesh was bared.

Bryan's hands moved from her breasts to her stomach. He laid his palms flat against her belly while his lips slipped over her shoulders and back. She ignored the tickling sensation and played on. He slid one hand from her belly to cup her mound, heat radiating into her pussy and making it ache for more than the light pressure.

His lips lingered at her nape then moved down between her shoulder blades. He could kiss her no farther as he'd reached the bunched material of her dress.

"Stand, but don't stop playing." The deep rumble of his voice was so sexy he could have been commanding her to kneel at his feet and suck his cock.

The desire to submit shot through her. Sylvia rose from the bench. He pulled it out of the way and moved in close behind her, his body tight to hers. His heavy erection pressed into the groove of her buttocks. His hand still cupped her mound, sending tendrils of desire sizzling through her. She wished he'd stimulate her clit, but he didn't.

Playing in a standing position was awkward. Her fingers tripped over notes. He moved his hand to her leg, sliding his palm slowly higher beneath the hem of her dress. When his fingers reached her dripping cunt, she found herself playing faster.

His long forefinger slipped inside her, and she gasped, missing more notes and struggling to get back on track. Sylvia gathered her willpower and concentrated on dulling her senses to Bryan's stroking fingers and focusing only on the music. She'd learned that self-discipline from Gary's tortures. If she could withstand the searing pain of pinning, she could certainly maintain her composure enough to keep playing while Bryan gave her pleasure.

He tormented her clit, tapping it lightly, flicking it hard then circling it until sparks of pleasure shot through her. An unexpected sharp pinch of the tender bud made her cry out and jerk her hips. The music slowed as she recovered from the little climax and plowed on into the second movement.

Bryan abandoned her clit and returned to fucking her with

his fingers, one, two then three stretching her and plunging deep. He rubbed his cock against her ass, holding her hip with one hand so she wouldn't lose her balance.

"I'm going to fuck you now," he growled against her nape. Taking his fingers from inside her, he flipped up her skirt, exposing her bottom. He guided his erection to her dripping entrance and pushed inside. Both of his hands clutched her hips now, keeping her steady as he entered her with a hard push.

"Keep playing no matter what," he commanded. "I want to hear your music when I come."

Another pang of lust swept through her at his challenge. God, the room was hot, and Bryan's big body was like a furnace blazing against her backside. Sweat dripped down her face, stinging her eyes and rolling down her neck. Sylvia flashed briefly on a moment with Gary at the piano after one of her command performances. Her repertoire completed, he'd bent her over, arms wide, breasts flattened against the instrument, and fucked her for his friends' enjoyment. It had been humiliating but perversely exciting being degraded that way.

She deleted the memory, not wanting it to taint the present erotic moment with Bryan—a world away from Gary's use of exhibitionist sex as a punishment.

Finishing the allegro passage, she slowed to an andante as Bryan pulled his length from her and thrust inside again with a soft grunt. Despite her firmly planted feet and his stabilizing hands, she rocked forward. Still she played, determined to finish the piece before losing control.

Conscious of her effort, Bryan filled her slow and easy. She loved the care he took with her even when the sex was a little rough, and right now he was being utterly gentle. After that first spearing thrust, he pulled out in increments and eased back in, a slow, slick slide. Her body welcomed the tender ebb and flow that matched the music. Her inner muscles gripped and pulled him into her each time then let him go with a caress.

Her eyes drifted nearly closed as her pleasure grew and the sweet emotion burning inside her emerged in her music. Bryan slid a hand around her waist, back to her pussy and resumed rubbing her clit. Good God, how could he expect her to keep playing through his climax if he brought her to her own? She inhaled sharply and played an intricate series of notes on the keyboard.

"Beautiful, baby. You play like an angel," he panted, pulling out then filling her again. "And you look like one."

It was a lovely distraction, hearing Bryan whisper endearments near her ear. "Sweetheart, you're so hot and tight. God, I can't get enough of you. You feel so good around me."

At his praise, so different from Gary's demeaning epithets during sex, her desire mounted. His words, his cock filling her and his relentless finger on her clit drove her to the very edge. And his caring was the most erotic part of all. She loved how he loved her. Her heart swelled and expanded along with her mounting arousal.

Only a few more bars and the piece would climax, but would her increasingly ragged playing hold out until the end? Her sweaty fingers slipped on the keys, her legs trembled and her knees threatened to give way.

"Yes, now! Right now!" Bryan's words ended in a shout. His fingers dug into her hips, and he froze. Warm jets of come spurted inside her. His body curved around hers, his pelvis fitting to her buttocks as if made to cup them and his finger never ceasing its movement on her clit.

Sylvia cried out as her own orgasm erupted. She gripped the edge of the keyboard, ending the song in a discordant crash of notes. Her head dropped forward, eyes closing. She wailed as the tension released, spiraling from her sex through her entire body like a glissando shimmering up the keyboard to end in a powerful chord.

When the last wave of bliss had shuddered through her, Sylvia opened her eyes and gazed at the ancient piano with its battered body and stained keys. It was more beautiful than any glossy, black Steinway, and she'd never forget the melody she'd played on it today or the exquisite union of their two bodies, their two souls.

Bryan was wrapped around her back. Now he drew a deep breath and pulled out of her then turned her to face him. He drew her into his arms, rocking her body. "Thank you. That was...beyond amazing."

Sylvia pressed her cheek against his chest, listening to his racing heart. "I didn't quite finish the piece."

He laughed. "It sounded like a good ending to me. I think I heard a choir of angels join in."

"Mm." She held him tighter, snuggling against him. "Will it always be like this?" The sex was fantastic, but she wanted to hear his assurance that he needed her for more than that.

He seemed to know what she was asking. "I'll be here for you...with you...for as long as you want." He pulled away and tipped her chin with his finger so he could look into her eyes. "This isn't just about sex, Sylvia. You feel that, too, don't you? I love you."

He paused and swallowed. "If it wasn't too damn soon, I'd ask you to live with me permanently, but after what you've been through, I want to make sure it's a decision you make for yourself."

She nodded. He was right. She shouldn't go lightly into living with him. After they moved to Phoenix, she should consider getting her own place at some point, just so she'd know what being completely on her own was like. It didn't mean they had to break up. But it would be all too easy for her to slip into the habit of deferring to the man in her life, and she wanted a full, true partnership with Bryan.

Still, in her heart, she couldn't help but be thrilled he wanted her for always. Resting her head on his chest once more, she sighed in contentment. They were together now, in this moment, and that was enough.

Epilogue

As Bryan pulled into the lot in front of the tribal hall, he was surprised at how nervous he felt at the prospect of attending this sing. Sure, he'd seen almost everyone at Grandpa's funeral, but this was different. Part social event, part spiritual—a sing was like stepping back in time. The event concerned spirit and healing, topics he'd sidestepped for too long.

No matter how far he'd traveled, physically or mentally, he'd never really broken his connection to his roots. So, here he was again, helping Grandma Naomi out of the car and offering to carry in her casserole as he had many times in his youth. Except there was no Grandpa Butch by their side. Instead, Mom was there, carrying a cake pan, and Sylvia, leaning against the side of the car, looking nervous at the prospect of facing strangers.

"We'll catch up with you." Bryan put a hand on his mom's arm and kissed her cheek. It still felt awkward after spending so many years denying he felt anything but disgust for her.

Her smile made him glad he'd bothered. "Okay. We'll see you inside." She touched his cheek. "I'm glad you're here. Both of you." She nodded at Sylvia then turned to walk with Grandma toward the building.

Bryan leaned on the side of his grandmother's car beside Sylvia and stared at the dusty lot mostly full of beat-up pickups. Since they'd arrived late, they were parked on the farthest edge of the field of vehicles. The sun had nearly set and orange light reflected from every windshield in a blinding blaze.

"Lots of people here tonight. Are you feeling uncomfortable?"

Sylvia smiled. "Yes, but no. It's not the sing I'm thinking about. It's just... Watching you and your mom together these past few days has me thinking about my own mom. I'll put off calling her forever if I let myself. I need to do it right now."

Bryan reached into his jacket pocket. "I don't know what kind of reception you're going to get. It's pretty spotty out here, but this is probably a better place than most, slightly higher elevation, nothing to block the signal."

He handed her his cell phone and walked away through the saw-grass at the side of the lot to give her some privacy. Standing at the edge of the desert, he gazed at the layers of gold, purple, rose and indigo that striped the horizon and the similar colors that banded the rocky outcroppings. The sheer beauty of the land made his heart ache.

Behind him, the sound of drums and chanting drifted from the tribal hall, songs his people had sung for generations before he was born and would continue to sing long after he was dust.

A loud whoop of joy cut across the chanting. He turned toward Sylvia. She ran across the open space between them with her arms outstretched like she was flying. She leaped in the air, yelling again then whirled around in circles that brought her closer and closer to him, her skirt winding around her legs with each twirl.

"I did it! I called! Got her answering machine, but at least I did it! I left a message."

He grinned at her exuberance. She was a completely different person than the silent girl with downcast eyes he'd first met. Yet her essence was unchanged, that special glimmer that had set her apart and drawn him to her above all the other women in Gary's house. She was simply Sylvia, the woman he adored.

"I'm proud of you." He captured her as she spun by and dragged her up against him. "You've come such a long way so quickly. Or maybe you were always braver and stronger than you thought."

"Maybe." Her eyes were sparkling, her smile enchanting, and he couldn't resist kissing her.

One long, lingering kiss turned into two, three, four, and by the time Bryan pulled away, both of them were breathless.

"We'd better go inside before we never make it." His breathing was ragged and his voice husky. He linked hands with her, and together they walked toward the hall—until his phone rang in his pocket where Sylvia had returned it. Bryan took it out and looked at the unfamiliar number. "I think this is it."

"Oh." She exhaled a shaky breath and reached for the phone, swallowed hard and pressed the button to answer.

"Hello?" Her fingers squeezed his hand tight as though drawing strength from him. Bryan was happy to give it.

"Hi, Mom," she said softly. "How are you?"

There was a long pause as she listened then Sylvia looked into Bryan's eyes, her own glowing with light.

"Yes, I'm fine, Mom. I'm fine now." She smiled at Bryan. "In fact, I've never been better."

About the Authors

To learn more about Bonnie Dee please visit http://bonniedee.com. Send an email to Bonnie Dee at bondav40@yahoo.com or join her Yahoo! group at http://groups.yahoo.com/group/bonniedee. Stop by Erotic Muses group blog any Friday to read Bonnie's posts, http://eroticmuses.blogspot.com.

Award-winning author Laura Bacchi can usually be found at the computer maniacally typing out plots before they evaporate from her brain or bribing the muses to please, please come back so she can finish what she starts. When not writing, she enjoys looking for four-leaf clovers and painting.

To learn more about Laura Bacchi, please visit www.laurabacchi.com. For reader feedback, email laura@laurabacchi.com.

So she wasn't wearing a two-piece and she didn't plan to skinny dip, but the bright pink one-piece wasn't anything to sneeze at, either. Full, round breasts filled out the top half, and long shapely legs tempted him beyond reason. He wanted to pull the straps of her suit down her shoulders and watch her pretty tits spring free. His mouth watered as he imagined tasting her soft skin and sucking on her perky nipples.

As he stood in the grass and concentrated on not getting a hard-on, Sapphire slowly descended into the water. The surrounding trees and wild flowers made the little round pond seem more like a private oasis. They were completely alone. Anything could happen.

"Come on," she enticed, "the water's just right."

He walked to the very edge and was about to step in when she splashed him a good one. He sucked in his breath as the cold water hit his bare chest. "Damn, that's freezing!"

She splashed him again, before ducking under the water and out of sight. Adam took the plunge and dove in. When he resurfaced, she was staring at him, a wicked gleam in her eyes.

He stalked toward her, noting the way she firmed her shoulders. Her nipples were stiff little peaks that he wanted to nibble on for hours. Her dark, wet hair was smoothed back, giving him a good view of her oval-shaped face and those mesmerizing blue eyes. Adam all but drooled. "You're a little minx."

"What are you going to do about it?"

Within inches now, Adam made a grab for her, just barely catching her upper arms before she ducked under the surface again. He drew her against his chest, aligning their curves. Damn, she felt good against him.

"If you aren't careful, you might get more than you bargained for, baby," He growled as he kissed her. He teased her lips and coaxed her to open for him so he could play with her tongue. She tasted like warm chocolate, creamy and sweet and much too addicting.

Adam pulled his lips from hers before ducking under the water. He grabbed her ankle and tickled her foot, careful not to irritate her cut. She squirmed and tried to wiggle her foot out of his grasp. He took pity and released her. When he resurfaced, the sound of her laughter filled the air. She made an attempt to swim away, but he caught her easily. "You want more or do you surrender?"

"I surrender," she said in a husky voice, sending a very clear signal to his cock that she was aroused.

Adam attempted to tame the beast and released her. She put a few feet between them, he wasn't sure if that was a good thing or not. "This place is like a small oasis," he said as he took in the Black-Eyed Susans and mature walnut trees. "It's so quiet, as if we're the only people on earth. Do you like living out here, away from everyone?"

Sapphire drifted closer to him, her hands moving back and forth just below the surface. "I get a little stir-crazy sometimes, but for the most part I don't mind the solitude."

"I'm so used to having neighbors. Hell, I don't know what I'd do with all this quiet."

"I know what you mean. In college I lived in a dorm. It was noisy twenty-four hours a day. Moving here was a serious adjustment."

Adam moved closer, enjoying the sexual tension growing between them. "I've never lived anywhere but the city. I think I might need to change that some day. For now, living a few minutes from my work is handy."

"I can understand. I miss the city some, but I don't think I could go back now. I'm too used to having my privacy."

Adam was close enough now to touch. He reached out and played with a wet curl. "You and I started something last night that we never got to finish."

"I wanted you desperately," she admitted. "I couldn't sleep for the ache."

"Sending you away wasn't the easiest thing to do, baby."

"Why did you?"

"I wanted to get to know you a little first and I didn't want you to wake up regretting sleeping with me."

"I wouldn't have."

As much as he wanted that to be true, Adam wasn't sure. He didn't think Sapphire was the type for casual sex. "I don't sleep around," he confessed. "I'm no virgin, but I'm no player either. I want you to know that."

Her fingers trailed over his chest and Adam had to suck in his breath when her thumb teased his nipple. "I'm not a virgin either, Adam. I'm a grown woman and I know exactly what I'm doing. Stop protecting me."

"My stay isn't permanent," he reminded her. "I can't offer permanent, Sapphire." He didn't want her seeing things that weren't there. Again he was reminded of the real reason he'd come to Waverly, the real reason he'd been on their land. He pushed down the guilt slowly eating away at him. He'd tell her. Soon. And while he worked to convince her this thing between them would be a casual summer fling, he wasn't sure he was buying it himself. The thought of leaving, of never seeing her again, already didn't sit well.

"I know. It's okay, I'm not asking for permanent." Her fingers moved below the surface, just barely grazing the waistband of his swim trunks. "I need you. I ache for it."

Adam's control snapped. He swung her into his arms, licked a droplet of water from her cheek and kissed her forehead. "Hmm, we certainly can't have that, now can we?"

"No, it could prove very inconvenient."

He held her close to his chest as he left the water and covered the distance to the house. He entered through a back door and took the steps to the upstairs bedroom two at a time. Her lips caressed his throat and his knees nearly buckled. Hell, falling down the stairs really wasn't the way to impress a woman. He forced his feet to keep moving even as her tongue teased his skin. She was so open and uninhibited. It was all he could do to make it to the bed.

He placed her carefully on top of the yellow quilts. The soft light from the lace-covered window illuminated the room. He let her watch as he stripped out of the black swim trunks she'd let him borrow. Her eyes, those magnificent sapphire pools, ate him up. His cock flexed, eager to sink inside the little beauty.

"Come here," she coaxed, a smile curving her lips.

The outline of her pussy lips and the tempting bud of her clitoris beneath the wet suit had him starving for a sip of her tangy juice. Her succulent tits spilled out of the top half, and Adam's hands itched to fondle and squeeze.

He moved closer, unable to deny her sensual request. "What are you planning to do with me, sweetheart?"

"I think I'd rather show you what I want to do," she purred as she leaned forward and kissed the head of his cock.

GREAT CHEAP FUN

Discover eBooks!

THE FASTEST WAY TO GET THE HOTTEST NAMES

Get your favorite authors on your favorite reader, long before they're out in print! Ebooks from Samhain go wherever you go, and work with whatever you carry—Palm, PDF, Mobi, and more.

WWW.SAMHAINPUBLISHING.COM

LaVergne, TN USA
01 March 2010
174582LV00004B/2/P